CW00495936

MOTHER OF DARKNESS

MOTHER OF DARKNESS

VENETIA WELBY

QUARTET

First published in 2017 by
Quartet Books Limited
A member of the Namara Group
27 Goodge Street, London W1T 2LD

A catalogue record for this book
is available from the British Library

ISBN 9780704374294

Typeset by Josh Bryson
Printed and bound in Great Britain by
T J International Ltd, Padstow, Cornwall

For

Suzanna,

Charles

and Charlie

Over the one who is made our sacrifice
this is our song: derangement,
distraction, ruination of the mind
in a hymn from the Furies
which binds the mind, no lyre's music,
withering mortal men dry.

Eumenides, Aeschylus

The banks of the Nile heave and strain to contain the tumultuous swell. The reeds sicken and die, their vibrant green fading to fragile tan, brittle as the herd of starving cows which bellow plaintively nearby. The sky is red; the moon already visible threatens like the rising Oriental sun. The eclipse is imminent, the climate bizarre.

Matty knows this place well, the recurring dream familiar as the womb. It's how his father used to describe his son's birth in more lyrical drunken moments.

Desert extends, barren and bare in all directions and the woman, his mother, screams into it, torn in two as the tornado rages through her guts, snake twists in her womb. It is as if the very elements have conspired to sabotage her meticulously planned journey to the hospital in Cairo. The nurse who has tended the woman for the past eight months has vanished with no warning. The broken journey by rickshaw from the diplomatic quarter has met hindrance after hindrance. It is too late now. Just the mother and the father, just an Arab and his donkey, just a herd of starving cows.

His mother shivers and shudders on the ghastly sand as the pain subsides, then roars through her.

But up ahead, a head! A living creature; wet, dark and sticky as a cowlick. Sweat creeps across the woman's forehead as with one final tortuous push she ushers the boy Matthew into the world.

A scream. But who is screaming? The moon begins its rampant passage of darkness and for one split second of fear, the father tastes the metallic taste of evil. Blood in his mouth. He is kissing the woman. Something is wrong. Why is she still screaming? The boy Matthew lies naked on the sands. Makes no sound. The rickshaw driver is frantically making cutting symbols, gesturing at the umbilical cord. It is strangling the child. The father leaps forward, fumbling in the darkness. Makes the break. More screams, wilder, younger, transit from death to life dragging what demons.

Rosy fingers savage the false night. The crazy sun glares again, sees the four strange creatures arranged in the form of a cross. His mother is silent now. She will not move from this appointed position.

But Matty is still screaming.

I

Matty hangs out of the window gasping lungfuls of London air until he feels the snake crushing his chest begin to slacken. Another Valium and he is able to slow his system long enough to admire his shaking hands cease their frenzied conduction. The night sweat of panic dries saltily upon his body and rational thought returns to battle the visions in his nightmare.

'What are you doing?'

The voice is sleepy. Female but unfamiliar. Shit, he'd forgotten that. No matter what Matty's intentions in the early evening, no matter how acute his remorse from the night before, there always came that point.

Last night it had happened around two: the beer was out and the dope was waning and the flesh felt old and empty. He was awake and itchy and the hours lined up in an endless assault course before him. What happened after that, he can barely remember, but once again he is empty of pocket and full of anonymous girl.

There was a time when Soho never slept. It was a haven for insomniacs, or those who could sleep but would sooner avoid the terrors that their dreams threw up. That party's over now, Soho's suited and booted: Matty is the last man standing from an age he never knew.

The edges of fear melt into fuzzier, less brutal warmth like butter fizzing at the edges of a frying pan.

'Go back to sleep, doll,' he says, trying to avoid the reality of her face as much as her name.

But she's behind him now, embracing his bare back as if they are people in love. It's more than he can stand. He disentangles her, a simian bundle of scratchy hair and smudgy makeup, and forces himself to engage her bloodshot eyes with his.

'Now look,' he begins, realising that he can see two of her, 'I'm sorry to do this, I really am, but you've gotta go. It's nearly dawn and my—ah—girlfriend's on her way back from New York. On the red-eye, you know? I—'

But she's already scrabbling her stuff together as he's talking. She must, he thinks gratefully, do this kind of thing quite often then. She probably expects men to behave as he's doing now. What she doesn't realise, of course, is the huge favour he's doing her, releasing her from the loser he is before any real damage can be caused.

The door slams.

Matty returns to the window. He watches her skitter down the street. She turns the corner then, with one last flash of too much skin, vanishes forever.

Maybe she's carrying my child, he thinks idly. Who'd bring a kid into a world like this?

These brief encounters with humans who seem to expect so little bring it home to him just how much he once had. How could anyone have been so truly blessed? It is such an alien state to him now. It is not, he thinks, running his hand up and down the curtainless window frame, in any way better to have loved and lost. That is the cruellest blow of all, to have knowledge of a soul-twisting love. Once you've been a member of that secret society, you know what you're missing. You know you'll never find it again.

He wonders, with predicable circularity, how it all went so wrong with Tera.

Thinking about it now, it's clear that their 'meet-the-mad-parent' mini-break had been an error.

He wonders whether family dysfunction is contagious in some way. Tera was not from eccentric stock; her parents were narrow-minded and smothering, but there were none of the Corani sort of skeletons in her genetic wardrobe. Had his own infected her, made her behave the way she did? Or is it just human nature to tire of perfection, tire of treating it with the reverence it deserves?

For it had been perfection, in the beginning at least.

And he's not sure when it turned sour, because, for him, it never really did.

But clearly he should have kept his lover locked away from his family. Matty had forgotten his father Daniel's brutality. He'd forgotten the patterns of the hierarchy, his own seamless failure to please and unwitting ability to provoke. Of course he'd wanted Tera and his father to meet. God, he'd been so proud of her, of himself for having her. But happiness is false fuel for optimism and the inevitable vitriol had unfurled over that first weekend when they'd so diligently trotted off to Havana to pay homage to the great statesman.

As always, it had been his brother, Ben, who'd been the peacemaker, the diplomat, his father's son. Ben had defended Tera as Matty, catatonic and tempted to run away, could never have done.

Was that when she fell for his brother?

The sense of betrayal punches him afresh, relentless in its capacity for shock, though the story is, by now, painfully familiar. Nevertheless, primitive human instinct brings a protective hand to the clawing, aching gap where his ribcage divides.

Such silence shrouding it all. All he wants is an explanation. Or some sort of apology. Or just some words from someone else to take the event outside his own head. He'd make them beg for forgiveness, they would tell him it was all a big misunderstanding then everything would go back to normal. Tera and Matty together, two halves made whole and the natural order restored.

There's a knock at the door.

A knock on the door at any time of day or night will most likely be Fix.

Matty draws back from the open window and pulls on the tight black jeans and sleeveless top from the night before, evidently discarded in haste. Crossing his small room, he opens his door and grunts some unintelligible greeting. Six in the morning. Not a time for niceties.

'Good night?' asks Matty.

Fix looks at him carefully. 'Mate,' he says slowly, as one might address an imbecile, 'we were only talking about "our night" a couple of hours ago. Seconds before you left with my ex.'

What? Matty's swift calculations can do nothing to accommodate this new twist in the timetable. He decides just to go with it. Figure it out later.

Things were always a little unpredictable when Fix was about, anyway. Half-man, half-animal, he would descend upon parties in a flurry of eyeliner and cocaine, a stream of manic beauties in his wake. Drinking buddy and purveyor of exotic substances, Fix was a man for all seasons.

'Why would you not want to try everything there is to try?' Fix had asked Matty the first time they met, still reeling with incredulity at a girl who'd turned down his offer to split a pill. Now Matty uses that question as a sort of mantra any time he finds himself wavering in a new situation.

'So, here's the gear you asked for,' says Fix. 'You wanna pay me now or bring it to the gig later?'

Why did this always seem to happen? Matty can't remember asking—a sure sign that he'd reached that level of drunkenness where drinking was no longer sufficient: time to diversify.

But now he thinks about it, actually not a bad idea.

He sees a morning of shooting the breeze with Fix, replacing the memory of that fucking girl, fucking that girl. Fuck, that *girl*.

8

'Bring it later, man. Let's have a line now, shall we?'

'Sure.'

The gram's nearly gone and Matty's just beginning to come back to himself when Fix's mobile rings.

'Yeah,' he says. 'Yeah. Uh-huh. Yeah.'

Matty knows this as delivery speak. He sees a morning on his own, too high to do anything but jitter.

Sure enough, 'Gotta head,' says Fix. 'Couple of drop-offs.'

'Okay,' says Matty, trying not to sound dejected. You should always try and be upbeat around people like Fix, otherwise they won't want to hang out with you. 'See you later then?'

He pads barefoot back to the window, climbs out on to the ledge and sits with his back against the pane, his legs dangling down the side of the building. They are crossed loosely at the ankle and he swings them back and forth, watching his neighbours at work. Where are the freaks and junkies, the hookers and perverts? They are harder to find these days—in their place, men wearing hard hats working machinery. The bulldozers are coming. From his ledge, he looks down upon what was once the iconic Intrepid Fox, now a burger chain, and beyond to Peter Street and Walker's Court, where the last vestiges of old Soho await their execution.

Matty takes the joint he's rolled from behind his ear as the final scene of his nightmare rips across his mind again. Time and time again, he is forced to replay the story of his mother's death, his own birth in Egypt. The dream inevitably turns to Tera's death in Ben's car, what he imagines happened in that fatal accident last year. First his mother morphs into Tera, and then he sees his brother, Ben. Ben at the wheel, Tera in the passenger seat, Tera's face in Ben's lap. His face, her face, obscene sculpture cut from the car wreckage, sexual gargoyles—he imagines the paramedics grimacing, one

9

vomiting, saying, 'Shit, we're going to have to cut him out of her.' Had he seen photographs of the scene, or had the police described it to him? He simply can't remember. The horror shut down his faculties.

Matty straightens his back and quietens his legs. He looks at his little toe and tries to bring himself into the present. Then he focuses intently on the Mexican street food chain on the opposite side of Meard Street.

But he can hear the squeal of brakes, can hear Tera cry out, can hear agony smother ecstasy as the car collapses around them, crushing flesh into flesh into flesh into dust, jumble of meat as the cold metal juts in. Some climax.

Police on the phone. Police everywhere. Police, ambulance, hospital, morgue. How did the police know that Matty was the one they should call? His photo, his texts would have been on Tera's phone, he reasons, fossil-like survivor of the devastation. The only thing he really remembers is that at some point Fix was there with him, a sort of *deus ex machina* making everything okay. Fix was like a father to him; he could be relied upon to spoon-feed him brandy and diazepam until he passed out.

Tera is buried in Brompton Cemetery, a mound of soil spiked with stone all that remains of her beauty. Matty did not go to her funeral; of course he didn't. He hadn't even known at the time whether it was day or night, whether he was dead or alive, who he was. The Day of Discovery sent him spiralling into oblivion of such depth and removal that vast tracts of time and space had been permanently erased, lost to some amnesiac chasm. Drifts in and out of consciousness—a dirty floor here, a cracked bone there—which threatened to haul him back to lucidity, were swiftly crushed before the scent of panic could hit.

Ben, by some miracle, survived the crash. Barely though— he is a tessellation of organs strapped to a pristine bed. Con-

10

suming cash. In Matty's mind's eye the life-support system appears as a giant fruit machine, constantly flashing three lined-up hospital beds, the sound effects bellowing on repeat, 'You've hit the jackpot!', as more and more money slaps flaccidly into the slot below.

It was largely under Fix's roof that Matty's unconscious time had played itself out, punctuated by brief visits to the police station. Fix always picked him up, though he feared 'the pigs' as he did conformity and salad. Matty had tried to spend as much time away from reality as he could, lost in a trance harnessed and honed by a steady stream of uppers and downers. Fix was the gatekeeper; he could open or close the portal to that dream life.

Fix was the only friend he had time for then. And now, actually. He was the reason Matty had sold his father's flat and was renting the 'micro-studio'—a bedsit—on the corner of Meard Street and Wardour Street. It was just down the road from Fix's rent-capped den on the other side of Tottenham Court Road. Matty's old family flat was crawling with corrupted memories and fake loyalties anyway.

Fix seemed to recognise the drifting nihilism at Matty's core. When Matty had no job, no energy or inclination to do anything, Fix didn't push. By day Matty eked out time and fended off anxiety however he could. When he grew calm, he grew sad. And the more he fought misery and consciousness, the greater the venom of the delayed fear when the circle came full again. Matty's undergraduate course—Philosophy and Greek—had long been abandoned. That left a legacy of haunting young men whose fates to fear—Oedipus, Orestes and their like—and unhelpful thoughts such as: is he, perhaps, merely a brain in a vat, in some laboratory? Is he a brain in a vat with electrodes attached to him, and scientists tampering with those electrodes to induce virtual experiences identical to those he is now experiencing? The answer to this naturally is, 'No. No he's not'. But how does he know that he's not a brain in a vat? How can he prove it? Answering this is more challenging than expected. And he didn't stay at UCL long enough to find out how, or even if there is an answer. A little bit of philosophy is a dangerous thing.

'You're paranoid, man,' Fix would say. 'You think too much.'

It was around that time, it must have been, that his stepmother Katya told him to go and see a shrink, one Dr Julia Sykes. Said she'd pay—no, really, she insisted on it. But Matty did not go, had continued not to go until very recently, the day before the night before began, and only then because Fix told him there'd be pharmaceuticals as far as the eye could see.

'Shrinking's less about talking these days and more about narcotics,' Fix said sagely. An occasional porter at Mile End Hospital, he'd taken an interest in the locked controlled drugs cabinets of the mental health unit in Bancroft Road.

The thought of psychiatric wards makes Matty shudder.

'You can tell her everything, you know. You must tell her everything. She's not there to judge,' texted Katya.

'Don't tell her anything you don't have to,' urged Fix. 'You don't know what could be used against you. Just say you've got ADHD or whatever, she'll prescribe you Ritalin and we can have some fun—or make some cash.'

Fix was mistaken. Sadly Dr J. Sykes was neither a psychiatrist nor capable of doling out anything harder than herbal tea. Cracking legs though. She had a PhD in something or other, hence being *Dr* Psycho. She was an academic turned psychotherapist. She wanted to talk *a lot*, something that immediately made Matty's alarm bells ring. Ask a question, get an answer. Don't keep digging, looking at him for clues. She seemed to find his answers as sketchy as he found his own memory. So he won't go back.

Matty fingers the little ridge of scar tissue hidden in his hair and exhales greenish smoke, a toxic sigh for the streets below. He feels a secret kinship flicker as he watches a handshake—a transaction—take place a little way down Peter Street. He's in on that. He knows what's going on.

An unexpected swerve of euphoria comes at him as if from the outside. For someone who devotes so much time to controlling his moods through chemical means, he seems to have remarkably little control over them. He can merely indicate to his body which direction he'd like to go in please. Up, down or the sideways zigzag. The rest is out of his hands. Twisting, Matty holds on to the window frame with his left hand and jumps back down into the semi-darkness of his flat.

His eyes adjust to the light and he breathes relief that the jangling fear is ebbing. As if sadness were a physical thing in retreat, he feels his chest lift a little, involuntarily. His eyes open slightly wider as if there were something beautiful to see. His heart sings as if maybe there could be if he only explored… something was demanding a new adventure of him, for him. He feels taller, like a hero—or a god, perhaps. Sitting on the side of the bed, Matty puts on the first socks that come to hand and his Chelsea boots. With vigour, he grabs his slender black blazer from the back of the door and skips to the life he knows is here still, hidden.

Dr J. Sykes BACP (accred.)
Psychotherapist

Private Room
36 Harley Street
London W1G 9PG

Date: Tuesday 6 October 2015	**Time:** 2PM		**Patient Initials:** MEC	**DOB:** 18.12.1993
Gender: M	**Ethnic Group:** White British		**Referral:** Private	**Attendance:** Y

GP:
Soho Square General Practice, First Floor, 1 Frith Street, London W1D 3HZ
Tel: 020 3405 6570

Health Issues/Medication:
Anxiety/insomnia. GP prescribed 0.5mg alprazolam, 10mg diazepam, 7.5mg zopiclone. Taken when needed.

Education:
Boarding school from age 7. Was studying Philosophy and Greek at UCL — left spring 2014. Considering next move.

Living Arrangements:
Lives alone in rented bedsit in Meard Street, Soho.

Family Dynamic:
Mother died in childbirth. Father (Daniel), ambassador in Havana, Beijing, Moscow, hence nomadic childhood. Father suicide spring 2014. Father abusive? First stepmother (Luisa) kind but had son of own (Ben, M.'s half-brother). She stayed in Cuba when father left Havana. Both sons went to british boarding school. Second stepmother Katya still on scene, recommended M. see me. Archetypal wicked stepmother acc. to M. Lives in France but 'interfering'.

First Impression:
M. late, a little sweaty but when arrived was polite, charming. Slightly red eyes, dilated pupils; firm (overly firm?) eye contact. Bit shaky, increased

SWALLOWING RATE, PARTICULARLY WHEN TALKING ABOUT CRASH. CLOTHES: DISHEVELLED BUT STYLISH (ROCK 'N' ROLL DANDY ASPIRATIONS?). STRONG SMELL OF TOBACCO SMOKE.

TRANSFERENCE:

MADE ME FEEL INITIALLY LIKE I WANTED TO MOTHER HIM. THEN AT OTHER TIMES FELT A LITTLE LIKE MC WAS FLIRTING — AND LIKE I MIGHT HAVE WANTED TO RESPOND UNDER DIFFERENT CIRCS.

PRESENTING PROBLEM:

ANXIETY, DEPRESSION, INSOMNIA, PANIC ATTACKS, AMNESIA, GUILT.

DESCRIPTION OF INTERVIEW:

M. ANSWERED Qs ABOUT FEELINGS ARTICULATELY; LESS COHERENTLY/COHESIVELY ABOUT EVENTS.

-SPOKE OF OVERWHELMING GRIEF AND LOSS SINCE CAR ACCIDENT KILLED GIRLFRIEND (TERA) AND HOSPITALISED BROTHER (BEN), WHO WAS DRIVING.

-ACCIDENT REVEALED THEY'D BEEN HAVING AN AFFAIR. FEELINGS OF BETRAYAL, TRUST ISSUES. ISOLATION.

-M. REPORTED INABILITY TO FUNCTION OR SEE A FUTURE FOR HIMSELF WITHOUT TERA.

-SAID DOES NOT TAKE DRUGS RECREATIONALLY — BUT TENDENCY TO GLAMORISE STREET LIFE. REPORTS ERRATIC MOOD. OBSESSIVE/CIRCULAR. BLOODSHOT EYES, SALLOW COMPLEXION. KEEP AN EYE ON THIS.

-RECURRING NIGHTMARES OF MOTHER'S DEATH AND TERA'S DEATH.

-EVANGELISING/DEIFYING MOTHER. MOTHER COMPLEX. TERA REPLACEMENT ATTACHMENT FIGURE? SOMETHING OEDIPAL HERE?

-HOT/COLD ATTITUDE TO OTHER WOMEN SUGGESTS AMBIVALENT ATTACHMENT — SEE BOWLBY ON ATTACHMENT THEORY.[1] FEAR OF ABANDONMENT DUE TO MOTHER TRAUMA? PROVEN RIGHT WITH TERA LOSS? DID HE PUSH HER AWAY?

-BUT FEAR/REVERENCE OF DOMINANT (BULLYING?) FATHER MIGHT INDICATE DISORGANISED ATTACHMENT[2] HENCE THE TROUBLE FORMING A COHERENT NARRATIVE, FRAGMENTED STORIES ETC.

---

[1] JOHN BOWLBY, PIONEER OF ATTACHMENT THEORY, WHEREBY A PERSON'S RELATIONSHIP WITH THEIR PRIMARY CAREGIVER SHAPES ALL SUBSEQUENT RELATIONSHIPS.

[2] SEE DAVID J. WALLIN, ATTACHMENT IN PSYCHOTHERAPY: 'PATIENTS LIKE THESE ARE TORN BY CONFLICTING IMPULSES (TO AVOID OTHERS OUT OF FEAR OF ATTACK, TO TURN DESPERATELY TO OTHERS OUT OF FEAR OF BEING ALONE) AND OFTEN EXPERIENCE THEIR FEELINGS AS OVERPOWERING AND CHAOTIC. AS THERAPISTS IT CAN BE VERY HELPFUL TO REALISE THAT THE APPARENTLY SELF-DESTRUCTIVE BEHAVIOUR OF SUCH PATIENTS REPRESENTS THEIR PAST AND PRESENT ATTEMPTS TO CONTEND AS SELF-PROTECTIVELY AS POSSIBLE WITH THESE CONTRADICTORY IMPULSES AND OVERWHELMING FEELINGS.' (P. 103)

THOUGHTS/TO RESEARCH:

TERRIBLE SHOCK OF ACCIDENT — PTSD RESPONSIBLE FOR DISTORTED/ABSENT MEMORIES OF THIS TIME? T-MINUS 1?[3] WONDER IF THIS DOESN'T STRETCH FURTHER BACK TO TRAUMA OF MOTHER'S STRUGGLE FOR LIFE. MATTY APPEARS TO BE IN A CHRONIC STATE OF STRESS AROUSAL, SUFFERING ALMOST CONSTANT 'FEAR STATE' (DUE TO RELEASE OF CORTISOL IN HIS SYSTEM). FEELS GUILT FOR MOTHER'S DEATH?

-COSMIC, SOMETIMES RELIGIOUS IMAGERY. MORE FORTHCOMING TALKING ABOUT DREAMS, MYTH, VISIONS, POETRY. EXPLORE SYMBOLS, ARCHETYPES. MAY BE KEY HERE.

-SELF AS GOD/SELF HATRED; NARCISSISTIC PERSONALITY DISORDER??

-IMPRISONMENT FEARS. OBSESSED WITH 'BRAIN IN VAT' QUESTION WHICH, I THINK, IS A MODERN VERSION OF RENÉ DESCARTES' DECEIVING DEMON/PLATO'S PRISONERS IN THE CAVE ALLEGORY — SITUATIONS WHERE IT'S HARD TO KNOW WHAT'S REAL AND WHAT'S NOT.

-PRISON BREAKOUT DREAMS, REBELLION AGAINST AUTHORITY, MOTHER FIXATION, PUER AETERNUS COMPLEX, ETERNAL CHILD? PURSUIT OF ECSTASY, UNCONSCIOUS DRIVE TO RETURN TO THE WOMB, THE SAFE LOVE OF THE MOTHER. SEE MARIE-LOUISE VON FRANZ.[4] FITS WITH EMOTIONALLY ABSENT FATHER/MOTHER VACUUM IN FORMATIVE YEARS.

'SUCH PATIENTS FEEL PERPETUALLY THREATENED FROM WITHIN AND WITHOUT, BURDENED BY AN ONGOING VULNERABILITY TO DISSOCIATION, OVERWHELMING EMOTION, AND AN EXTERNAL WORLD MADE DANGEROUS BY THE PROJECTION OUTWARDS OF UNBEARABLE INTERNAL EXPERIENCE. IN ADDITION, THEIR CAPACITY FOR METACOGNITIVE MONITORING IS PROFOUNDLY LIMITED — BECAUSE LOOKING DEEPLY INTO THEMSELVES OR OTHERS RISKS BRINGING TO LIGHT WHAT MUST, OF EMOTIONAL NECESSITY, REMAIN HIDDEN.' (P. 96)

[3] LANGUAGE RICH IN METAPHOR AND GERUNDS SUGGESTS THAT A 'FRAGMENT' OF SELF IS 'FROZEN IN TIME' IN A MOMENT IN HIS LIFE - REFERRED TO BY DAVID GROVE (SEE WWW.CLEANLANGUAGE.CO.UK) AS 'T-1'. THIS, IN BRIEF, IS A MOMENT JUST PRIOR TO THE POTENTIAL WORST MOMENT OF TRAUMA. THE MIND UNCONSCIOUSLY 'FREEZES' HERE (IN 'T-MINUS ONE') IN AN ATTEMPT TO PROTECT ITSELF FROM THE POSSIBLE ONSLAUGHT, AND POSSIBLE 'DANGER' AND TOXICITY OF THE NEXT MOMENT. 'T-MINUS ONE', RIGHT ON THE EDGE OF TRAUMA IS 'FEAR', AND THE FROZEN FRAGMENT OF PERSONA/SELF IS STUCK, CONTINUOUSLY IN 'FEAR'. JULIA SYKES, WORKING PAPER PUBLISHED ONLINE FOR PEER REVIEW, SEE: 'T-MINUS ONE', 2013.

[4] MARIE-LOUISE VON FRANZ, THE PROBLEM OF THE PUER AETERNUS:'PUER AETERNUS IS THE NAME OF A GOD OF ANTIQUITY. THE WORDS THEMSELVES COME FROM OVID'S METAMORPHOSES AND ARE THERE APPLIED TO THE CHILD-GOD IN THE ELEUSINIAN MYSTERIES. OVID SPEAKS OF THE CHILD-GOD IACCHUS, ADDRESSING HIM AS PUER AETERNUS AND PRAISING HIM IN HIS ROLE IN THESE MYSTERIES. IN LATER TIMES, THE CHILD-GOD WAS IDENTIFIED WITH DIONYSUS AND THE GOD EROS. HE IS THE DIVINE YOUTH WHO IS BORN IN THE NIGHT IN THIS TYPICAL MOTHER-CULT MYSTERY OF ELEUSIS AND WHO IS A KIND OF REDEEMER... THE TITLE PUER AETERNUS THEREFORE MEANS ETERNAL YOUTH, BUT WE ALSO USE IT SOMETIMES TO INDICATE A CERTAIN TYPE OF YOUNG MAN WHO HAS AN OUTSTANDING MOTHER COMPLEX AND WHO THEREFORE BEHAVES IN CERTAIN TYPICAL WAYS...' (P.7)

-AMNESIA. WHEN TRIED TO FIND OUT MORE HE COULDN'T SAY MUCH TO PUT THIS IN CONTEXT; THINKS STRESS MAY BE A TRIGGER BUT SAYS HAD AMNESIAC EPISODES ALL HIS LIFE; MENTIONED FEELING LIKE DIFFERENT PEOPLE AT DIFFERENT TIMES. DISSOCIATIVE IDENTITY DISORDER?[5] NOT NECESSARILY. LOOK AT JUNG ON INDIVIDUATION[6] AGAIN BEFORE NEXT WEEK.

-GAPS/INCONSISTENCY IN ACCOUNTS. DYSNARRATIVIA?[7] OR HE'S DELIBERATELY HOLDING SOMETHING BACK.

THERAPY:

SUGGESTED HE TRY TO WRITE LIFE STORY FROM AS FAR BACK AS HE CAN REMEMBER AND EMAIL IT TO ME (TO USE NEXT WEEK — NEXT SESSION 13 OCTOBER).

-CREATIVITY WILL HONOUR POSITIVE SIDE OF PUER AETERNUS ARCHETYPE (ALSO SEE ANTHONY STORR, ART OF PSYCHOTHERAPY, FOR BENEFITS OF WRITING FOR THE SCHIZOID PERSONALITY).

-MAY HELP TO LOCATE PART OF SELF STUCK IN 'T-MINUS ONE'.

---

[5]   KNOWN PREVIOUSLY AS MULTIPLE PERSONALITY DISORDER.

[6]   'I USE THE TERM "INDIVIDUATION" TO DENOTE THE PROCESS BY WHICH A PERSON BECOMES A PSYCHOLOGICAL "IN-DIVIDUAL", THAT IS, A SEPARATE, INDIVISIBLE UNITY OR "WHOLE"', SEE C. G. JUNG, CONSCIOUS, UNCONSCIOUS AND INDIVIDUATION, IN THE ESSENTIAL JUNG, (P. 212).

[7]   'IT IS MORE THAN AN IMPAIRMENT OF MEMORY ABOUT THE PAST, WHICH IS ITSELF HIGHLY DISRUPTIVE OF ONE'S SENSE OF SELF [...] THE EMERGING VIEW IS THAT DYSNARRATIVIA IS DEADLY FOR SELFHOOD. EAKIN CITES THE CONCLUSION OF AN UNPUBLISHED PAPER BY KAY YOUNG AND JEFFREY SAVER: "INDIVIDUALS WHO HAVE LOST THE ABILITY TO CONSTRUCT NARRATIVES HAVE LOST THEIR SELVES." THE CONSTRUCTION OF SELFHOOD, IT SEEMS, CANNOT PROCEED WITHOUT A CAPACITY TO NARRATE.' SEE JEROME BRUNER, MAKING STORIES: LAW, LITERATURE, LIFE, (P.86).

II

Rain beats against the glass facade of the telephone cubicle. It is exposed like the nerve gnarled beneath a dodgy tooth. When did that happen? When were red phone boxes usurped by transparent plastic hoods? They let in the rain when the wind blows the wrong way. And who doesn't have a mobile? Quick check: he doesn't. Lost it, must have.

There's a bottle in Matty's hand and a numbness in his palate, a wetness round his nose. A touch of his fingers smears ruby jewels, red ants marching across the back of his hand. Soho lights glitter. A couple is jitterbugging in an alley. There's a half-naked girl in a doorway, heroic survivor of the last strip joints of Soho. The light from the sign screaming neon 'Girls Girls Girls' illuminates the rosy tan of flesh beneath rubber. Reminds Matty why he's there, beneath the plastic hood, redundant and leaky as a split condom.

He speaks into the mute black receiver, curved and somehow sensual beneath his caress. Everything prickles and shivers. Everything turns him on.

'Where are you? I want to ravish you. Come on, baby, you owe me that, you bitch, you—'

'The number you have dialled has not been rec—'

'How could you do this to me, you fucking whore?'

'The number you have dialled has not been rec—'

'Fuck!'

Blank, numb dial tone.

'Don't go. I'm sorry, I'm so sorry. We can work it out, Tera. I love you. I—'

Tears. Tera. Terror.

There's a girl dancing in front of him. Where is he? Is he dancing? Should he be?

A slick of lipstick flashes through the confusion. 'Hey, you,' it whispers, 'come round the back with me and I'll show you something.'

Feels good, so good.

Zones in. Naked flesh. Creeping dirt.

You're not Tera.

Heart hammering haywire. Just get the fuck out. Run.

'No such thing as a free lunch, angel.'

Can't see straight. Take it. Presses note against her. Red mouth. Gaping. Sticky. Got to get away. Running through the light streets.

Here's his door. Keys don't work. Fumbling. Fucking thing, work! Footsteps inside—what? There's someone inside his flat! Door opens. Fix! Eyes red. He's rubbing them.

'Matty, mate—what the fuck?'

He takes in the strange, shaking boy in his doorway, the wide, wired eyes scared, and pulls him inside. It's not great for business having casualties like this hanging around outside your house.

There are a few faces he recognises still there from the night before, just sitting around on the floor, staring at their smartphones, a sitcom of snails. Matty is safe. Here are his friends.

Fix hands him a joint and the smoke curls round him like a mother's goodnight kiss. His breathing slows and he can think linear sentences once more, the circular anxiety ironed out into chains of logic. Everything is fine. Fine! Suddenly he can't imagine why he was so worried. It's all just a bit of a laugh isn't it?

You're only young once.

The blur of time and space falls into order and he can see now where he fits into it. Clearly the day after he was here

19

before, but does the clock mean four in the morning or four in the afternoon? He can't tell by the quality of light as there is only one small window in Fix's place and a standard greyness doing the opposite of shining through it. A single light bulb hangs naked from the ceiling, its dingy emissions barely illuminating the debris. Matty always feels at home here, surrounded by people who can think of more important issues than fucking tidiness.

'What the hell are you doing?' A needle drags a sharp thread of panic through his lower abdomen.

'Chill, Matty, we just need a roach,' says a face he recognises but does not know, waving a piece of card at him. He has taken it from the little heap of stuff Matty has removed from his pockets and placed on the low table before him. He always does this. He says it's so he might sit on the floor with less discomfort but it's just habit, really.

'It's a photo, arsehole.' Matty's on his feet, snatching it back, checking it briefly for signs of damage. The black and white image of his mother remains intact, if a little frayed. But that's his fault for not carrying it in a proper holder or something. He really should sort that out. She looks a bit like Tera, leaning against a pyramid with a cat-like sense of ownership. She still has that innocence, though, that old, posed, sepia-stained photographs seem to convey. If he lost that one reminder that he came from some original goodness, he himself would be lost. He likes the way his mother was smiling, not as if amused by some wry statement, but with genuine joy for the world, for life, presumably for her prick of a husband, Matty's father. But then maybe he was different in those days. The misery of loss does funny things to people.

'Gear's here,' says Fix, and Matty feels the familiar guilty lunge in his gut as he wrestles with the idea of *just saying no*. There's a spike of hope poking at him; if he can just get some sleep now, there's the slenderest chance he might wake up tomorrow feeling normal. All is not lost. He can write off the hazy memories of the night before and begin again, do something productive. He is on the verge of standing back from the self of yesterday that jitters and gnaws, insatiate for drugs and sex that he does not want, does not need.

'You okay, mate?'

Matty is touched by Fix's concern. Someone in this hostile world looking out for him.

In the aftermath of disaster, Fix was the only one who had not tried to drown him in sympathy, a deluge of suggesting, nagging, pitying. Everyone had an answer, an explanation; everyone required him to do something proactive. Matty hadn't wanted to dig himself out of the hole. It was dark and safe and he had wanted to sit inside it, quiet, undisturbed, and gather the pieces of himself together again.

He had gone to great lengths to hide, to free himself from those connections which pursued him with their relentless, energetic concern. They'd been hard to lose, the police in particular, but he'd managed to disappear in the end. He always managed to disappear eventually. The corporeal world is an easy place to lie hidden. Doors and walls block intrusion. Changes of address thwart those who seek. The world is full of nooks and crannies where one might live out one's days incognito, a floating island adrift from the mainland.

If you could make a desert of your mental life, you'd be laughing. But the internal self's never busier, never buzzier than when you're physically deserted. It's in the silence of his flat that he's most vulnerable to the voices. Now he tries not to be alone too often and Fix, who has little respect for sleep or the other mundane concerns of humans, is his oasis.

Fix asks, 'You in?' and waggles a little packet in front of him and Matty sees the pendulous grey darkening outside and knows immediately that he is, that he'll always be in for whatever removal from himself Fix is offering him.

21

'Sure,' he says. 'What is it?'

He floats home embalmed in a warm glow as he watches London's youth heading out to bars, to restaurants, to plays, to galleries, to pubs and clubs. So much fun to be had, so much life to be lived, laughs to be laughed. This self is calm, a relaxed, almost impartial observer who sees life happen around him and sees that it is good.

This mood pervades as he enters the flat that is his, all his, nothing to share, no one to witness. The buzz flexes its fist inside him as he sees shatters of his creation around him— here scattered sheaves of paper, here shards of a broken bong, here some shells he once shaw, saw on a shaw, sore on... ah, fuck it.

The walls shine and spin as Matty falls upon his bed, paper in hand to pen the lyrics he'd promised Fix at some point. He tries to conjure the muse, ever Tera, but the letters of her name begin to dance; the kingfisher rocks him steadily to sleep.

And she is there. Only she moves before him. Fluid,
elemental as a river.
Another summer and the hot rays of August have
streaked Matty's tarnished hair with gold and stripped
his pallor. Another field, another rave, another strain of
bass rocks his rangy body to its irresistible rhythm.
Time speeds and only the dance can follow it, swifter
and swifter into the lull and void.
Time stops.
Musical statues.
Tera watches Matty drowning in her dance. Snake
charmer, she feels like she is slipping into a dream,
drawing him with her. Her blue eyes lock with his green
electricity, demonically ringed, winged in kohl. Her

first sight of Matty paints an image on her unconscious
which will resurface on the insides of her eyelids,
reanimate in the dreamlands of each sleep.
They stare, entranced, at one another. Now they are
still as the music crescendos and the dancing demons of
Heaven and Hell fade to blur, cacophony of colours.
The slender shoulder revealed by her displaced dress
strap blinds him, as bold, as shocking to his senses as if
she stands before him entirely naked. He is lost to the
curve and swell of breast, the flawless flat expanse
above scarred by a single white flower. They move,
unthinking, towards each other, twirled together by a
gravitational pull as undeniable as the double helix of
fate and death.
Looking back on that moment through the purple haze,
Matty is unable to place the shifting scene in a static
context. He cannot tether the ethereal nature of falling
for Tera to a base of real settings, to time and space.
But he can feel it. He can feel the amphetamine thrill
sing in his bones, in his blood, adrenalin and love. He
can feel the quasi-painful pull within his chest, the
winded sensation just below, can feel the vibration of
the music beating through him, the flashing lights, the
whirls and colours. He can feel the crush of the people
around him, the heaving, dancing mass, living, leaping,
one body acknowledging its place in the universal
order.
In a sea of writhing cosmic creatures, human emblems
of every faith, every interpretation of good and evil,
Tera glows before him, an angel, yes an angel in
dazzling white. Clarity, as if for the first time. Matty
sees that Tera is the goddess at the centre of this
twilight dimension, a world hanging gently to the side
of reality, yet in its absolute beauty more real, more

*true than any shadow of it visible in the grey monotony
of the day-to-day. He watches, awed, as the vital colours
of the trees glare with animation behind her, framing
her. The silver sliver of moon swings in and out, in and
out, mirroring each breath she takes. He can hear her.
He can feel her. He must have her.*

*Tera sees the slashed torso, the satanic horns, the wide,
wide green-eyed flare of the devil dancing before her.
Matty, one half of his face illuminated by the Roman
candles exploding in the forest behind, is all she can
see. The background fades, time spins and the two are
all that remains, looking, looking not daring to touch,
each humbled before the sheer power of the other. The
music is thumping an eternal tattoo and the pair falls
easily into its pattern, never breaking eye contact,
moving closer and closer.*

*It is one of those times when both the rising sun and the
waning moon are visible, confusing cousins. Dew kisses
skin as they run into the pathways of the green, green
forest bordering the field. They stumble upon a
clearing, stubs of candles illuminating where the red
dawn cannot pierce through the high canopy of trees.
They are not the first to come to this sacred den, that
much is clear from the debris, the disturbed cushions.
They are part of a long venerated tradition, the very
essence of Earth, humanity, the universe. They sit cross-
legged facing each other, minion of hell and celestial
seraph. Matty touches Tera's impeccable face lightly
and as her halo slips aside, he leans towards her and
kisses her.*

*Light filters in from the ravaging streaks of the dawn. It
splits into fragments of every hue the world has hidden
as it strikes the prism of their shelter. Tera's eyes
expand and reflect, crystal orbs of time and space. She*

24

*moans in colours as he pushes the white dress away and
beyond the angelic flesh, luminescent against the damp,
mossy bed. Gazes melt and the world shuffles on its
axis as Matty enters her. Smells, strange and brooding,
speak into ears which, imbued with new sensitivity,
channel the orbits of the Milky Way, small against the
backdrop of infinite galaxies. One pulse, his, hers,
Earth's heartbeat. He can taste the morning sky, feel
the animal scent of her, see the sensation of his touch
upon her skin as he slides into and upon her.
Breath upon breath, stark sighs in, out, in, out, the
forest moving with them. A night dance in celebration
of the morning.
Flower flames.
Sigh subsides.
Pulse beats.
Matty feels the lifeblood course through him, through
Tera, and into the earth beneath them. The eternal
cycle of life. All is one, all is calm.
They lie beneath molten sunrise, head nestled in inner
elbow, mould of muscle mingling flesh with flesh, one
body, soul within soul. The green grass curls around
Tera's left breast as she curves her sleek physique
around Matty's diabolical torso like a vine. Paralysed,
complete, the marble statue of the lovers allows itself to
be painted by the dawn's lurid orange spillage. Shards
of innocence, they lie in the sweet, sweaty chill of the
morning light. Darkened by sun and dust, Yang curls
round s-curved Yin, a perfect fit. A bird looking down
on them sees this holy symbol and flits away in fear and
awe. Matty yawns and smiles.
Slowly the sky clarifies, the airy blue skimming the rosy
mist from the surface. Cold, fresh, real. In the stark
daylight, Tera still sends his senses spinning with her*

*peculiar beauty. Angelic wings poke out from her back
at the disarming angle of a dislocated limb. Her halo
sits aslant the dip of her right temple, a cherubic beret.
Moss and mud adorn the pale hair, falling in complex
tangles around her disrobed shoulders. She tries to
edge her dress up, smiling nervously at him, newly self-
aware, Eve in her nudity. Paradise found, paradise
lost? But Matty's hand prevents the dress's movement
as he smiles lazily into her dark eyes, no longer so
innocent, the black abyss of her pupils so deep, so black
as to consume any light from the surrounding blue.
Another level of understanding; two humans
vulnerable, flawed, see their reflection in each other.
The bravado of the dancing nymph, the predatory god,
theatrical fade to black and the surprise comes in the
continued pleasure of reality. The mundane has been
transformed into something of value. Laughter
dissolves the intensity of the night, of what lies
unspoken between them. The world opens up before
them, revealing layer upon layer of new experiences to
be shared.*

Matty wakes up. He gravely wishes he had not as the great
weight of pain crashes back upon him. For a split second he's
still half there, back in the holy glade, back at the rave, kissing
Tera, making love to her—it's not sustainable. He's all too
aware of what's going on outside those closed eyelids. And it's
only going to get worse if he's not there.

Tears sneak down his chest, familiar snail trails of sludge
and despair. He cannot endure it. He wants to run to Ben's
hospital bedside and kill him. He should have died. He could
have forgiven Tera, if only she had lived. He's not dreaming
now but he can't bring himself to leave the memory, to live
there and not here.

Dr J. Sykes BACP (accred.)
Psychotherapist

Private Room
36 Harley Street
London W1G 9PG

Date:	Time:	Patient Initials:	Attendance:
Tuesday 13 October 2015	2pm	MEC	DNA

Notes:

Am re-reading Marie-Louise von Franz, The Problem of the Puer Aeternus:
'He is looking for a mother goddess, so that each time he is fascinated by a woman he has later to discover that she is an ordinary human being. Once he has been intimate with her the whole fascination vanishes and he turns away disappointed, only to project the image anew on to one woman after another. He eternally longs for the maternal woman who will enfold him in her arms and satisfy his every need. This is often accompanied by the romantic attitude of the adolescent.' (p. 7)

-Also David J. Wallin, Attachment in Psychotherapy, on disorganised attachment — to be my focus should MC return to therapy:
'The integration we are called on to facilitate here has multiple dimensions, including (but not limited to) the integration of traumatic experience and dissociated effects, as well as the mending of splits in these patients' images of self and others. Making this integration possible depends upon our ability to generate an increasingly secure attachment — a haven of safety and secure base — that can itself become the primary source of the patient's ability to tolerate, modulate, and communicate feelings that were previously unbearable.' (p. 103)

Finally, this — because MC told me I should look it up when we talked about writing one's life story: Galen Strawson, 'Against Narrativity':
Extract 1: (A person) 'creates his identity [only] by forming an autobiographical narrative — a story of his life', and must be in possession of a full and 'explicit narrative [of his life] to develop fully as a person'. (Marya Schechtman) (p. 428)

EXTRACT 2: 'IF ONE IS NARRATIVE ONE WILL ALSO HAVE A TENDENCY TO ENGAGE UNCONSCIOUSLY IN INVENTION, FICTION OF SOME SORT — FALSIFICATION, CONFABULATION, REVISIONISM — WHEN IT COMES TO ONE'S APPREHENSION OF ONE'S OWN LIFE.' (P. 443)
AND I LIKED THIS BY MARY MIDGLEY, QUOTED IN ANOTHER ESSAY BY THE SAME MAN, 'I AM NOT A STORY':
'(DOCTOR JEKYLL) WAS PARTLY RIGHT: WE ARE EACH NOT ONLY ONE BUT ALSO MANY... SOME OF US HAVE TO HOLD A MEETING EVERY TIME WE WANT TO DO SOMETHING ONLY SLIGHTLY DIFFICULT, IN ORDER TO FIND THE SELF THAT IS CAPABLE OF UNDERTAKING IT... WE SPEND A LOT OF TIME AND INGENUITY ON DEVELOPING WAYS OF ORGANISING THE INNER CROWD, SECURING CONSENT AMONG IT, AND ARRANGING FOR IT TO ACT AS A WHOLE. LITERATURE SHOWS THAT THE CONDITION IS NOT RARE.' (P. 7)

III

FURIES: A curse, inescapable and heavy,
Has locked onto the head of Orestes,
And wherever he goes, it goes.
His head is the iron cage
Of that curse.
Wherever he stands, or sits, his eyes
Peer out through those bars.
He is held in that cage, his own prisoner,
Till an avenger comes—[†]

Matty makes his accustomed journey from bed to window, tries to gauge the time outside, considers smoking something which might take the edge off the day and keep him in the realm of memories and dreams. The (limited) appeal of the attic flat is the large window overlooking Meard Street; it's the first thing you notice as you walk through the door, directly opposite it. The light from this north-facing window, should you arrive at the right time of day, will throw the rest of the room into shadowy relief. On the right, a bed, woefully single, beneath a sloping roof. At its end, a sink-cum-washbasin and small raw mirror. Above, shelves, two jutting lengths of wood containing ephemera and some books: he liked the B's most—Burroughs, Berryman, *The Book of Disquiet*—worlds where insanity is more logical than reason. But these once beloved books are relics now, from the days Matty used to read more than the tea leaves of his own head, the scribbles that emerge from it. Meard Street has changed and so has Matty. The house on the street where Sebastian Horsley once

---

[†] Aeschylus, *Eumenides*, trans. Ted Hughes p. 158.

lived now bears a plaque that bellows THIS IS NOT A BROTHEL. Horsley is no more; likewise Matty is no longer a student.

Under the sink, collecting drips and beard hair is *The Oresteia*—that had been a degree-time favourite. Matty had every sympathy for Orestes, the mother-killer. What choice did he have? Matty's father had called him that once. He'd liked Oedipus the father-killer too—and he feels that he probably did bring on his father's suicide, just by being a disappointing son. There are a few old philosophy texts under there too: Plato, Aristotle, Locke and a series of papers on personal identity: there's a particular sort of girl, easily spotted, that rips her knickers off for this kind of stuff. And Matty had been, at one point, genuinely interested in it. It's just that university was too straitjacketing, way too structuring.

On the left of the room, there's a kitchenette—miniature fridge, microwave, toaster, kettle, hob—in the corner by the door. Next to this, a laptop on a long, thin table masquerading as a desk. This had been a present from Daniel for getting into UCL: 'Share it with your brother—he'll need it for his A-level coursework.' Beneath the desk his turntable and record collection, mocked frequently by Fix whose place is kitted out with cutting-edge DJ paraphernalia. A wardrobe and a broken chair fill the remaining floor space of the left; several ashtrays of incense cones and ash dot the room randomly here and there. A television on an arm overhead, to the left of the window, has been turned to face the wall.

A bathroom shared with the rest of the building is not really a problem in this tiny pocket of old-world Soho. Nobody complains at these prices. Nobody complains because the landlord has a history of kneecapping complainers. But it's good that some grit sticks to stop the rot of clinical Soho. Where are the Cardinal and Colony clubs now? Why are the cafes, steeped in literary history, being knocked down for chains of coffee outlets that have spread through the area like an outbreak of cholera? Where do the pubs go when they've been demolished, when the last person who remembers the last person to have drunk there dies? Where are the whores? Matty does not want a luxury flat in a 'stunning new apartment block'. He wants Soho to be as it was.

Matty often feels out of time, as if he belongs to a different era. Though he has replaced the mobile phone he lost, he yearns for a world in which actual conversations are not interrupted by virtual ones, mundane events do not call for selfies and Soho still roils with the revels of velvet-jacketed libertine poets. He's got the debauchery down, but Matty's poetry is at best deranged, at worst illegible. Or vice versa. And you fit in where you can, don't you?

The *Bacchae*, used mainly for roaches in the sleepless nights, is on the window ledge, open and face down. When he picks it up he sees that someone, presumably him, has highlighted, 'And they say that some foreigner, some wizard sorcerer, has come here from the land of Lydia, his fragrant hair falling in golden locks, his complexion wine-coloured.'[†] Dionysus, ignored deity of wine, ecstasy and group sex, is certainly a god whom Matty can get behind, though he can't imagine what made him highlight that part last night. He chucks it on the bed, sweeps some other papers off the ledge, inspects one of the sheets and as quickly screws it up and flings it away. A theory of life he remembers thinking was the missing link last night. Or the night before. He climbs out. There's so much paper in there he could make a home within his home from it, a smaller bedsit of papier mâché, in which he could hide like a child in a wigwam or an igloo. He tends to veer from frustration at confinement to terror of wide open spaces, depending on the time of day or his choice of breakfast.

[†]   Euripides, *Bacchae*, lines 232–4.

Meard Street below smells of Soho grinding; preparing its first coffee beans. Matty's still half in his dream—partly because it's such a nice place to be—mostly because Tera's ghost floats around this area of London. It's where he'd brought her after the rave for breakfast, to a venerable greasy spoon, now extinct. Here their neon war stripes, whistles and apocalyptic attire drew only the most cursory of glances.

He remembers it as if it were yesterday. The post-rave high had followed them back to London. With the self-absorbed intuition of lovers, they had happily forgotten the friends they had come with as they joined the carnival of heaven and hell on its journey back to civilisation.

Unable to eat, they had gazed at each other, hands and legs entwined beneath the screen of the sticky Formica table. At each point of connection, a blazing heat wanted to melt and weld them together, to forge a new sculpture.

It was not a morning for intellectual debates. There were too many small yet vitally important details about each other which needed to be discovered and stored until a complete profile had been constructed. It came in fits and starts, laced in giggles and flirtation, freed by the vodka in the Bloody Marys they'd ordered once the time had been established as wildly inappropriate for such things.

It was late August 2012, the end of a glorious summer. Matty was eighteen, and about to embark on his degree course at UCL. London felt like the centre of the universe, still buzzing with Olympic excitement. Tera was also enjoying a post A-level summer of liberty. She was, she revealed, excited about a life less dominated by structure and stringent rules. She was an artist and though people said she was pretty good, she wasn't convinced she was ready to abandon herself to a life of penury and lack of recognition. So she was taking a year's course at Camberwell College of Arts and if it went well, and they thought she had potential, well, she'd carry on.

Otherwise, well… she hadn't really thought that far ahead but she expected it would have to involve a degree of some sort.

She'd rather travel though. South East Asia. She had implausible images of herself crossing seas and deserts draped in eastern silks and dragging an easel, embraced by the key figures of each new culture she encountered and immortalised in art.

'Not in China,' Matty had snorted. 'The only culture left there's of the encephalitic variety.'

'And how would you know?' she asked.

'Lived there for six years when my father was British ambassador.'

She was impressed. Not just Beijing but Havana, St Petersburg too… she felt jealous. She'd always lived in London, in Putney to be precise. Her family—yes, what was her surname by the way? Oh that's fairly unexciting too. Cotta? Ha ha, sadly not. It was Martial. Her family, as she was saying, moved once in her whole upbringing and that was only to an identical house two streets farther back from the main road.

She was an only child, but thought Matty was lucky to have a brother.

Half-brother. Same father, different mothers.

It took Tera an extra beat to see that Matty was not comfortable talking about his family. Just as she was deciding not to press it, he'd said: she's dead, my mother. Her eyes widened. No, no, it's not like a recent tragedy or anything. He never knew her. She died giving birth to him.

But still.

Changed the subject.

Rush of relief. Back on course.

Favourite colour? Blue. Both.

Favourite food? Noodles. Steak. Her. Him.

33

Favourite cocktail? He'd rather have a beer, really. Boring. Had he ever tried a Black Russian?

Time was playing tricks again; the dusk was falling and there was still so much left to learn…

Leaving the cafe, laughing at nothing, they walked hand in hand to a place Matty had in mind, three streets through the Soho web, where his friend, Alex, was working to fund a gap-year road trip across the States. They settled down to more serious discussion in The Cock and Bull over a shared bowl of Thai beef noodles and the sickly sweet Kahlua kick of Black Russians.

Matty's flat awaited them in blissful solitude. They tumbled through the doorway, a messy jigsaw of tongue and tooth, fingers and clothes.

She never really left.

In the street beneath, Matty sees a girl shivering in the morning cold, poking an apparently unresponsive phone. She is wearing very little; no doubt she and her gold sequin hot pants have made one of his neighbours very happy. What did she cost? She reminds him of a girl he used to see in front of a brothel in Peter Street, her grandmother behind her keeping the books.

'All girls are prostitutes,' he recalls some shadowy figure telling him in Havana, 'if the price is right.' At once an essay title appears on his mental whiteboard, a tweed-clad geriatric tapping it with a cane: 'All females are inherently sluts.' Discuss.

After a month of camping at his flat, Tera had become as essential, as elemental to Matty as the hand on the end of his arm or the breath in his body. He'd never felt anything like it. Though solitude continued to be his firmest friend, for the first time that was compatible with the company of his lover. Like a white blood cell he had eaten her, engulfed her and made her part of him. A chemical change had, he felt, occurred once the one had slid into the other. Though they could be physically separated into two entities, this superficial parting disguised the different, combined blend of blood which now ran through the veins of each. And as soon as the forces holding them apart should ease, the two would magnetically intermingle again, indistinguishable. His love for her felt too large to contain yet too transcendent to express. A physical weight he carried in his chest which threatened to explode with fear if he dared to contemplate a life in which he had not found her.

Matty drifts farther into that intense time. The last time he felt alive. He closes his eyes and imagines Tera there, the warm violin curve of his sleeping girl, if he were only to turn around and look towards the bed.

When Matty stops floating in scenes of the past, it is as if he has been elsewhere. Respite from himself, to a hole in time. He cannot immediately remember where he has travelled.

He tips his angular frame back through the window, muscle memory reminding him to concertina his too-tall body past the dangling light bulb. He lets his eyes readjust to the dinge.

For as long as Matty has been aware of memory, there have been gaps in his. Always it dawns on him much later that there's time unaccounted for. And where was he? What was he doing? Was he asleep, in a stupor, on 'autopilot'? And if he can't remember it, was it the same he who was present at that time? He's interested in who is to blame if not.

The one time he'd tried to explain these amnesiac black spots to Tera she had laughed, stroked him maternally, said it was hardly surprising given the amount of weed he smoked.

He'd shrugged it off, but realised that unlike most things about him which Tera—though perhaps not the rest of the world—understood, these peculiar mental holidays were his own solitary burden. The irony was that, though he doubted dope did much to enhance the clarity of his short-term recall, it was the first medium he'd found which could unlock the buried treasure chests of past memories.

It is the main reason Matty follows the lure of the dancing smoke. It restores him to a better time, when everything was different, less ugly, more innocent. The world to which he is relentlessly forced to return is a dirty, defiled one, tainted and taunting with Matty festering in the very nucleus of all the mess, radiating rot.

As reality swims about him, he turns back to the scrawls of poetry littering his floor, hoping one might jog another memory. One piece of paper does—a court summons. No need to think about that right now. It joins his scrumpled theorising in the non-bin, the area of his four-walled cave designated 'rubbish'. It's lucky he doesn't have his own bathroom. Another thing he'd only fail to keep in order.

He flicks through leaf upon leaf of paper full of the late-night ravings of forgotten highs, the sketchy records of dreams which feel complete until one tries to describe them. Some of them so happy they make him sad, some so bitter they bite:

> you fuck how could you have left me to this?
> all your always. all your this is it, this is love.
> still crippled i curse i cough where you kiss
> i beg of myself enough now enough

There are reams of the things. In most, the scratchy writing, misshapen letters, make little sense to him. But each thought seems to tally with something elusively familiar. The recognition itself has the quality of a dream, but a dream where you think, I've already dreamed this. He feels an aching sense of belonging, a knowledge of its history.

He cannot remember writing these things. He cannot remember dreaming them. But as he reads, his confusion settles and he is calmer. Each fragment of abandoned poem leads to another chamber of his labyrinthine mind, a place to escape the present. But the deception is finite. You can't lose yourself in a four-line poem forever. Before long he is thinking about the correspondence beneath the poems, the bills, the letter from loathsome Katya, his stepmother, the nagging pain in his skull—oh God... And beneath that something worse, elusive, lurking.

Like the map of vanished dives and dens he so admires, Matty knows there's a whole world lurking beneath these paper-committed shards of consciousness. They are just the doorways, the many bare portals inside unassuming Soho corridors. The right knock, name, password and the previous reality falls away. You're in.

He wishes he could join up the dots of his jumbled story and stop feeling so removed, so confused. He wishes he could figure out how it has come to this. Have some sort of clarity or control over his life. He'd like a written world in which he can lose himself more completely. He'd like to write a parallel but happier universe into existence, one so comprehensive, so credible that he will be able to trick himself into knowing it as his true reality. And in writing his own path through it, he will find the thread of his own role, a scattered self linking all these episodes and emotions. He'll do what thousands go to Goa to do. Find himself. He'll have to lose himself to do it, of course.

Maybe the Sykes woman had a point: 'Have you heard of dysnarrativia, Matthew?' she'd asked, crossing and uncrossing her legs seductively.

'Is it a drug?' he'd asked.

'Er, no,' Dr Psychosis had replied. 'No.'

'Oh. Right. No then.'

'Sometimes, for a great number of reasons—trauma, amnesia, brain damage, child abuse—people don't have the ability to tell their life stories.'

'Hmmm.'

'Life-writing therapy has much to recommend it. It's very hard to see the patterns when you're living your life, episode to episode. But write it all down in chronological order and we can start to make some sense of it, and of you.'

He'd thought it sounded appealing, but somehow dangerous.

'So let's make a start this week, shall we? Let's call it homework. I'd like you to write an account of your life, starting with your earliest memories.'

When they said goodbye, he'd thought maybe she would hug him. He wondered if she wanted to write a book about him.

Walking back into the street from the side entrance reserved for patients leaving, he'd suddenly remembered the debacle of his first year exams. He'd produced four papers which began and ended with some promise. The middle, however, was a different story. 'This part,' wrote the course professor, 'seems to have been written by an entirely different candidate. Does the candidate have a history of possession?' A letter had been sent to his father expressing concern about the Tourette's explosions within each paper. Matty couldn't explain it, though he recognised the part of him that had protested mid-paper; the tone, the language were familiar to him as another anarchic part of himself, a part as fundamental as the one diligently beginning and ending the papers. A different, male Dr Psycho had been located; instructions to see him issued from France by Daniel and Katya. But Matty had been nineteen and time had been short. Too short for sessions with a quack, too short for contemplation of the black holes within himself, and eventually too short for the degree itself.

Now, at twenty-one with no degree and no job, there is too much time. And if he is condemned to spend most of it inside his own head, he must make that a nicer place to be.

He'd been, he realises, afraid to look too closely at it all, at himself. He'd worried that giving mental space to something is like giving it some kind of objective truth. Writing something into existence so much more so. But it keeps going wrong, his life. He keeps getting it so wrong. Maybe it's the very act of stifling the stuff that's happened which gives it such force. He'll be a good boy and do his homework for Dr Psycho.

Transcription: extract from conversation between Dr J. Sykes, BACP (accred.) and Matthew Corani

JS: What was your mother's name, Matty? I realise I didn't get that from you last time.

MC: Her name was Ruth. My father said that wasn't exotic enough. He called her Freya — the Norse goddess of love. And death.

JS: And it's a biblical name, Ruth, isn't it? Was her family religious, do you know? Was she?

MC: I don't know.

JS: Last time we met you told me about a dream you had, about your mother. Do you remember?

MC: No.

JS: It seemed to me to be referring to something in the Bible? The donkey, the desert.

MC: The whole world's becoming a desert, isn't that what the scientists are saying? Everything's closing in and drying up. I don't think there would have been anything religious about it.

JS: Do you have anxieties about the environment, Matty?

MC: I think the world's going to end if we don't change our ideas about it. We'll be like the dinosaurs — only the microbes will survive.

JS: I agree, there are certainly concerns there. Maybe doing something practical to help might alleviate —

MC: Do you know where she was born?

JS: Who? Sorry, I'm confused.

MC: My mother.

JS: No, why don't you tell me?

MC: I can't. I don't know. I think Britain. My father didn't talk about her very much. All I know is they met in an airport; he'd missed his flight.

JS: Did you ask him to talk about her?

MC: Mmmm.

JS: Are your maternal grandparents alive?

MC: No.

JS: Do you know what she, your mother, looked like?

MC: I have this one photo. Here look — she's blonde, like a Viking you see. And beautiful.

JS: Your father was a well-travelled man?

MC: It was his job to be. He worked for the Foreign Office.

JS: Did you want to be like him when you were growing up?

MC: [pause] I'd rather die.

JS: Why do you think that?

MC: He was a very unhappy man. A brutal man. And a bit mad, I think — or maybe that's the same as grief.

JS: That must have been very difficult for you as a child?

MC: Well, he could be amazing as well. I didn't see that much of him. He had Ben, my brother.

41

JS: And you think he preferred your brother?

MC: Oh he didn't. It was a Cain and Abel situation, you know. He tells me that sometimes.

JS: How does he tell you?

MC: He comes back in dreams sometimes. Sometimes he's just standing there in front of me.

IV

It's the afternoon and the light bulb flickers. Matty is writing—or at the very least, thinking about writing. Propped up by one elbow, the rest of his six-foot length stretched out takes up most of the vacant floor space. The broken chair which usually occupies about a square foot of this space (should Fix drop by) has been folded up and slotted under the bed. Matty is listening to an old Cuban album that takes him back to his expat childhood, panicking a little and trying to sync his jumpy heart with the slower bolero. *Dos Gardenias Para Ti*—the romantic lilt is hardly his thing, though he once heard an admirable remix at a rave in Elephant and Castle.

The record takes him back to Luisa and memories of mothers. Not his own mother of course. After she'd died in childbirth near Cairo, Daniel's diplomatic work took him and his son and a nanny Matty can't remember to Havana a year later. When he thinks of Luisa, as now, he feels the warmth of filial love, a slight but defined umbilical pull. Stupid really. Wasn't as if she were any kind of mother to her real son, his brother Ben. She certainly wouldn't know where he was now. Or what he'd become.

They'd called him Benedicto, 'the blessed one', after Luisa's grandfather. Whenever Matty scuffles around for his earliest memory, as instructed by Dr Psycho, it's Ben's birth which spews up. It seems to mark the point at which Matty became conscious of his own existence. Can you remember your own birth? Maybe under hypnosis. It must be in there somewhere, in the unconscious that is. It's all in there somewhere, that's the problem.

Gazing up he remembers a half-smoked joint in the ashtray, which he'd moved off the chair and put on a shelf. *Waste not want not.* Had that been one of the nanny's sayings? One of Daniel's? It could have been. Sage advice. He draws deeply on the relit remains, initially ashen, later fragrant. The Sommelier, white-glove clad and snooty, struts into his frontal lobe. *Can you detect, sir, the subtle note of wet compost on the nose, the astringent strains of bonfire and toffee apple on the palate?*

'Oh certainly,' Matty says to himself. 'The body of a very fain wain indeed. Such a wain might best be appreciated with a little nibble or two, don't you think?'

As he reaches for a pill, it dawns on him that not much has changed since his days of conjuring up soldiers and heroes to play with.

He turns the record over and settles back down on the floor on his back. Images pour out of the music. Sunny days, sprays of seawater, running naked and unashamed in the swimming pool of the embassy. He closes his eyes as head spin envelops him, the grey smoke lifts the blackness from his heart. Luisa sits before him, an intoxicating mash of plantain, avocado and black beans on a spoon, the water of a green coconut splashing from its regal goblet.

Life consisted of simple pleasures back then. He wasn't born with tin foil and a Bunsen burner in his hand and this crushing misery in his head. How did he get here? Psycho is right. He needs to go back to the very beginning of his life and work out exactly what has happened. A book would tie it all together—immortalise the happy memories and make sense of the bad. He will write his life. It will be a mighty catharsis.

At the moment his past is all so very sketchy. When he tries to remember his relationship with Tera, to trace some tangible progression from beginning to betrayal, he can't do it in any linear, logical way. It's all scenes and themes and feelings revolving. Like a lost weekend, like the blanks in his memory of the night before, it's the missing bits that sing louder. And it's the same with these childhood flashes of memory—as if he's seeing many static snapshots flicked through very quickly. Absolute familiarity… yet with gaping chasms in the path of time, no continuity in the characters, there, and in the many other places he lived as a child.

This writing will bridge the gaps. He'll pour everything into writing the book: all the pain, the confusion, the paranoia, thoughts, fears, theories and the vagaries of emotion which swim through his head. He will impose order on the chaos, logic on the irrational, hope on fear. And maybe by doing so, he'll transcend the parochial whining of his mortal soul and heal not only himself but all those searching for something. His readers and followers can learn from his mistakes.

For what sort of a world is this? Where family counts for nothing and the kindest person he knows is his drug dealer? Where Isis is no goddess of fertility but a gang of death and destruction. Everywhere he looks, people are looking for something, the answer, the remedy. Cults, drugs, whores. Ashrams, travel, raves. All of it, Matty sees with dazzling clarity, misses the point. These are *symptoms* of a diseased society, not the answers to it. Humans have moved so far from their original form, they have lost sight of their essence, their purpose. They cling to archaic systems of belief, no longer pertinent to their situations. The twenty-first century is a bleak void in which individuals struggle to act as they think best, without reference to each other or any central ethical core. Like a blind species, humans shuffle around crashing into one another, politely excusing themselves, doing it again. It is only in a world such as this that brother would betray brother, that true love could be chucked away, that father and son should be separated by a gulf of resentment and blame. And does a sick world make such tragedies acceptable?

No, Matty answers himself, statesmanlike. It is precisely this state of drifting ice which makes our relationships with one another so crucial.

Never has humanity been more in need of guidance.

He gets up and regards humanity from his window. With a sudden rush from the pill, he scents hope rising from the drains below. His mind is racing now. He feels a roaring course through his body as the idea takes shape. He chooses life. He will flush away the fragments of his shattered life and begin again. The slate is clean here. The world is his for the taking. He, Matty Corani, will yet achieve something with this life and make his mark, reinvented. He will set muddled, damaged Earth the right way up again with his writing. The time is right for a new way of thinking.

He steps up on to the window ledge, feeling higher and higher. Enough! New beginnings! He will mend himself, a patchwork of impenetrable scar tissue!

His eye is caught by a look he knows. Fix, beneath a rakish hat, is walking down Wardour Street with a girl on his arm.

'Mate,' he calls out and Fix, who is in fact mates with a number of people in Soho, turns around.

'Coffee,' says Fix. 'That's what we're hunting. Come if you want.'

'I'll catch up with you. Just working on something.'

Fix looks at him curiously and Matty realises it's the 'work' element of that, that's struck him. But he can't leave the LP unplayed to the very end, to the point where the needle clicks up and the arm swings back to its base. Superstition, or something.

The tables outside Bar Italia are very close together. When the tables are full as they are now, it's difficult to navigate to the middle to join Fix and his latest groupie. At least four people stand up to let him through and the scrape of metal on pavement is heavy on his ear.

Fix is looking particularly feral this morning, bruised of eye, tangles of hair around his pretty, hollow face. Feral in Fix is no bad thing. It makes him look the part, the rock star. Certainly the beauty next to him looks unconcerned by the grime beneath his fingernails, his evident antipathy for baths.

'This,' says Fix, gesturing idly, 'is Sasha. She's a model.'

'I'm actually an actress,' she says quickly. 'Modelling's so shallow. I'm just doing it because I can really. Just picking up a bit of cash before I go to Hollywood.'

'Nice to meet you, Sasha.' Matty thinks he recognises her from a billboard or a shop window or something. She's public school like him. No question. But her mockney accent would convince a less keen critic.

'I'm Matty.' A pause. 'I'm a writer,' he continues with an air of enigma.

A waiter calls across to take their order, one Matty feels compelled to change to a triple espresso in honour of his new gruff, artistic identity. He will speak frequently of his life as 'a Creative' now.

'Oh cool,' says Sasha. 'I love to read. Where can I buy your stuff?'

'Uh it's not out yet.'

'What kind of stuff is it?'

'Yeah,' says Fix, 'what kind of stuff?'

Matty shifts uncomfortably. 'It's sort of a life story.'

'An autobiography? Wow, you must really have lived if you can write your memoirs at—how old are you, twenty-five, twenty-six?'

'Twenty-one, actually.'

Is she being sarcastic or is she not? He decides not. She's so chippy about being seen as vapid, she's trying to impress Fix with some sort of literary depth.

Fix is unlikely to be impressed by literary depth.

'No,' he says, 'it's more objective than that. It's more like a novel.'

'Oh I see,' she says. Her puzzled expression suggests that she does not.

He waits for it.

It comes. 'I'm clearly being really stupid, yeah, but how is the story of your life told by you not subjective?' she asks, flicking her blonde hair over to the right to make way for the incoming coffees.

'Well it's like this,' he says, summoning up his powers of bullshit, honed by unprepared philosophy seminars. 'All writing's a little bit subjective, sure. So I draw on my life for inspiration but within my life is a whole load of imagination too. At least half my life is lived through potential dream scenarios—to me those are as real as me sitting here with you. So it's a sort of exploration of my imaginary life as well as my real one with all the characters and situations they both involve.

'And you know what?' he adds as an inspired afterthought, 'Do you remember how huge things seemed when you were little—how cities and tables and humans towered over you and everything was wondrous? Your perspective changes as you grow up, things equalise with you, then suddenly you're bigger than it, the magic goes, you learn to look for amazement and beauty in the little features, you're not just awed by the enormity of the big, wide world around you…'

He's aware that Fix and Sasha are waiting for him to stop talking.

'I'm just saying that sometimes you need the unobjective writing with all its flights of fancy to tell the whole story. And to find your way back to wonder.'

Fix flicks him an amused smirk.

But Sasha's sold. 'We're all in the gutter,' she says with the dreamy look of a luvvy acting a poet, 'but some of us are looking up at the stars.'

And just like that, the conversation turns and the pressure is off.

Why is it so hard to chat with others, just to feel like he's not the last member of some obscure alien race trying to communicate?

It's probably, sir, because you're too busy analysing every last excruciating detail. The Sommelier has crept back in.

'And talking to you.'

Well, quite, sir. It's difficult to connect with others if you're always yabbering on with figments of your imagination.

'MATTY?'

Fix is looking at him with some intent.

'Yes.'

Because the answer is always 'Yes'. Isn't it?

V

The answer is not always 'Yes'.

Matty has little idea how he got home but he clearly did. The Cuban music's playing again. Whatever's beneath him is hard and he can smell the sweet burnt something of, of smoked crack? No, it's more bleachy than that.

Must he open his eyes?

So this is your life now, snorts his father in some remote part of his aching brain. *Yes, ambassador, he is indeed a son of whom one can be proud.*

What were you thinking, baby? A lovely face appears, a strange amalgam of Tera and his mother as she looks in his photograph, Viking-haired and icy-eyed. The slight mental kindness makes him want to cry. *You can't keep doing this to yourself.*

The music's so soft and incongruous he suddenly wants to laugh, lying here in his own dirt, a million miles from this man in the song offering some beautiful Cuban girl flowers. No gardenias here, man. Chance of life sprouting in this room's about as slim as him feeling better when he sits up.

He sits up. Reels with some sort of acid upsurge in his throat and nostrils.

That is IT. That's enough. Let's draw the line here, old boy.

The Mental Master has spoken. His authority is usually reassuring at times like this but today it throws Matty off course, the term of affection reminding him of a Korean film in which, he is now certain, a man is compelled for some reason to cut off his own tongue. Like in the stories he was given as a child. There was one where an evil barber cut the tongues out of naughty, talkative children. He kept them in a jar in the shop window, writhing around like so many fat grey slugs. And the parents never twigged. They thought this barber was brilliant. They didn't notice that their children came home from their short back and sides tongueless. For fuck's sake.

He tries to bring himself back to the music. He feels in his pocket for the photograph of his mother. All's well that ends well. He made it home safely one way or another.

But he's dreaming if he thinks he's escaped the Jitterer. It's the Jitterer who lingers darkly beneath the surface, always aware of the full horror of the situation. And all its horrific potential. The promise of the Jitterer is there even in the first sip of a night out.

Matty can feel him about to blaze on to the mental scene and sure enough, lo and behold, he screams in with a cold wind of shaky hand and shivery limb. Panic drenches him. *What did you do? What did you say? Where did you go?* He can't really remember anything beyond Fix and that quite annoying girl and someone else coming along and, at some point, being in another place, being kind of out of it... then shots of Soho lights, Soho streets... are these memories of last night or just from his photo album of wrecked days and nights of the past few years?

It's the Jitterer who clocks the searing pain that shoots through Matty's abdomen as he shuffles around the room. It's the Jitterer who won't let him look himself in the eye in the fragmented mirror above the basin. It's the Jitterer who sees blood where his floor served as a pillow and more bills on the mat where a day ago lay Katya's cash.

The stage is set for the Barrister. He can argue his way out of anything. *Actually,* the Barrister says, *actually... think about this... it's a good thing you went out, exorcised all your vices at once, got them out of the system... And you were celebrating, man. You'd just found your novel idea! You're on your way!*

51

The Barrister always becomes more pally, more jubilant and self-congratulatory as he warms to his theme. He doesn't sound like any barrister Matty's ever heard. He likes him much more than his own lawyer, the indefatigable Squales, who's helping him in his upcoming trial for selling skunk as a student.

The Jitterer, fortunately, is easily calmed by the Barrister. The Mental Master respects the Barrister. Matty respects the Master. He creates mental harmony by harnessing the other two. And as Fernando Pessoa says, 'In the vast colony of our being there are many different kinds of people, all thinking and feeling differently.'[†] The trick is divide and rule... it's a martial art.

It would be foolish, says the Mental Master, with authority, *to worry too much about this. No harm done. You've over-stimulated your nervous system, that's all. Let's just concentrate on getting you healthy again, shall we?*

Silly boy, slap on the wrist!

The Barrister has just become incredibly camp. It makes Matty uncomfortable.

His attention is caught by a drawing on the floor. *Did you draw that? What is it? It's terribly good.*

Think! What must you do to make yourself feel better?

Whatever strain of thought constitutes his mental make-up, it is to his body as a mother is to a crying baby. His body whines and he tries to guess what ailment is troubling it this time—is he hungry, perhaps, or will a cigarette pacify it? Is this anxiety linked to withdrawal or is it a symptom of hypochondria? Is he restless or horny? It seems to be a body unusually intolerant of discomfort. Matty is almost constantly offering it a bottle, a nappy change, a teat, floundering in a physical world one step removed from his mental controls.

[†]   Fernando Pessoa, *The Book of Disquiet,* p. 14.

He longs for some point of reference outside his own distorted self. A self so easily swayed by its own conflicting components is unable to stand firm in the drifts and volleys.

Well, says the Master, *isn't that the point of writing it down?*

Yes, for God's sake do something productive with your life, boy. Matty thinks he must hear more from his father in death than he ever did in life.

He lights a cigarette and inspects the drawing. Seems to be an attempt to communicate his last apocalyptic nightmare, a ghastly London where the Thames was blood and the east had overcome the west in some phenomenal world war, a prophecy his father had been keen on. 'Looking Up At The Gutter by Matthew Corani' is painted over it in red. Seems horribly familiar. Did he try to impress someone by quoting drunkenly at them?

You nasty little guttersnipe.

What an odd word to choose to immortalise in his title. And that—ha—nothing's more ephemeral than the pages people write. Suspend it beyond your grave for your children, their children, whatever. It's a physical certainty that Earth will die, the sun will burn out, the universe will end. And your silly little stories will be the first in the cosmic fire.

He turns the drawing over. 'I dedicate this book to Tera Martial,' he writes, 'the bitch who broke my heart'.

It doesn't feel quite right. He crosses it out. He can dedicate it later. Maybe by the time he's finished the story, he'll have forgiven her. Or he'll have manipulated her into someone who didn't ruin his life. Regressed her, maybe, to the woman she was before she seduced his brother. Such power. His book, his game. On paper, his father's just a chess piece, his brother just a vegetable and he, Matty, can be the healthy bonny child of Cuban frolics forever.

Looking Up At The Stars, then. He tries to summon the spirit of yesterday, the tiniest spark of excitement but it's as if the despair that hangs around him is made of clay. He's breathing it.

Tears on Tuesday. Suicide Tuesday. Tuesday Blues. Everyone knows the midweek after-effects of a weekend getting high. Monday's fine. He can't believe he's got away with it. Tuesday, the world caves in on him.

Except it's… what? Friday? Sunday? He really has no idea.

The urgency to be held, to hear just a word of kindness in this bleak abyss is not a new feeling. *Please help me. I'm trapped in this body. I don't belong here.*

Come on, Matty. You create your own reality with your thoughts, you know. Had it been Katya, self-help whore, who'd said this to him at his father's funeral?

She's due to come to London—he panics—at some stage, or so she keeps threatening in her letters. To check up on him, on the him of whom more funds will no doubt be divested for the upkeep of his encrypted brother.

What must it be like for Ben lying there all the time, comatose? Is he trapped in his own whirring thoughts unable to speak, to move a muscle?

Is he sorry?

So this is where his novel must start. Now he is starting to remember why he wanted to write it in the first place.

PRIVATE AND CONFIDENTIAL
DR J. SYKES

CONTENTS: MEC EMAILS AND LIFE-WRITING WITH MY COMMENTS AND QUESTIONS WRITTEN AS FOOTNOTES - FOR MY USE ONLY.

From: Matty Corani <matzcorani@gmail.com>
Subject: Life-writing (Looking Up At The Stars)
Date: 27 October 2015 11:19:58 GMT+01:00
To: Julia Sykes <juliasykes@mail.com>

Hey Julia, here's the first chapter. Matty

LOOKING UP AT THE STARS

Chapter 1

-It's a boy! came the shout of one of the la-dies-in-waiting.

My father, Darius, was a king and we lived in a palace. We were all about being really, really rich in a country where not many people were rich at all.[1] The shout came after some months of Mami growing rounder and rounder until the brown skin of her belly was so ripe I thought it might burst into flower. Mami is my mummy[2] but she's not the queen though because she was never married to the king.

There'd been a great deal of screaming for a very long time. My first thought had been that my father was trying to kill Mami.[3] But he'd gone out

---

[1]   GRANDIOSITY? NARCISSISTIC? OR IS FANTASY MORE BEARABLE WAY OF GETTING AT THE TRUTH? ASK NEXT SESSION (28/10) — AND FIND OUT ABOUT TITLE.
[2]   INNER CHILD? SEEMS TO MAKE M. FEEL SAFE RECALLING THESE TIMES DESPITE PRESENCE OF FATHER?
[3]   FATHER VIOLENT?

on kingly business. He was here now though, in the courtyard which overlooks the restless sea. He was pacing up and down the shady walkways, the dark amber of well-aged rum ever-replenished in his hand[4] and a nervy cigarette ever-lit.

-About bloody time,[5] said Darius and went to meet his new son.

-Come and meet your baby brother, Maxi sweet-heart. My nanny[6] scooped me up from where I was wobbling, eyes and ears on stalks.

-A real child, a child of our own,[7] *querida*, said my father to Leya,[8] looking hard at me.

-Don't be such a brute, said Mami, all sweaty with the effort of bringing this tiny human into the world. It had now taken over the screaming job, fists balled up in rage and old man's face wide open in protest. Maxi is as much our child as this one will be, she said, you know I think of him as my own.

In that moment, gazing up at the three of them, Darius the king leaning over Mami and this new thing, I knew I'd been usurped. Whatever I had to offer had been majorly trumped.[9]

-D'you think we could call him Benedicto after my grandfather, Leya asked Darius, tenderly holding her hand now. It means 'blessed'.

---

4   ALCOHOLIC? EXPLAIN ERRATIC MOOD?
5   CHARMER.
6   WHO IS M.'S PRIMARY CARER? 'MAMI' OR NANNY?
7   WHAT DID M. MEAN BY CAIN AND ABEL SITUATION? FATHER LIKE GOD? EXPLORE RELATIONSHIP WITH BROTHER.
8   THIS IS LUISA? 'LEYA' LIKE HIS FATHER'S NAME FOR HIS MOTHER, 'FREYA'. WHY THE NEED TO CHANGE NAMES LIKE THIS? DISTANCE?
9   AMBIVALENT ATTACHMENT. ENVY OF BROTHER.

I crawled out of the room and down the corridor. Toddling was too tiring after all the drama.

-We must all give Max plenty of attention too, otherwise we'll have terrible trouble with him, I could hear Leya telling the assembly.

I picked up the pace, feeling the pleasant burn on my knees. A hiding place, irritating and obscure. That was what I needed.

-Maxi, darling, come to Mami.

Dick seemed a decent shortening for my little brother's name and I rallied for it, yelling it at all times of the day and night.

-Awww he can't say Benedicto, the members of the royal household would say.

But maybe I just knew with the sixth sense[10] of children what he would become.

I'd been right about the usurping. I had to share everything. Benedicto, the blessed, seemed then to fulfil the prophecy of his name in almost every way. It was Dick, not I, who snuggled clamped around Leya's inviting bosom. I'd watch my father in amazement as I realised he was not made of stone. It just took Dick to excite him.[11]

It was Ruben[12] who could enchant my surly father with his huge, dark Cuban eyes and gurgly chuckle.

I can't remember the point at which jealousy turned to gratitude. Perhaps it was a gradual

---

[10] WHAT DOES HE MEAN BY THIS? IS IT LIKE DEAD FATHER VISITING HIM?
[11] HUMOUR AS DEFENCE?
[12] WHO'S RUBEN? BENEDICTO? WHY HAS M. CHANGED THIS NOW?

recognition that with Ruben doing all that baby charm stuff, I was free to do what I wanted.

And life was good. For me, life was sunshine and Leya's kindness and the energetic company of the royal staff if I wanted it. I began to play more by myself and in my own imagination. As I grew up, I learned only to seek out attention when I had something genuinely impressive to show. And always to Mami - impressing Darius was just too hard. And I was too awkward to amuse him for long; I could leave off that losing battle. Occasionally other children came to play, usually those of other very important, if not royal, families. Occasionally one of Leya's myriad Cuban cousins came for the afternoon. These afternoons were never much of a success.

I preferred the unconditional adoration[13] of my little brother to the demands of my peers. I could control Ruben.[14] It was a fun game to see his reactions. Poke him and he cried; tickle him and he burbled with delight. Such power, such manipulation![15] But children my own age were of less interest to me. Their motivations were more complex and I found it harder to gauge how to make them act in the way I required.

When one of Darius's diplomats brought his son, William, over to play one afternoon, I was able to identify the reason these episodes made me so cross. I did not, I realised then, want to spend the whole afternoon creating a tree house with someone who would then claim co-ownership of it, want equal praise for it and demand to spend his share of time in it. Far more gratifying would

---

[13] NARCISSISTIC PERSONALITY DISORDER?
[14] TALK ABOUT CONTROL. SEEMS TO BE KEY ISSUE.
[15] STRONGLY POINTS TO NPD. ASK MORE QUESTIONS.

be to undertake such a project alone, to do it perfectly, no matter how much time it might take, how much preparation it might require nor how many times I might have to review its progress. And then, when it was complete, when it was the tree house which complied with all my wishes, desires and dreams,[16] then I would invite Leya and Ruben and the staff to view it, to praise it and, if they wanted, to play in it.

Thoughts like that ruined my afternoon with William and he never came over again.[17]

---

[16] PERFECTIONISM; OCD? WHOSE VERY HIGH STANDARDS ARE THESE? FATHER'S? OR M.'S OWN? ANXIETY PREVENTION OR SIMPLY PRIDE IN WORK?

[17] WHO ARE FRIENDS NOW?

Dr J. Sykes BACP (accred.)
Psychotherapist

Private Room
36 Harley Street
London W1G 9PG

Date:	Time:	Patient Initials:	Attendance:
Wednesday 28 October 2015	4pm	MEC	Y

Notes:

-M. clearer of eye today.

-Said had found writing generally a positive experience but fury and hurt at Ben's betrayal had grown worse.

-Said life-writing easier changing names, mythologising it a bit. Also wants to achieve something, not just use as therapy. Talked a bit about losing control. M. claimed to like it. Not sure that's true.

-Attachment issues raging, provoked by mother/father memories. M. presenting signs of NPD,[1] 'special' one minute (e.g. writing), full of self-loathing the next,[2] envy of brother. Mother, Leya, Nanny, Tera (co-dependency?) all left him. Trust a problem. Katya really so dreadful or is this all part of it? Lack of empathy.

-Asked about father's drinking. 'No more than you or me' said initially.

-Spoke of father's hedonistic, womanising tendencies, manifestations of grief after mother died (or perhaps always – how would he know?). M. said not drinking himself for next two weeks. Wonder if there's a pattern of self-destructive behaviour here – father puer aeternus/Peter Pan complex too, M. showing identification with the aggressor?

---

[1] 'Narcissistic Personality Disorder: (patient) swings between seeing themselves as special and fearing they are worthless. They may act as if they have an inflated sense of their own importance and show an intense need for other people to look up to them.' (NHS.uk).

[2] 'There is an arrogant attitude toward other people due to both an inferiority complex and false feelings of superiority... Generally great difficulty is experienced in adaptation to the social situation and, in some cases, there is a kind of false individualism, namely that, being something special one has no need to adapt, for that would be impossible for such a hidden genius, and so on.' Marie-Louise von Franz, The Problem of the Puer Aeternus, (p. 7-8.)

-Talked about relations in lead-up to what he calls 'The Day of Discovery' ie car crash – more religious overtones (though I can't place this as a reference). Says he and Tera were happy, Ben busy. No signs of anything wrong.

-M. has names for voices/motivating forces within him – the Jitterer, the Barrister, etc. These are conflicting elements of his personality. M. said: Plato divides psyche into three parts – reason, spirit and appetite. A soul is healthiest and happiest when reason rules, keeping the other two in check. But makes me think more of Freud – id, ego and superego. Or are they archetypes? Primordial elements of the psyche and part of our collective unconscious.

-Concerned with what makes a good person – carries burden of guilt. Explained Aristotle's function argument to me – a thing's essence can be defined in terms of its function: e.g. the function/essence of a knife is cutting. A good knife is one that cuts well. M. v. worried about what makes a good human?

-Talked about managing PTSD. Mindfulness/meditation.

-More writing set. Next session 3.11.

VI

Idly searching the internet for the name 'Ruben', Matty feels a grim satisfaction when it turns out to mean, 'Behold, a son!' in four different languages including Hebrew and Spanish. As if his parents had discounted the one they already had.

One week into this new and wholesome regime and Matty is feeling purged, pure, itchy to undo this potential redemption before it takes up permanent residence in his psyche. The trouble with abandoning bad habits is the new sense of guilt when one invariably returns to them. Even the simplest vice must be newly adorned with the unpleasant recognition that this is not the only option, is certainly not the best one.

Matty thinks this is because during these abstinent periods when the Jitterer looms large, he expends all his energy building up the Personal Trainer: *You're doing so well*—and—*Come on, you've done forty-eight hours without polluting your body with mind-altering chemicals*—and—*Quitters are winners!*

This rambunctious creature he has created to bark orders and congratulations at him is hard to dismiss once he is *in situ*. But when the Jitterer's in retreat, the Personal Trainer loses all conviction. When temptation arises, the silver-tongued Barrister makes the Personal Trainer appear brutish and crude. It becomes apparent that the Trainer is at heart a thug; how could he begin to understand Matty's fragile artistic temperament? Nevertheless, his weak and desirous side is never quite comfortably free from him. Not until a meaningful amount of drugs have gagged him.

Time is an expanding circle.

Every minute feels like ten.

The clock grins and ticks backwards.

Four hours until his solitude is broken by Dr Psycho. He'll go out. He'll go and see his blessed brother in Marylebone on his way. It'll help him remember his childhood. It's research. *Many drugs in hospitals.*

Matty! The Personal Trainer has an Australian accent today. *Mate! What are you thinking! No pain, no gai—*

Go fuck yourself.

He rakes a hand through his dusty bronze hair, noticing how wild it has grown again. He can see its tawniness creeping past his shoulder from the corner of his eye. It's a mystery to him that the same girl could stroke his brazen mane with such adoration and yet go off with Ben, with his smart, dark short back and sides. It was barely hair at all, frankly.

He walks through Soho, dull grey and urban by daylight, towards the Princess Grace Hospital, Marylebone, where Katya insists Ben be treated. It's an expensive business keeping a dead man alive, privately.

Even now, in his coma, Ben is immaculately tonsured and clipped. The hospital is overwhelmingly white. A blank void for people whose lives hang in limbo. When Matty approaches Ben's room, the nurses hanging around reception scuttle nervously for security but Matty holds up his hands. The pacifist.

'I just want to see him,' he says. 'I'm not going to cause any trouble.'

It may well be the first time he's entered the hospital with anything other than trouble at the front of his mind. He is sober and looking for answers.

Compassion springs up but it must be crushed. It's just a natural physiological response to a fellow human's suffering. Inappropriate here. Ben is less than human, he reminds himself. And not so blessed now, it would seem.

Wires coil from every orifice, a technicolour fiesta mocking the blank white bed, the blank white Ben. His face, static for once, looks different unanimated. Almost a different man without cheeks lifted by smiling and eyes open, glinting with whatever thought leaps behind them. It's the first time Matty has been calm enough to actually see Ben. He takes in the unmarked body, the perfectly attached limbs, the gashless head—and thinks of Tera: mangled, mutilated.

He could have forgiven her. Tera was half of him. He was sewn into her on a cellular level. Brothers can make their own way. He looks down at Ben, so peaceful, so utterly oblivious to the misery he's left behind and he thinks, why the fuck didn't you die instead? He'll never forgive him.

He sits down slowly on the bed, feeling the misery of his unselfmedicated state of mind settle like snow on all his systems. A nurse is hovering in the corner, a paragon of private deportment. Matty's not given up on his mission to move Ben on to National Health. What difference would it make to him?

More than you think, mate.

Matty nearly falls off the bed in shock.

Oh what? You think you can stumble in here out of your skull and hurl abuse at me week after week and I'll just take it lying down?

Matty looks wildly round at the nurse. She looks back, slightly wary.

Sleeping Beauty remains in position, packed away for storage.

Matty leans in very close to Ben's ear and whispers, 'Can you hear me?'

But Ben doesn't reply this time.

'Um, excuse me,' he says to the nurse. 'Have there been any signs of recovery at all?'

'Nothing, so far as I know. Perhaps you'd like to speak to the doctor?'

He'd quite like to speak to the nurse, he realises, now he takes a closer look. 'Speak', of course, being defined in the loosest possible terms. He has a sudden image of taking her from behind in the meds cupboard. She'd be clinical but generous. Kind but firm. He's had nurses before; they're great, they really are. Open to all kinds of trippy kinkiness and a little bit vulnerable, what with all the tiredness. But closed to the involuntary horrors of the human body and bossily maternal. Best of all, she looks nothing like Tera. She's a small, bouncy thing; pretty, not violently beautiful.

You treat women like shit. Let her be.

Matty looks sharply back at Ben.

'Now hang the fuck on—I hardly think you're in a position to moralise.'

The noise of his voice draws more nurses to the open door of Ben's room. Matty is quiet in the interest of finding out what's going on. He talks his face into numbness.

'I would like to speak to the doctor if that's possible,' he says. The cloud outside the door dissipates to let the foxy one trot through to set this up. He can hear her heels clip the corridor over and over with their peculiar unechoing beat. Matty is alone with his brother, his mind unclouded by narcotics for the first time since the crash.

He rallies himself. Ben wanted to be a barrister; he's strong with words. You, then be stronger. Stay strong.

How easily you put down our long friendship.

Matty closes his eyes and lays his head on Ben's wasted chest, breathing in tandem with the ventilator. In, out, in, out, in, out. Little molecules of Tera sprinkle on his skin.

'I'm sorry,' he begins to say but before he can, he realises in terror that he's let his guard down. In a world where everyone's against him this is unwise. Ben's off. It's time to leave.

Have you any idea what it's like in here, in the shell of my own head fizzing with live wires trapped in a corpse? I thought it was purgatory at first, some sort of torture. I live a whole life in here. In my mind I've housed people in a universe of new galaxies

65

and solar systems. I've had to trick myself into creating rooms of love and friendship, happiness, dreams, children, brotherhood…

Is an eyelid flickering? No, there's nothing.

Matty, it's like being buried alive. You know they keep finding fingerprints on the roofs of coffins? People would be certified, dead, funeralled, mourned, whatever, then they'd wake up six-feet under clawing at the wooden box containing them! Medicine knows fuck all, mate. The clever ones know the limitations of humans to know anything.

'You slept with my girl!'

It sounds facile up against purgatory.

Oh for Christ's sake, Matty, why couldn't you see it coming? She wasn't yours to lose. I was doing you a favour.

He needs to be away from here. The digital display on Ben's life-support machine is flashing. Hurts his eyes. He is walking very quickly out of the door, down the endless sports-hall-like corridors with their stripy lines and their *Alice in Wonderland* sense of geography. Exit? Exit? Exit?

Ben's yelling down the corridor,

You thought love was some organ-throbbing, pulsing gut union, liver and lover as one. You suffocated her. If it hadn't been me, it would have been somebody else…

The voice tails off as Matty pushes through the revolving doors to exit the hospital, fumbles for a cigarette and walks at speed down the street. He inhales furiously and it's as if the smoke smothers the sound in his head and he can see straight again.

It's not a healthy place to be, that hospital. It's not good for him.

Should he, he wonders, ditch Dr Psycho? Should he, perhaps, give Fix a call instead? It's Tuesday afternoon. If he goes to see Fix now, that'll blow out the rest of the week. And besides, Fix is becoming increasingly tight about the money he owes him.

And besides, the Aussie Personal Trainer pops up helpfully, *you're a changed man! Look, there's a juice bar. What you need, dude, is a spinach and ginger juice. A Spinger! Nothing like it, mate.*

Matty has a sudden yearning for easy company, for a choice of company. Anything but his own noise. Truth is, it's been so long since he's made contact with any of his university friends that the process would require just too much effort.

But this detachment is what he wants, isn't it? Freedom from having to explain, having to justify himself, from being answerable and found lacking. He has a sudden inner plummet as he remembers the wedding last year of his former school pal, Guy. Or rather, half-remembers. What he does remember clearly is that nobody had found his impromptu speech about *Gay* witty or endearing. Also that the decision to invite elderly women of the congregation to play a round or two of 'Cock or Ball' had not been well-received.

He trudges on to Harley Street in time for his appointment with Julia Sykes, despite the fact that he has nothing to show for himself. His hands are empty of novelly masterpiece. Sobriety really isn't good for his creativity, he reflects.

Transcription: EXTRACT FROM CONVERSATION BETWEEN DR J. SYKES, BACP (ACCRED.) AND MATTHEW CORANI

JS: SO, JUST TO BE CLEAR, YOU THINK YOU HEARD YOUR BROTHER SPEAKING TO YOU?

MC: NO. I DON'T 'THINK' I HEARD HIM. I ACTUALLY HEARD HIM. THAT IS FACT.

JS: BUT HE DID NOT AT ANY POINT OPEN HIS MOUTH OR EMERGE FROM THE COMA HE'S BEEN IN SINCE THE CAR ACCIDENT.

MC: YES, I KNOW IT SOUNDS STRANGE...

JS: AND DID IT SEEM STRANGE TO YOU AT THE TIME?

MC: YES, BUT IN A GOOD WAY. IT WAS NICE TO HEAR HIS VOICE, FOR ONE THING. I MISS HIM, DESPITE WHAT HE DID. BUT IT WAS ALSO NICE TO HEAR THAT HE'S BEING PUNISHED. HE KNOWS EVERYTHING IN THERE, HEARS EVERYTHING — BUT HE'S TRAPPED, LIKE A BRAIN IN A VAT.

JS: HOW DO YOU THINK HE MANAGED TO COMMUNICATE WITH YOU?

MC: I DON'T KNOW. THERE'S A LOT OF STUFF IN THE WORLD THAT'S INEXPLICABLE, DOESN'T MEAN IT'S NOT REAL.

JS: HAVE YOU BEEN SLEEPING ANY BETTER WITH THE DETOX?

MC: WHY? DO YOU THINK I'M LOSING IT?

JS: NO. BUT SOMETIMES LACK OF SLEEP CAN MAKE US SEE OR HEAR THINGS THAT AREN'T THERE.

MC: THIS WAS AS REAL AS YOU TALKING TO ME NOW IS REAL. I LIKE YOUR HAIRCUT.

VII

Another week later and the flat is bare and soulless.

Is this all there is? All day? All evening and, given that he probably won't be able to sleep, all night too? Unbroken time stretches insufferably before him.

He must do something.

He unearths Chapter 1 of *Looking Up At The Stars* on his laptop. His heart sinks still further as he reads his own dumb hand at work.

He wonders if perhaps some elusive little speck of something or other might have escaped the manic spring clean which ushered in the Age of Detox two weeks ago. But little flickers of worry prickle whichever way he looks—an unopened gas bill before the door, a stain of red beneath the sink where he vomited this morning (red wine?). But he has not drunk for a while now. *Blood?* His heart speeds beneath his T-shirt as the walls close in and the Jitterer can be contained no longer.

He could really do with a drink.

Just as he's preparing to argue with himself, the answer rushes at him. The Barrister is in the house.

He should get a bar job! Some form of income would free him from the tyranny of Katya. And it would put him in touch with people—with life. It would force him to say words out loud to people who weren't Fix or his brain-dead brother. Yes, this is an excellent idea. He might even pick up a girl or two.

With renewed energy, he doffs an imaginary cap to the Barrister and steps purposefully out into Soho. The light hangs grey, the air temperatureless and for a moment he cannot remember whether it is summer or winter.

He heads straight to The Cock and Bull. Good to lay new memories to replace his first date with Tera.

As he has with songs which remind him of her, so he must inure himself to places which bring it all back.

The manager's not there, but the girl behind the bar tells him that yes, they are looking for someone. She is slight and Slavic, with bleached-blonde hair raked into dreadlocks and a great many silver studs and rings poking out of various punctures. Matty would be the last person to judge a book by its cover, but he takes her appearance as sign of a kindred spirit. He'd be surprised if he couldn't tell exactly how she spent her weekends.

'Why don't you come back at six?' she suggests. 'John's always here then to check the stock.'

Well Matty's here now. It's already three. He might as well wait.

He orders a lager and takes it over to a seat by the window. Then he remembers that beer makes him feel woolly when he's not drunk for a while, so he orders a double whisky too, to sharpen him up for his meeting with John. 'Have one on me, sweetheart,' he tells the barmaid, brandishing his debit card. She happily does so but does not initiate any kind of introduction.

'I'm Felix,' he says, though he is not really sure why. He feels a little foolish passing over the card, evidence that his name is, in fact, Matthew, but she does not seem to notice.

'Silja,' she replies with a wary smile.

The whisky rumbles through him, a miniature sun blazing a trail of light and warmth. Almost instantly his disparate thoughts unify into one coherent train. Maybe his book's not that awful. Suddenly he can begin to see positive 'what-ifs' creeping out of the woodwork. He wants to unfold their trails. He smiles winningly at the barmaid, who is fiddling with her phone, and asks whether she happens to have any scrap paper behind the bar.

She's surprisingly helpful and hands some straight over. It is as if she has a stash of A4 on her at all times precisely for this purpose. He sits down again and writes.

LOOKING UP AT THE STARS
Chapter 2

Above all it was the heavy sun I loved. Of course, growing up in Cuba I didn't know anything else but now I realise it was an electric light bulb in my body, a troop of fireflies warming pliant young muscles and making the world glow for me. It was the September after I'd celebrated my seventh birthday. Ruben was five. The weight of maturity lay heavily upon me, the trailblazer, as I set off in the back of the black Chevy, an unaccompanied minor on my way to Havana airport.

I'd tried to explain to Ruben, as Leya had explained to me, exactly what I was to expect, what fun it will be, why it must be so. All little boys should go to school and England was full of funner, better places than could be found near our Cuban palace.

The dry cold of the air-con braced me as we drove, the chauffeur in silent reverence for my big adventure. It was important that I was alone. Such things were too grown-up for Ruben. It was the beginning of a new phase in my life. My trunk was packed full of smart new clothes and I would, Leya had said, be back in Havana before I knew it, in time to celebrate Christmas. She'd said I'd be able to write home from Rockwell House and I was already planning my first letter full of imagined boasts to Ruben. She'd said you play games literally *all* the time and eat 'tuck' and have outings to palaces of other very important people, like the queen.

-I'll send you parcels every week, she'd said.
-I'll make you toys to play with, Ruben had said.

Matty swallows the last of his lager and stares at what he has written. He sees himself peering out of that aeroplane on to Havanan tarmac, undersized frame dwarfed by its seat, sees himself seeing Leya and Cuba for the last time. This omniscient narrator, this older Matty, knows that the next time his younger self boards an aeroplane, it will indeed be in time for Christmas, but the aeroplane will be routed for Beijing and his family will be reduced to three again.

The fury attacks him afresh, does not know where to direct itself as, voyeur, he sees the small boy sent across seas to endure the torment of an English boarding school. Sandwiched like a French-calf-to-the-slaughter with others collected from the ambassadorial globe, school was a catalogue of misery.

He had been unpopular at Rockwell House from the outset. The insular tendencies which had been accepted, even encouraged, in Cuba marked him as the school outsider. He had no problems with understanding or completing the work, but in it he'd found a way of occupying and thereby losing himself, of removing himself from the company which surrounded him. Team activities simply did not appeal. This was due to a mixture of incompetence—he found the idea of inadequacy unbearable—and a fierce terror of sharing the kudos of accomplishment.

Although these traits had undoubtedly become more pronounced as he grew older, Matty could identify the seeds of his character as firmly sown by the age of seven. One which continued to dog him was an inability to sieve his thought processes before they reached his mouth. Matty spent a large proportion of his formative years regretting the exit from his person of things which should never have been said. He had always, however, been fascinated by the chains of events they sparked off, watching the trail of cause and effect unfold, scrabbling their way to cataclysmic consequences.

Matty's memory of early childhood is divided neatly into the white of Cuba and the black of school—and the even bleaker black of Beijing. And all of it coloured by envy of Ben. For all Ben's blessings the one which still grated was that his father allowed him to stay in China, to go to school there, while Matty was sent into exile in England.

He orders another pint, another whisky, another drink for Silja who is notably more friendly this time.

Returns to base. Thinks about writing; just as valuable a pursuit as the actual writing. More, perhaps.

Matty had been twelve when Ben joined him on the much-dreaded Beijing-London flight. Why, he wonders even now, had Ben been given five years' grace? Had Ben perhaps slotted more perfectly into life in Beijing than Matty had in Havana? Beijing had scarcely been deemed safe enough for Matty to return for his summer holidays. Yet Ben had been allowed to remain there with his father, not shipped off, evacuated, dumped in an alien system. Matty remembers the couple of photos slotted into the grooves in the wooden bottom of the bunk bed above him. Cuba, palm trees, Leya, sea smiled down upon him, all in varying shades of blue and green. None of them dated beyond 2001. He doesn't have any of them now, just the stolen image of his real mother.

Whatever worries Matty had about Ben joining him, and like most worries in Matty's world they were consuming, were dispelled magnificently within a couple of weeks of the first winter term. A smile personified, Ben charmed all who encountered him. Even those who had planned to give him hell, related to Matty as he was, were charmed, as Ben set about wooing the black-market customers of the older years with his proliferation of Chinese fakes, fags and fornication mags. Whatever social intuition Matty lacked, Ben had gained in triple portions. Magnetic, he offered new heights of daring to the boys he met; incandescently diverting, teachers and authority were hypnotised into unprecedented states of lightheartedness and distraction. Matty's school life, until this point unremittingly grim, met some respite when Ben arrived. He could not quite bring himself to assert that his world had improved. He could, however, acknowledge that the elements which had bullied, afflicted, plagued and seemed set to destroy him for the past six years, had receded. He was free, finally, to do as he pleased.

Does anyone really know what makes them happy before they have ridden the lows and highs of experience? Matty did not, but he was certain of the circumstances in which such happiness might best be achieved. The solitude that Ben's presence enabled him to acquire was key to all of it. For that, as in Cuba, Ben was indispensable.

The relationship between the two brothers was similar, Matty thinks now, to that between a schizophrenic and his medication. Dependency, denial and defiance intermingled with rapid and alarming irregularity. The journey home, wherever home happened to be that year, reasserted the hierarchy.

Matty hated China. The icy needles of Beijing-chill cut into him with an unanticipated venom as he got off the plane; 'home' again, still half-expecting a blast of Cuban humidity, though he knew by this point that he was heading east, not west. December was drawing the year to a close and Matty had never experienced such savagery of snow and searing cold. All the eagerly anticipated elements of home, charted nightly in a plaintive diary and letters to Leya, were melted and expelled in this strange land of impenetrable mystery. Serene landscape, frenetic people. Given the run of a courtyard house and the attention of several nursemaids, Matty felt equally the pain of loss and stifling claustrophobia. He saw his father, Daniel, the British ambassador, on only three occasions for the duration of that particular winter holiday. He picks up his pen again.

The most memorable occasion I saw my father was on Christmas Day, when Ruben and I were brought in to the drawing room before a selection of very important men and their wives. The air in this room was suffocating with cigar smoke. The air outside wasn't much better, painful with bitter cold.

King Darius must have been very drunk indeed; I hadn't really noticed that he drank a lot until we came to China. I suppose you only notice these things when there are contrasting situations, like my stint in a school where there were male adults who weren't all surgically attached to a glass of rum by day and night.

Here in Beijing, away from Leya's gentle protection, the bottle was allowed to take hold; my father was lonely, I suppose, and surrounded by men for whom booze was the only redeeming feature of an unelected life.

Men barked their views on communism, intoxicated vocal chords reverberating with competitive intensity. To one corner, the women subtly extricated themselves to discuss the many benefits of Chinese tailors and craftsmen. Brandy was making Darius morose. I knew the warning signs.

He was peering at me and Ruben through the smudged glass of his brandy balloon.

Darius smiled slowly. Ahaaa, he said. He placed his glass carefully on an imaginary tray as a nearby member of staff swept in to catch it and clapped his hands together, commanding the attention of the room. Ladies, gentlemen, he said, my sons: Maxi and Ruben.

I shuffled awkwardly, not sure what was expected of me but not liking the way this was going. Ruben was beginning to approach, naturally more gregarious, more trusting. Possibly more stupid.

And now Darius was laughing, a sound that might feasibly come out of a crocodile's splayed jaws, laying a heavy hand on Ruben's shoulder, some considerable distance beneath his own.

-Dear God man, he said, turning to me, why in hell are you dressed like a girl?

Matty squirms in embarrassment at the memory. Remembers too some faceless man laying a warning hand on his father's arm. 'Come on, old boy—lay off the little chap,' he says, or some similar mindless platitude. God, they must have been fascinated by Daniel, drunkard appearing from nowhere, complete with a roving eye for the ladies and two sons from conspicuously different origins.

At the age of seven Matty was as concerned as he is now with matters of gender and sexual orientation. They are of less than no importance. He knows what he is and if that veers towards omnivorous, that is fine. He has come to see that what is beautiful in a girl can, upon occasion, be similarly compelling in a boy. Any Freudian inferences traced back to this time in Matty's childhood would be misguided. Looking back, he cannot see much feminine about his Chinese robe anyway. Ben had been dressed in almost identical attire, but because his centre of gravity was nearer the ground the skirted bottom fell in pleats which resembled loose trousers, a miniature version of Thai fisherman's trousers. Then again, Ben had not been tarred with responsibility for the death of his father's wife.

-I'm glad she's dead. She could never have stood such a disappointment for a son.

That's what he said. In front of all those people. Then he just turned away and plucked a conversation out of the air with the nearest red-faced diplomat as if nothing had ever happened.

I ran and ran but in the maze of the courtyard house I ran nowhere. Ruben came to look for me, his hand on my shoulder, tacit kindness, the first I'd experienced since Leya's farewell, since the loss of Cuba, the onslaught of hostility at school. Ruben crouched, unconditional embrace stretched over and around my back, and I realised that Ruben too must feel the loss of a mother, of a home. It was the beginning of an alliance. When I returned to school after that first Christmas, it was the wrench of leaving Ruben that had been difficult to bear.

He still feels that. It's what keeps drawing him back to his brother's bedside. Even when he looks down with revulsion upon the lifeless quasi-corpse which stole Tera, which killed her, some deep, unfathomable part of him is calling out for Ben—the Ben he grew up knowing, not this one. He can feel the betrayal in his heart, but he cannot retrain his body to respond in any other way than it does, crippled by habit.

Matty feels a hand lightly touch his shoulder. It's the pretty barmaid. 'Hey,' she says, 'you look kind of occupied but I could really do with a hand if you fancy a trial run behind the bar tonight. Can you make a cocktail? It's going to get even busier soon and the guy who takes the six o'clock shift with me has just called in sick.'

'Uh, yes, sure,' Matty replies. What a very successful day. Had he maintained his silly sobriety kick none of this, not the book, not the job, not this girl, would have transpired.

'Oh thanks.' She gives a grateful little sigh. 'That's really great of you. And it could work out well, you know—if John comes in and sees his pub full of punters and you keeping the bar queues happy and under control, he's bound to give you the job.'

Matty can't think of anywhere he'd rather spend this Tuesday night.

Dr J. Sykes BACP (accred.)
Psychotherapist

Private Room
36 Harley Street
London W1G 9PG

Date:	Time:	Patient Initials:	Attendance:
Tuesday 10 November 2015	5pm	MEC	DNA

Notes:

In M.'s absence (avoidant behaviour — worried about being examined too closely? Or just scatty?) read more from David J. Wallin, Attachment in Psychotherapy: 'Let's start with "dissociation" a term that has two distinct meanings. It refers to "disintegration" of various kinds, including the self-protective splitting off of an unbearable state of mind (in which, for example, one's father has murdered one's mother) from other states of mind that are more tolerable and readily integrated with one's ongoing sense of self. Dissociation also refers to a defensively altered, trance-like state of consciousness.' (p. 247)

'The same altered state that keeps painful realities at bay also makes it impossible for those realities to be confronted effectively. The result is that unresolved patients live as if refusing to identify the smell of rising smoke in the basement... Moreover, dissociation as an altered state usually entails experiences of "leaving the body" which can have a number of very problematic consequences.' (p. 248)

And Galen Strawson, 'I Am Not a Story':

'But many of us aren't Narrative in this sense. We're naturally — deeply — non-Narrative. We're anti-Narrative by fundamental constitution. It's not just that the deliverances of memory are, for us, hopelessly piecemeal and disordered, even when we're trying to remember a temporally extended sequence of events. The point is more general. It concerns all parts of life, life's "great shambles," in the American novelist Henry James's expression. This seems a much better characterisation of the large-scale structure of human existence as we find it. Life simply never assumes a story-like shape for us. And neither, from a moral point of view, should it.' (p. 3)

VIII

'You lost me my job.' Husky. Female. A fingernail traces the lines of muscle which form a grid upon Matty's thin torso.

Where is he? This sense of confusion, this suspension of despair until he knows the situation, is familiar. He is reluctant to open his eyes. He forces his brain, dormant and lazy, to recall where he has been, what he has done. Futile. Stops short at cock and balls and oh God, some sort of bar-top jig. Fix. Fix was there. Fix and some beer and some bright lights and some coke, probably. Some sort of energetic movement, sure. But with a girl? *Think.*

'Fe-lix,' the voice is sing-song, the form of address odd. She sounds Russian, Polish perhaps.

Whoever it is has made herself at home with his body. Her naked legs are curled through his, but she has pulled herself up on to her elbow. She is observing him from this elevated position. It is the girl from The Cock and Bull. Silja. The name leaps back into his mind and with it a flood of new and nameless shapes and sounds. The roar of a club, the hiss of sex. Booze bottles shatter, pill bottles rattle. Wraps unwrapped and then there had been coke and, yes, almost certainly MDMA and—

'Are you hungry, Felix?'

Who the fuck is Felix?

He swallows, a bitter chemical tang at the back of his throat, and forces one eyelid open. She is not unbeautiful. She is not Tera. Gone are the days when he wakes to that. What does beauty have to do with it, anyway? Silja's eyes are grey, not blue. She is almost aggressively lean where Tera's body softened into curves. Her hair is silvery and her skin

80

flecked with studs. It is not good skin, he can see that now he is at such close quarters. But she is striking. It is her bones which make her so striking. His eye is drawn from cheekbone to collarbone, both too prominent. An illusion of ill health, yet they draw him.

'I could be. Where are we?'

'In your flat. Do you not recognise your own flat, Felix? Or have you broken into someone's house and pretended it's yours in order to impress me?'

Lucky. He's as good as home. He's in Fix's flat. And it's not a bed they're lying on, it's the floor.

Fix is not there though, that much is clear.

Why on earth did he tell her his name was Felix? He has no idea.

'Of course it's my flat, silly. Look, let's try and sleep a bit, shall we, and then we'll go out or… something…'

His voice becomes fainter with each syllable, reduced to a whisper as he trails off. Tiptoe, he begs her silently, around the precipice of my consciousness for as long as might be possible, please.

'Sure,' she says soothingly, stroking his hair. 'Do you want a line, though?'

Matty comes to as if she has hotwired his brain.

Reality does not have to launch its hellish siege of recrimination just yet.

He can sense a niggling something, just out of reach, just round the corner of his mental faculties—the reason he is not in his own flat, something to do with his…? *Don't think about it.*

After a chemical breakfast, meticulously arrayed by this small metallic girl, Matty is back in the moment, primed and ready for serendipity.

He thinks there must be some meaning in finding Silja in the very place where he spent his first day with Tera. Maybe this is a new dawn for him. Maybe he could love this girl. She seems more amusingly wry, more cool and flirty now. They're having fun, playing with Fix's decks and Matty's doing a passable impression of one who DJs from time to time. He's a happy-go-lucky kind of guy. Doesn't take things too seriously. At the same time he's aware of a tightening swell of excitement in his chest, anticipating what he has no idea. But it feels better than the pendulous apathy, better than the jittery panic by far. He's cruising on the surface of things, feeling things momentarily and unjadedly; childlike.

So when the real Fix comes back from God knows where with some mescaline, Matty is all for it.

When Silja expresses dissent, Fix says, 'But it's amazing! Honestly, I've done it and it's awesome. It'll expand your consciousness—like it did for Aldous Huxley—here, look, have you read this?'

Fix extracts *The Doors of Perception* from the bookshelf behind her head, flicks through it muttering something unintelligible, then reads, '"The urge to transcend self-conscious selfhood is, as I have said, a principal appetite of the soul." No, it's not that bit. Here. "To be shaken out of the ruts of ordinary perception, to be shown for a few timeless hours the outer and the inner world, not as they appear to an animal obsessed with survival or to a human being obsessed with words and notions, but as they are apprehended, directly and unconditionally, by Mind at Large—this is an experience of inestimable value to everyone and especially to the intellectual." Can't argue with that.'

Matty is suddenly far more interested in getting out of his head than into Silja.

For all her earlier bravado, she's looking a little tired and teary, suddenly talking about a bad ayahuasca experience, a fried friend in a nuthouse who took too much acid… So it goes.

'Go home, sweetie. Get some sleep,' says Fix.

'Okay,' she says, answering Fix but looking reproachfully at Matty, whereupon he realises it is his job to despatch her in a gentlemanly fashion.

He escorts her from Fix's flat, pausing just before the final door to pin her up against the wall and kiss her memorably. She's kittenish again as he sends her off with promises of phone calls and play dates.

Back to business.

'Because actually, this is the single best thing you could ever do for yourself as a writer, you know?' says Fix, strumming a guitar, when he returns. 'It's just going to unlock all those bits of your brain that take you to other worlds. It's going to show you the whole starry fucking firmament and everything beyond.'

'It's time to really focus on my writing, man. Like you and your music. This is going to be the making of me.'

Fix places the guitar against the wall and boils the kettle. Two mugs of brewed potion appear looking homely and nourishing. An evil steam floats from the top into the unwitting nostril.

Matty, thinking of the greater good, holds his nose and drinks.

'More tea, vicar?'

It tastes foul but Matty wants to ensure he does this properly. He holds out his mug, noticing it features a faded Daffy Duck on one side.

'It's not like acid. You can't take too much.'

'*Have* you had it before?'

'Probably.'

'I take it Sasha's off the scene, is she?'

'Certainly not, buddy. She's become one of my main crack whores.'

Fix's band is called, most recently, The Cracks, a name chosen primarily for pun capacity for its groupies. There are many, considering it is as yet unsigned. Matty knows they are there to hunt Fix, rather than for the 'thrash-melancholic harmonic charms' quoted on all their flyers. 'Quote' would imply some-one had once said it and indeed someone had. Fix.

'Is that all there is?' Matty asks. 'Do you think it's enough to have any effect?'

Fix looks at him with amusement. 'Ask me that tomorrow, man. You'll see. I've got some K to bring us down as well.'

Matty is sold. He feels the squirming in his stomach triple in strength, a pulse of compulsion beginning to heave.

But sometime later all he can feel is the coke beginning to wear off, the burden of being human returning.

'Nothing's happening,' he says.

'Be patient.' Fix replies. 'This is a spiritual experience so just relax. Let me be your shamanic guide. Or something.'

Fix, Matty knows, is open to a great many possibilities: aliens, ghosts, fourth dimensions, sixth senses… the list goes on.

'Anyway,' Fix goes on, 'it can take up to two hours to kick in. Have a beer.'

Matty likes the way Fix always sets his mind at rest. He's always taken care of him really. An excellent figure *in loco parentis*. Matty shivers back to the night in the cells, the one phone call he was allowed; Fix's majestic rescue and risk, high as a buzzard with forty grams of coke about his person, com-ing to bail him out.

They're true brothers, in this adventure together. There's usually a crowd of hangers-on milling around Fix's place, smoking dope or buying it, playing in the band or wanting to. They have no part to play in this sort of undertaking. Matty's mind is open and waiting.

'Are you seeing something?' he asks Fix some minutes later, when Fix appears to have developed a sudden fetish for the table leg.

'*It's just so intricate*,' he keeps saying. 'Look at it!'

But Matty is more interested in Fix's eyes, huge black holes pitted in a landscape of purest purple. The most perfect, most purple instance of purple he has ever seen. In its simplicity, its purpleness, he sees the very essence of what purple really is, the standard by which all purple things might be measured and found lacking. He cannot tear his eyes away.

'Look at this,' Fix is saying, but his voice sounds angular and distant and suddenly Matty finds himself sucked at speed into those purple eyes, through those black windows down, down deep into Fix's soul, falling and flailing like Alice down the rabbit hole.

He tries to take some control over his body but there is no hand to hold, no cartoon branch to clutch as he drifts from the cliff aloft on an airy, feathery levity. Sensation roars like a white-hot blast from the top of his head and his heart swells with the burden of omniscience, the shock of divinity around and within him.

He lands gently, cushioned in a fleshy bed. Peering cautiously around him, he sees Stonehenge and, beyond, flashes of a strawberry sky. He is, he realises, nestling in the lily pad of Fix's gum, in the place where a premolar once resided until a fight led to its untimely eviction.

Matty attempts to lever himself up so as to get a better look at the world beyond the enamel, but finds himself transfixed by the softly mutating cellular pattern of the flesh on the inside of Fix's lower lip. Like the purple of his eyes, the redness of this red, the geometric symmetry of its arrangement blazes with the power of perfection. This red is the essence of red, being and doing all that red should, by virtue of being red. What is the essence of a human, wonders Matty? What is the perfect human by whose standard we all fall short?

He realises with a shock, as he leans out over Fix's teeth, the rocks of dazzling whiteness, that he is seeing the real world for the very first time. In its jewel-like splendour and magnificence it would be too much for mortals to contend with. It would distract them from the mundane duty of perpetuating biological existence. Mescaline has removed these bodily safety nets, these veils, and allowed him to see what actually is outside ourselves, rather than the dumbed down version which is as much as we can cope with in our limited mortal bodies.

He never wants to go back.

But already he can feel the veils reinstating themselves, dulling the colours, halting the dance of the patterned curtains, removing him from Fix's mouth. He fights it, tells Fix he needs more time there. He eats what Fix holds out but this is different. If he can just be given enough time to see human reality, the definitive form of the human, then he will hold the key to all human understanding.

As space and time creep back to anchor him, he has one pervasive thought: the men of history who saw 'God' and were awed by the majesty, the brightness, the perfection, had seen the form of man, what man really is; what His essence is. Matty would go back, would seek it out and the knowledge of it would be his contribution in life. Then he would know the point of it all. Why we're here. What we're for. Right and wrong, good and bad. The universal truths of existence, so elusive, are all around him, just imperceptible until the veils were lifted.

The thought circles and circles growing in intensity until it is his whole mind. But something is at work on his body, newly returned to his consciousness. A woozy haze is dissolving the knots in his muscles, steadily unfocusing his gaze. He likes it. He wants more.

Fix is lying across the chair with his head and feet on the floor but Matty can see the little wrap of ketamine and does not need to disturb him. Ignoring the tiny spoon next to it, he shakes all the powder on to the smeared mirror lying prone on the kitchen table, crushes it and separates it into six neat lines, four of which he inhales in quick succession. He sinks back into the chair and almost immediately feels a creeping paralysis sneak up his right leg, then his left, up and up until even his jaw is rigid. He tries to speak, but can say nothing. Just as panic is beginning to radiate its waves, his brain lurches backwards and the rock at the front of the cave is rolled away, letting the blinding sunshine stream in.

Matty is Coleridge, smoking his way to visions of exotic beauty. He is Plato, fighting off imposters of the truth, seeking the clarity of what really exists beyond the limited filters of human perception. Then, without warning, he is lying beneath Tera in his bed, in the flat they had shared. He cries out at the unexpected pain of coming home. He looks to his left. The bed segues into sand, its pale camouflage illuminating his father outstretched in post-coital bliss, his mother curled foetus-like in the crook beneath his arm. He looks to his right. The edges of the bed shimmer into Ben's hospital bed, Silja bound to him by the various wires and tubes of drips and machines plugged into him. The three scenarios depict various stages of the same act, like a stained glass window triptych showing the story of the murder of a saint. The creatures slither out of their own third and writhe over and around him, a heaving orgy suffocating and strangling him.

Fix! He tries to yell but he can't move his mouth. He's paralysed. There are bars on all sides. He is in some sort of prison with his tyrannical father, his treacherous brother, eternal sin.

But something is coming towards him, rising out of the earth before him like a combatant helicopter. Holographic, its outline shimmers in different, reflective colours. A man. No, bigger than a man. He is ten-feet tall and beautiful as the day, with his purple flashing eyes and his black hair. A chorus of Maenads, the raving ones, chant:

O secret chamber of the Couretes
and all-sacred haunts of Crete
where Zeus was born,
where the triple-breasted Corybantes
invented this circle of stretched hide
in the cave for me.
And in the intense rites
they mingled its noise with the sweetly-calling breath
of Phrygian pipes and placed it in the hand
of mother Rhea to beat time for the bacchae's shouts of
joy.
And the maddened satyrs
borrowed it from the mother goddess
and added it to the dances
of the biennial festivals
in which Dionysus rejoices.[†]

The god unlocks the cell door and pulls Matty from the other vile bodies saying, *I see you, Mandrax, in the wilderness. Imprisoned by your own father, Divitus the king, sold down the river by your own brother, Benzo. Well I'm here now, Mandrax. It's okay, Man.*

'Who are you?' Matty asks as the prison door swings open and his hand is grabbed.

You, O scribulous Mandrake, shall know me by my new name, Feracor.

'Matty, can you hear me?'

Fix is shaking his shoulder.

'Hey! Matty! Come on, man. It's time to go home.'

'Do you see him?' Matty tries to say, dazzled by the divine. 'Do you see?'

'I don't know what you're on about but you owe me for that K, okay? Okay? Matty?'

[†] Euripides, *Bacchae*, lines 120-34.

But Matty's miles away, running hand in hand with his rescuer through a land lurking in its own dying embers, rotting in its own filth, unfolding before him. Comets come thick and fast. Meteorites desecrate the landscape but he feels safe. He's in the presence of real power.

You humans, you see, have forgotten what it is to be human. Feracor is saying, and Matty recognises him now. He has come in different form but he is Dionysus. The Eternal Child, 'has the charms of Aphrodite in his eyes and keeps company day and night with young girls, dangling them before his Bacchic mysteries.'[†] Feracor's purple eyes flash with conviction. *You have forgotten and if you do not allow yourselves to remember your essence you shall become as obsolete as the race of dinosaurs before you…*

[†] Euripides, *Bacchae*, lines 235-9.

I, Feracor, have come to take you forward, Mandrax, with your fellow humans into the Fifth Age. Not all of you will make it through the good fight, but those of you who do shall rule as kings, as gods even. Once the corn is scraped from the sides, the kernel, full of goodness, vitality, life, shall flourish unhampered by its little yellow buds, sweet and parasitic.

Many years ago, when the Third Age of man was drawing to a close, a man named Jesus Christ was born to herald the Fourth Age, ushered by portents, stars, foreign majesty. This man, let me tell you right now, is the reason you are suffering, the reason you will have to fight to make it through to the Fifth and most glorious of ages.

History, Mandrax my friend, is written by winners, by those who survive. The punished, the oppressed, the losers disappear by the wayside and their story is never told. So has it been in this, the Age which those who survive will call forever 'The Lost Age'. It could have turned out one of two ways. This is the path you chose, so that now you are defending yourselves against a topsy-turvy nature. The elements are haywire; the planet is merely decades away from implosion; the nations are no longer split according to common creed and race but, jumbled and sectioned and warring, the human race is riddled with plague, filth, corruption. Even those less intellectually gifted than you may suspect that something has occurred to incur divine displeasure.

A simple misunderstanding, my fellow afflicted. Jesus Christ was not the man to lead the Age, to instruct you how to live. Jesus Christ and his watery-eyed philosophies have persuaded generation upon generation to abandon, to abjectly deny, their essential nature, the very essence of man which, if nurtured, perpetuates the species. But if it is rejected, in turn it rejects. The story of this Age lies buried with the losers. Christ was a most persuasive speaker.

But you, Mandrax, shall be my prophet. 'When the god comes upon the body in his might, he makes those he maddens tell the future.'[†]

[†] Euripides, *Bacchae*, lines 300–302.

Dr J. Sykes BACP (accred.)
Psychotherapist

Private Room
36 Harley Street
London W1G 9PG

Date:	Time:	Patient Initials:	Attendance:
Tuesday 17 November 2015	5pm	MEC	Y

Notes:

-MC very excitable, wondered if intoxicated. Eyes all over the place.

-Distractible, didn't realise he'd missed a session last week.

-When asked about sleeping said 'I've got bigger fish to fry.'

-Mood changed. Not grief-stricken but elated. V. odd, inappropriate response to Isis Bataclan attack in Paris, claimed to have been forewarned of human destruction in 'a vision'.

-Vision religious, mythological — a god called 'Feracor' who is Dionysus in new shape? Influenced by puer aeternus talk? I didn't talk to him directly about this — certainly didn't mention Dionysus association with the archetype.

-M. being made aware of his condition through mythological vision? Accessing collective unconscious?

-Found this:

'(The puer aeternus archetype) manifests itself as a mythological figure when it becomes perceived by the consciousness to any degree, but in the unconscious, where it resides, there can be no mental picture as all mental pictures are subjective and conscious. It can be understood, somewhat, as a potential, an energy pattern which can deliver the images and significances that might be understood by the consciousness. Mythology, itself, is the precursor to psychology: Unconscious patterns of energy can present conscious images that then can acquire a narrative... They can also be manifested in certain altered states of consciousness through drugs, extreme physical suffering or the shaman's practices which might include the previous two as well.' Source: www.pasttimesandpresenttensions.blogspot.co.uk.

THOUGHTS: Are drugs involved? Is Feracor simply a distorted version of 'Fix', Matty's best friend? Dream characters more likely to represent aspects of himself. He spoke of writer, Mandrax. Is that an aspect of himself? Mandrax a Quaalude-type drug in 1960s (ask Mum). Benzo is his brother Ben – benzodiazepine?

-Showed pity for me, claimed had to be there to understand – part of narcissism?

-Jumbled philosophical ideas. See Plato's Theory of Forms in The Republic: Forms are perfect ideas that are the essence of each object or quality. These Forms exist in a transcendent, intelligible realm – the true reality. Things in the material world can only mimic the Forms.

See too John Locke, An Essay Concerning Human Understanding: we are trapped behind a 'veil of perception' that prevents us from seeing things as they really are.

-And mythological ones. Left over from degree? Or distorted version of characters around him? Read The Bacchae.

-M. unclear about circs leading up to vision. 'Falling down rabbit hole.' Just a dream, concluded – and seemed much calmer by end of session. He is going to continue with life-writing homework. Said had written second chapter by hand but lost the paper.

-See Marie-Louise von Franz, The Problem of the Puer Aeternus: 'For the time being one is doing this or that, but whether it is a woman or a job, it is not yet what is really wanted, and there is always the fantasy that sometime in the future the real thing will come about [...] With this there is often, to a smaller or greater extent, a saviour complex, or a Messiah complex, with the secret thought that one day one will be able to save the world; the last word in philosophy, or religion, or politics, or art, or something else will be found. This can go so far as to be a typical pathological megalomania, or there may be minor traces of it in the idea that one's time 'has not yet come.'(p. 8)

CONCERNS: Apocalyptic dreams/visions frequent precursor to schizophrenic episodes. Refer to psychiatrist if necessary.

IX

Matty may or may not have had a few drinks, and/or other pick-me-ups, on the way home to ease his frustration after seeing Dr Psycho. She seemed to think he was drunk anyway, and he does hate to fall short of people's expectations. He was not drunk, merely excited; and that enlightened buzz continues this Wednesday morning as he lies in bed, still unable to sleep, hearing whatever mutant city birds dare to leave Soho Square to squawk at him as the dawn breaks. He feels he has accessed something genuinely new, something exciting—and isn't that what he's always been seeking? It has altered his entire perception of the world.

Matty marvels at the speeded passing of his life. Exempt from time and space for most of last week, he had slept all weekend, taking downers whenever the fragile membrane of sleep threatened to rupture; and when he woke up, aeons later, he discovered that his dreams had been actually happening in reality. He had seen the attack on Paris; had seen people revelling in the streets, then running for their lives.

He can't make sense of it all yet, that is true, but he could have begun to explore it further with Sykes's help, had she taken him seriously. It can't just be coincidence that one minute he is directly receiving prophecy of human death—and that the next all of Paris is in horror and tragedy. Is it possible that he could have averted it? That he could stop future disasters by learning the purpose of his visitation? He feels that he, Matty, might have a purpose beyond his understanding.

It sure beats this reality, he thinks, as he manoeuvres his disobedient body out of bed and locates a grey T-shirt on the broken chair, resurrected to take up nearly all of his floor space once again. He will face the daytime glare head on, not fester in bed seeing the sleepless hours accumulate before him, all lined up, no divisions, until his death. Looking for his jeans, he realises he is already wearing them, grabs a pair of sunglasses and stumbles noisily down the stairs and on to Meard Street.

Matty is momentarily disorientated. He turns right, towards Dean Street, thinking that he might lie in the sun in Soho Square and inhale the last of the Special K he'd bought the night before. Breakfast. But it is a little chilly. As he reaches the end of his street, he starts in surprise as his heinous stepmother, Katya, darts into focus, framed by the lurid backdrop of Burger and Lobster. She looks mutinous and immaculate in her knee-length skirt and smart little jacket. She too is wearing sunglasses. Hers are Prada, and Matty is suddenly aware that his own have horizontal neon blue bars across them and are designed for a man seven times his size, such as exist in fairytales only.

He stands rooted to the spot. No matter how still he tries to stand he is unable to stop his body swaying, his face droop-ing a little with a tired, lopsided kind of grimace.

'Where the bloody hell are you going?' she snaps.

'Uhh, hello, Katya. I'm just going for breakfasht.' His attempt at sprightly intonation is brutally slurred. O treacherous larynx.

'I suppose you know what day it is.' The fact that he can see her words hang in the air as a cartoon speech bubble sug-gests that he is still phenomenally high.

'Oh no. Oh no, don't tell me I've forgotten. Ish it your birthday?'

'It is Wednesday morning, Matthew, on 18 November 2015, and you are due to meet Mr Squales at 9.30am—*in precisely two hours.*'

Christ, not Squales the Squealer. That's all he needs.

'Chill, Katya, I'll go get ready now.'

Katya takes him by the arm and they walk back down Meard Street to No. 25. Evidently she is impatient to get going, carping and fidgeting; she seems blind to his tour guide attempts, neither glancing at the chalk outline of a door drawn on the wall beside her that Matty points out (he occasionally tries to open it, thinking it might be hiding an actual door to a secret Soho drinking club) nor the sculpted stone nose set high upon the wall above her.

He finds his front door, retrieves his keys from his pocket and leads the way up the many stairs.

'Give me a sec.' Matty steps elegantly over the threshold and falls over the laptop. He shuts the door behind him and does a quick whip-round of all things unlikely to impress Queen K.

Katya, upon being let in by his shaky hand some moments later, gulps.

'Please,' Matty urges, 'make yourself at home. Coffee?'

'I think we could all do with some coffee. Look, I'll make it. Can you have a shower? Shave? Please clean yourself up a bit. Christ, Matthew, how do you live in this pigsty?'

'Sure thing, Katy.'

She sighs.

It may be a pigsty but it is his pigsty and it gives him untold pleasure that Katya hadn't been able to enter it with her own keys, as had been the case with the Marylebone flat.

He takes his towel to the shared bathroom, locks the door and sniffs the rest of the ketamine. The shower is a Cuban rainstorm; Matty enjoys a little salsa dancing, kicking up Havanan puddles with his naked feet.

Back in the room, he shuffles on to the bed as Katya takes the chair, continuing on and on as he zones out, thinks of his strange dream—of the strange deific figure '…bail…' was it a dream? '…dependent…' or a vision? '…good behaviour…'

or a prophecy! '...drugs tests...'—and of the odd story and what it could possibly all mean for the world and humanity—and finally of Tera: they are sitting with arms and legs around each other rocking back and forth, back and forth. It is enough to have this most welcome and novel distraction, to see something of beauty and truth in his mind's eye.

'Yes,' he agrees, nodding at his stepmother, sipping the coffee and feeling terrifically grateful that there's enough stuff in his system to shield him from this ordeal and keep him in his own head until at least tomorrow.

He goes through the motions as if in a dream. Now he's in a suit. Now he's in a cab to Chancery Lane. Now he's talking to Squealer in his stark, clean office. Squales is speaking interminably about laws and court and pleas and loopholes. But all the time Matty's drawing the veil, he's somewhere else, marvelling at what he's seen. Revelation of one world, anaesthesia of another. He had looked, he now realises, for answers to his melancholy where there were none—in the dumb corpse of his brother, in his own busy, racing mind, in the photograph of his mother, in the memories of time with Tera. Awe and reverence have shaken him out of this introspection. Religion, as he knows it, is a bore, but what he saw that day with Fix was a different kind of thing altogether. Not puritanical parish teas but numinous ecstasy, an awakening. Transcendence. Philosophy had taught Matty to question religious beliefs and his tutors had openly mocked the credulity of churchgoers. He'd seen those tutors as gods of sorts.

But it seems facile now, that there should be nothing beyond this life and no explanation for anything. He feels that there are greater forces at work. Drugs or no drugs. He's not taking anything at face value. But it feels good, his mind not being his whole world and his failings not responsible for every misery everywhere. He is insignificant in the grand scheme of things. Gods and universes versus little Matty. It seems as if something bigger has found him.

'You would be well-advised to keep your nose clean for the next few months until the trial,' warns Squealer. 'The judge will not look kindly upon you if you blot your copybook while you're out on bail.'

'I haven't taken anything for months now. Don't worry. I'll be a good boy.'

'That's not what I mean. I can't see the relevance of…'

Matty never knows quite what Squales is on about. He drowns him out.

Katya purses her lips and fiddles in her handbag for a tissue.

Endless fucking charges. Matty can't see why it's such a problem for the rest of the world if he chooses to take drugs, occasionally. It's a private matter. Oblivion, occasionally, helps. And lucid oblivion helps his writing, no question. Lets him turn over the stories of his past with the detached emotions of another, with a child's frank eye. He wants a return to childish things.

This is strange, considering the nature of his childhood.

He starts to think about what he will write for next week's Psycho session. He thinks again of the unfairness of Ben's late arrival, *five years late*, at Rockwell House. Matty had been twelve, Ben ten, nearly eleven. Though Matty was by this point a veteran of the unaccompanied minor procedure, still Ben was the more confident of the two. The flight was an education in itself. Matty's eyes were opened to opportunity; so many *things*, so much pointless *stuff*, which Ben leapt on with enthusiasm. The journey from home to school and vice versa, with the exception of that first flight from London to Havana (via Paris), had been typically fraught for Matty with stealthy tears and dread. It had never occurred to him to try to alleviate this distress with material comforts. The two were distinct worlds and the one, he had mistakenly thought, could not touch the other.

The meeting with Squealer's over now, nothing new to report. He's sure there is much to be said for his good behaviour in this interim period before the trial but he can't bring himself to care. What's done is done. And if he's caught again, he now knows, since Fix has told him, that there are all sorts of tricks for getting drugs out of his system—downing loads of vinegar or something like that'd do the trick. Fix has a lot of vinegar in his flat but has never, to Matty's knowledge, pickled anything, except perhaps himself.

Katya's left him now, still keyless despite various attempts to wheedle one out of him.

'I worry about you, all alone,' she'd lied. 'What if you pass out one night and choke on your own vomit or something?'

She'd suggested dinner before she flew her broomstick back to France but Matty skilfully disengaged himself, feigning a prior commitment.

'Having dinner with an old friend,' he said, mentally chortling at the prospect of a dinner of herbs with himself, his very best old friend.

X

PRIVATE AND CONFIDENTIAL
DR J. SYKES

CONTENTS: SECOND EMAIL AND CHAPTER FROM MEC, WITH MY FOOTNOTES.

From: Matty Corani <matzcorani@gmail.com>
Subject: Life-writing (Looking Up At The Stars)
Date: 19 November 2015 02:12:48 GMT
To: Julia Sykes <juliasykes@mail.com>

Hi J, more of my life. Matty.

LOOKING UP AT THE STARS

Chapter 3

The first flight to school with Ben[1]

Ruben, full of life and laughter, drew the air hostesses to our seats like wasps to a slick of jam.[2] I remember wishing to God[3] they would leave us in peace. Incessant questions addressed first to Ruben, who chatted gregariously, seemingly oblivious of the age gap. These women were no different to Ruben, as potential pals, than the boys who came to play with him in the sandpit. Always they turned dutifully from Ruben to his pale, sullen shadow[4] to ask me the same questions.

---

[1] THAT FONT AGAIN - IS TYPEWRITER SOMEHOW MORE AUTHENTIC, WRITERLY?
[2] WOMEN ARE LIKE WASPS?
[3] FOR SOMEONE WHO SAYS HE'S NOT RELIGIOUS, THIS WORD COMES UP A LOT.
[4] M. AS SHADOW SIDE OF BEN. TALK ABOUT THIS.

They are so stupid,[5] I thought. Surely Ruben must realise this? I feigned sleep from the window seat, always my preference due to its capacity for seclusion. Through squinted eye and the slight suggestion of a snore, I stared contemptuously at their orange skin, fluorescent powder collecting in the crevices of saggy neck and under-eye bag. I despised their vacuous inquiries; surely they of all people should know where they were heading? What hope for their safety if the crew did not know where the aircraft planned to land?

As the smell of chicken stock, the one defining feature of all airline meals, pervaded my senses, I turned my head to the white blank canvas of sky beyond the window and my thoughts to what lay behind and ahead. Any relief I felt at freedom from my father and his entourage was swiftly transformed into panic at the entrapment of school. A surge of adrenalin shivered up my spine as my eye spun open just in time to see semi-lunar black prickles of air hostess eyebrows, surprised as a botox mannequin, bearing down upon me.

-Beef or fish?, asked the eyebrows.

-Neither, I said, teenage catatonia reducing my answer to a single indecipherable vowel.

-Both!, Ben cut in, eyes shining with glee.

I, glorying in the self-control my maturity had afforded me, enjoying the sudden sensation of hunger which tingled like fear in my extremities, shut my eyes properly and blocked my nose against the chicken offensive.

---

[5]   M. SENSE OF SUPERIORITY, SPECIALNESS - NPD. THIS FUELLING IDEA OF HIS COSMIC SIGNIFICANCE IN FERACOR VISION/DREAM? KEY MAY BE FINDING EMPATHY FOR BROTHER, FATHER?

I was convinced I had been asleep for a couple of hours at least, but when I opened my eyes again, awoken by Ruben moving from his seat, the two trays were still there. I quickly stuffed as much of the remains as I could into my mouth, not stopping to separate savoury from sweet, cold and congealed from dying heat. I could see the eyebrows wheeling a trolley, Ruben behind her returning from wherever he had been. Lowering my head so that it was concealed behind the headrest of the seat in front, I crammed the remainder of the food into my mouth, not tasting, merely feeling its satisfying bulk filling me.

Eyebrows was there before me, bundling the grey trays into their appointed grave.

-But I haven't finished; I just went to the loo, Ruben was saying.

I swallowed the last of the globulous mass, the giant ball in my throat like a bolus slithering through a snake's digestive tract.

Almost immediately, satiety was replaced by shaky guilt.[6] Revulsion at my behaviour saturated every cell of my being. But I knew that if another tray were placed within my reach, I would be powerless to resist polishing off that one's treasures too. Nothing to lose.

***

Matty delays emailing what he's written to Julia Sykes, sets the laptop aside and smokes a joint to soften the sadness that comes over him. He gets up and folds himself through the window to sit on his perch. There on the window ledge,

---

[6] M. BINGE/REMORSE CYCLE. SELF DESTRUCTIVE BEHAVIOUR. ASK HOW THE MINDFULNESS IS GOING.

watching moonlit Soho turn to dawn, his sense of the structure of time returns.

Heavy of heart he thinks of his brother. He remembers the flight landing at the other end, the whirl of transfers, pick-ups, buses and cars leaving Ben dizzy with excitement, Matty dizzy with nausea; the two entering the driveway of the school, Rockwell, Matty's second home for the past five years. This conferred on it the dubious status of being Matty's most stable home, just beating the embassy in Beijing by a term. His father was about to be relocated to Moscow, ending Beijing's entry into the longevity competition anyway.

Matty was furious to find his one advantage here, familiarity with Rockwell's layout, removed upon entry. The school had undergone extensive refurbishment over the summer and he was as disoriented as if he were entering it for the first time. Ill at ease, he was swept to a new building by his old matron; she had temporarily replaced hard-faced discipline with all-embracing tenderness for the benefit of the few local parents depositing offspring. The smell of new paint and raw furniture could not disguise the inimitable smell of school corridor.

Matty felt a flood of unidentifiable emotion as he was informed of the changes made to living arrangements. As of this year, each boarding house would contain a range of ages, with boys from every year. Boys from the same family would automatically be in the same house. This upheaval of his most consistent environment was mitigated by a fierce and secret gratitude that he would not be separated from Ben.

Rockwell was a school which prided itself on its firm Church of England foundations. The headmaster encouraged the upholding of these values with a tradition of chapel services at every available opportunity. This was, equally traditionally, met with resistance. On a nightly basis, busy matrons would patrol suspected dens of concealment, unearthing culprits.

Matty, however, had never been caught.

He'd come to revere this hallowed time of solitude as zealously as any churchgoer. Sunday afforded a particular bonus, bringing as it invariably did, the Eucharist: a multi-faceted extravaganza of humility and repentance which took up the best part of an hour, sometimes more if Matty was lucky. The tolling of bells announced its ending to Matty, crouched beneath the earth of the hideout he had dug in the outer reaches of the school's extensive grounds. Its fragile wooden lattice of a door was easily hidden from public view by a high hedge. Even so it never hurt to sweep a few twigs and leaves over it when he left, heavy of heart, to return to the throngs. Though he occasionally left belongings for his entertainment down there, tightly preserved in the waterproof casing of a Beijing Duty Free carrier bag, he never looked at them. He was just grateful for the earthy stillness, all-enveloping silence. Away from the flurry of activity, demands, noise and enthusiasm for once, like a fox going to ground, he could just be. Still. Silent.

As the first urban birds start to twitter, Matty climbs back inside and returns to his laptop.

***

This Sunday evening, however, was the first day of term and the whole school was expected to convene in the chapel for a sharp dose of welcoming vespers.[7] Dizzy with jetlag and the new layout, I was not sure I could locate my outdoor den if I tried. Nevertheless, it was the one thing I could show off to Ruben, certain of a receptive audience.

-But why?, Ruben asked, his dark eyes large with bewilderment.

-What, you'd rather go to chapel?

[7] DEVOUT UPBRINGING

-Well, yeah. It's cold out there and all my friends are going.

-Oh *all* your friends. Right. Have you even met anyone yet?

At that moment Ruben was prevented from answering by a wave of arms and legs which swept him up in their chatter and carried him off to chapel.

With an ever-increasing sense of foreboding I followed, spying more and more of the faces I had been praying might have been removed over the summer. Various disasters, both natural and manmade, had crossed my mind for the individual dooms of my peers. I had, in fact, conjured them up with such vividness that I'd actually managed to convince myself of their untimely demises. I was initially shocked at their continued survival. There, for example, smirked Philip Blackwater, the repellent son of the British ambassador in Barbados. Popular simply by virtue of the exotic holidays he could offer his friends, I had imagined him suffering at the claws of a rogue giant sea turtle, the likes of which I believed common in the Caribbean. Sadly, Philip looked unscathed by any such trauma.

The building was awash with stained glass and brightly-coloured cloth, punctuated by the odd statue. I took my position on one of the benches allotted to the first year of the senior school, jostling against the elbow skewers on each side of me. Tom and Peter. The former had been my friend for the very first term but had swiftly realised, once Peter had shown him the potential glories of an alliance, that he was backing a loser and would be shunned by the other pupils accordingly. I did not mind. Fewer friends, less need to entertain, still less to care.

Gazing at the sea of faces, trying to work out where Ruben was sitting, I felt an acute longing claw at my heart, the object of which, be it person or place, I could not put my finger on. Though the feeling was physical, tangible, the yearning was for something less obvious. It was as if I were homesick, though not for the home I had just left. Lost in analysis, the dirge-like prayers allowed me to drift inside myself.

My eyes jerked open as the pew three behind mine erupted into snorts of laughter, the sort of molten hysteria that comes only when suppressed to breaking point. This sort of behaviour was not taken lightly at Rockwell, but to my astonishment the giggles were not swallowed in coughs, but swelled and spread through the ranks of boys until the entire chapel was letting out bellows of laughter, the faces of the masters twitching, the contagion unstoppable.[8]

I, now laughing too, looked behind me at the grinning epicentre of the hilarity, Ruben. As we caught each other's eye, I felt something lift inside me. It was all going to be okay now.

***

Matty cannot help but smile at the memory. He saves the file and emails it to Dr Sykes. Finally, something is lifting. Some tiny fragment of light is creeping in. Almost imperceptibly, he senses a lightening of the suffocating blanket he had not been able to identify.

Well then, it's working. This is writing as therapy. He is following Dr Psychosis's prescription and will soon be master of his own thoughts, his own patterns of thought, surely. He wonders if it might be within his powers to persuade her to sleep with him.

---

[8] MAGICAL THINKING? ROOT OF PREOCCUPATION WITH RELIGION?

XI

Matty has every intention of seducing Dr Julia Psycho at five on the following Tuesday afternoon. But he sleeps through the appointment, and when he wakes, oppressed by guilt and thirst, he goes straight to Fix's flat.

To his surprise, Silja opens the door.

'Hi, sexy,' is her exuberant greeting.

He doesn't feel very sexy. He doesn't have much to say by way of reply.

She looks put out.

He scouts beyond her shoulder. Fix is there, not alone.

Not for the first time he marvels at the distance between two bodies and two souls. So easy to be underneath this girl naked, grinding teeth and genitalia. Why so awkward clad and sober?

'Wow,' he settles upon. 'Good to see you.'

This seems to ease the friction, slightly.

'You seem a little surprised, Felix!' says Silja. 'I was just passing your street. Looking for another bar job in Soho actually. Thought I'd drop by to say hi. Oh yeah and then Fix tells me this is his place, not yours. It's fine, by the way. I'm used to guys who make shit up. Where do you live?'

He really wants to see Fix. What is she, the door monitor?

'I'm sorry. Don't know why I said that: my name's Matty, not, er, Felix, and I live round the corner—in Meard Street. Come round sometime, if you want.'

He moves in for an ungainly hug and feels her wary body give into his.

'Can I come in?' he asks.

She steps aside. 'Doesn't matter,' she says. 'Let's start again. My name's Sylvie actually. And I'm not from Russia or Lithuania or whichever one I trotted out for your delectation. I'm from Chichester.'

Matty suddenly feels like laughing.

'Brilliant. Turns out I'm way more Slavic than you, then. My father was the British ambassador in Moscow until he died a couple of years ago. I've got a vile Russian stepmother to prove it and everything.'

'Lucky boy. Aren't they always Russian in the fairytales, wicked stepmothers?'

'Um, are they? Or do they just have amazing cheekbones in their evil faces?'

Enough of this. He moves inside and Fix drops him a naval salute from beside the fridge.

'Matty, hey man. You know Sasha, right?'

'Oh heeey,' she says, more beautiful than he remembers. 'You're the writer.'

'And I have indeed been writing!' he says. There seems to be nothing more to say.

'Have a beer, buddy,' says Fix, extracting a bottle from the fridge and handing it over. 'We've got a gig tonight in The Caves. The guys are coming here first—think we're on about nine.'

A ready-made crew of friends with cool credentials. Priceless.

He settles into being one of the gang, chatting with Sylvie and Sasha. This is what it used to be like with Tera. Easy.

But Tera had been more than that. She'd been a lifestyle choice, not just someone with whom he could comfortably kill time. She'd been all he'd needed, a thousand girls in one. Mother, sister, hooker. Lover, companion, partner. She'd been everything, and their time together had been his whole world. Yes he'd had Ben as his confidante, Fix for kicks but he'd been careful not to splinter himself, to give himself too freely to acquaintances. Why would he want to involve others when he had the perfect girlfriend? She was the standard, the ideal. Tera was the yardstick and all girls fell short of her perfection. Matty understood that Tera didn't match up to the universal form of 'girl'. But he knew equally that she had been the very definition of *his* girl, for he himself had created the criteria.

'Matty! What do *you* think?'

He realises he has zoned out of the conversation. Saved by the bell as The Cracks have arrived, clanging their way instrumentally into the kitchen. Blaze, Lude, Gingko, Soul and the Earthman, more hair between them than a herd of musk oxen. Soul, Matty notices, has painted his nails in some sort of fluorescent yellow, matching the horizontal stripes on Gingko's face.

'Highlighter,' says Gingko, catching Matty's curious glance.

'Striking yet cost-effective,' says Fix. 'I applaud you, my herbal friend.'

Matty always finds these men rather intimidating until the barriers have been broken down and they've all been reduced to silly, gurning children. Then they're his best mates. But for the moment, he'd rather get steadily tight with a girl, someone gentle.

Sylvie is next to him. They're sitting against the wall. He thinks he likes the freedom to be whoever he chooses with her, that the anonymity is another escape from reality. Plus it's not great chat to impart your misery to people you barely know. Nevertheless, suddenly he's talking about Ben, biting his tongue not to talk about Tera.

'Well, what are your brother's chances?' asks Sylvie after some time.

'Well, nobody's really prepared to give a straight answer. It's been a while now and not so much as an eyelid flicker.

And of course the worry is, even if he does wake up, there won't be much left of the Ben we knew…'

As he says it, it strikes Matty how infinitely preferable such a change would be. He could forgive a new version of Ben, one whose brain was chewed into a new shape, which might give rise to a new character and new actions.

'And no parents? Just you?' She sounds incredulous.

'Well, it's kind of always felt like that. My mother died giving birth to me—she was beautiful. Look, I've got a photo of her.'

'Yes, beautiful.' Sylvie presses on. 'And your father?'

'Retirement got him… He settled down in Provence and was dead within the year. I think the inactivity did for him, that, and his new wife.' He is becoming faintly paranoid that he's giving away too much. There's always an ulterior motive when people start grilling you about your family, childhood and the rest of it.

Oh let me psychoanalyse you, go on. There must be a reason why you're such a fuck-up.

He supposes he can always return the questions but frankly he does not think he can endure a breakdown of Sylvie's family tree. He does not see that it is of any relevance to understanding the girl before him, stroking his arm and muttering, 'Poor Matty. Matty the Orphan.'

The longer he spends with her, the more she reminds him of Tera. He is reluctant to smash that delusion by knowing more about Sylvie than is strictly necessary.

'Can I come with you to the hospital, Matty?'

'Why?'

'Well obviously I won't if you don't want me too. It's just—it must be quite lonely, living the way you do. And it might help, sharing it with someone.'

There is clearly some sort of morbid curiosity in the girl. Matty wonders whether emo tendencies lie beneath the punk hair and savage eyeliner. Suddenly, though, the idea of visiting Ben with her does not seem quite so unappealing. As usual, he feels the conditioned thrill of hope at the prospect of seeing his brother. He forgets, in that initial split second, that things have changed.

It might be that Sylvie's presence would change things in some other, better way.

'Yes, why not? We'll take a picnic. Fix, would you like to come too?'

'Love to, mate. Thought you'd never ask.'

Only Fix knows what really went on with Matty and his brother. Even Katya's been protected from the full extent of the truth. He is grateful he has Fix fighting his corner. Every time he sees Fix he feels more in awe of him. He's a free spirit yet has shown such tenderness to Matty, not just in those strange few months after the arrest but ever since he's known him. He makes him feel like a favourite son.

But you have to work at friendships. With Ben, the unconditional nature of their set-up had made it all so easy. But family does not entail unconditional love. He knows that much from his father. Fix's friendship is elective; there's more to it than biology and blood.

As they leave the flat and wander to The Caves, clanging and bashing their way to the gig, Matty realises he's slightly unsteady on his feet. He must have drunk more than he'd thought. If beer tasted like alcohol, he wouldn't have this problem.

You're a cartoon of a man. Face up to yourself for once, you fucking lush.

Matty's walking alone in the crowd. Sylvie's talking to Fix. He needs to speak soon as he can feel that awful sense of disconnection coming on. Like when he's been in his flat alone for too long and he's afraid to open his mouth in case he doesn't recognise the sound. In case the Jitterer's taken over and made it out of the introspective realm into his voice box.

As he walks through the Soho streets he feels he is a ghost, an observer observing life on the fringes, seeing stuff that no longer applies to him, is no longer available to him. It is a self-perpetuating state, of course.

He walks a little more quickly, dodging a guy handing out flyers, until he's walking level with Fix and Sylvie.

'No, I don't mean *I'm* lost, sweetheart,' Fix is saying to her. 'I just think there's something weird about the way we humans live now, the way it's all about the individual becoming really powerful and rich and successful. Not like eastern cultures, man, not like what I saw when I went to Cambodia or Laos or even India. Collaboration, yeah? That's what it's all about. Be the best you can be as part of a bigger whole. See the way *we* live, I mean our crowd, like we're part of a commune or something, is far closer to that. It's more like a Saxon village or a Chinese hill tribe than that whole corporate bigger better faster Western shit.'

Fix breaks off when he sees they've arrived at the door of The Caves. The group heads underground, where the arched walls and ceilings divide into rooms, alcoves and nooks. The stage must be at the far end of the labyrinth judging by the warped acoustics echoing through.

Fix looks around at his band, indigo eyes sparkling with fragments of light in the low-lit shadows, sweat sparkling on the walls. A blue bandanna is tied around his mass of ungroomed black hair. In appearance he is, thinks Matty, more akin to a strange panther than a regular human.

The bar clearly has a gay bent. Makes Matty feel both knowing and uncomfortable. It's dimly candled and pretty snug, a bit claustrophobic even. It irritates him that Sylvie's still hanging on to Fix's every word and so he moves slowly to a point behind her from where he can stroke her arm.

'Yes?' she says, melting back into him so he can put both arms around her.

'What'll you have to drink?' he asks, bringing his mouth to her ear, then her neck.

She turns round to face him and opens her bag to reveal a bottle of vodka. 'Just Coke please.'

'Good work! For that, sexy smuggler, you may have both liquid and solid forms,' says Matty. Fix, he is sure, will have something up his sleeve.

More horse tranquilliser, it turns out. 'Coke's such shit quality these days,' says Fix scornfully. 'It's not the eighties, man.'

Just take more K.

He supposes so, though sometimes you just really want both together; cocaine and ketamine, opposing forces, Yin and Yang: they complete each other and become so much greater than the sum of their parts. Matty is disappointed to miss that shattering white wake-up call shimmy through his face and bones. Ah well.

He takes Sylvie into one of the smaller, emptier caves where others are doing the same thing discreetly and offers her a bump of ketamine to inhale before taking some himself.

The process is repeated a few times, laced with vodka and chat, before The Cracks are up and by the time they are, the cave world is a wonky, sliding place to be. Fix is prowling provocatively around the front of the stage, trading too long on their one very good song. Not for the first time, Matty wonders if they have what it takes. He'd never say that to Fix, of course. Blaze is a talented bass player but the rest can't match Fix's charisma, nor, more importantly, his tempo or tune. Sasha doesn't seem to mind, dancing and singing along at the front. Matty grabs Sylvie by the hand and enters into the spirit of things.

Wonky is as wonky does and before long the gig is over and the party has begun. Turns out someone knows someone who knows whoever owns The Caves and a lock-in has been duly arranged.

Fix has clearly recovered from his disdain for the cocaine of this decade and is cutting lines, speaking esoterica quickly and urgently to anyone who will listen, which is everyone who wants a line.

'We can't begin to conceive of infinity, man, mortal minds are too limited to entertain the concept. The universe you do acknowledge is hard enough to get your head around. It's just one of a limitless number of spheres, universes, domains, planes. Of the doors which divide them, divide us, some are spiritual, some physical. Like death. But I reckon the same laws, eternal and unchanging, govern all of it.'

Sylvie's doing a bad impression of reverence.

Fix is undeterred.

'These laws are bigger than everything, bigger than infinity, bigger than gods. Gods are like slaves to the Universal Powers which transcend time and space. Gods and men are the same. It's just that one can stay in one dimension, stick around on the same plane though time ticks on. Being mortal eventually forces you to end your existence on one plane and cross into another. This is why the worship of gods appeals to humans. They hope they'll be rewarded with the same divine ability to endure the crossing of the divide.'

Matty has this overwhelming sense that somewhere else another Matty is battling the same issues, that every possible idea, action, thing, person and deity is contained within the cosmos, whether decomposed or recycled, split or reformed, present or inaccessible, all answerable to the great governing laws.

Sylvie is saying something about going home and Matty suspects she'd like him to go with her but now seems like a really good time to talk to Fix about the mescaline weirdness. Matty has been unable to break free of the vision and the voice, the persistent voice of the purple-eyed god, Feracor, that has lodged in his head. A strange arcane land has begun to replace the desert as his default dream, blessed relief from his recurring nightmare. Sometimes Matty sees this world's emperor, Divitus, who looks a little like his father, bursting with contained wrath, a string of concubines attending to him. The great despot sits on his gold and unwittingly awaits his doom at the hands of Feracor, like Montezuma expecting the return of the god Quetzalcoatl.

'Er, is that normal? Did you see something similar?' he asks Fix.

'Maybe you've just recognised what was always there,' Fix replies enigmatically. 'Don't look like that. Think about, oh I don't know, the first time you heard a new word, in a song lyric or something. As soon as you learned what it meant, bet you saw that word everywhere—in magazines, on buses, on the lips of actors in films. It's just that you wouldn't have noticed these instances had you not had that word explained to you, thought about it a bit.'

Fix is as garrulous as Matty's monotonous. The drugs have taken him inside himself, closed off from the outside.

'It's, like, lucid dreaming, man. You control the vision.' Fix adds.

As Fix chatters on about the unexplained phenomena of the world, Matty feels himself drifting happily within his mind, allowing the colours and shapes around him to blend and fuse and separate out again into new forms as he looks out of new eyes. Or rather the eyes of someone else.

He is floating within someone else's mind, seeing through their senses, though his body (and he is vaguely aware of it, tethered by gravity) remains where it was. This time when he feels the mental fetters begin to loosen, he enters the rabbit hole with interest and logic, not shock. Open mind. Open sesame. Open.

The scene changes rapidly into what he is looking for, as if it is waiting for him. And once again Matty has become

Mandrax, the scribe, eagerly awaiting wisdom from his god, Feracor.

The pair keep to the privacy of the farthest cave; Feracor tosses his head, throwing back black ropes of deific hair and the world seems to tremble in acknowledgement.

He speaks…

I am Feracor; I am Bacchus; I am the god that you humans offended when you all started playing nicely nicely and turning the other cheek. You think the Antichrist is some terrific devil. Let me tell you, it's just the other essential side of humans. The fierce-hearted side that if you would only acknowledge, revere, would enable you to survive.

Try and think of it in terms of balance. A happy cosmos exists when the forces within it, opposing, adjacent and symbiotic, exist in equal measure, none excessively strong and violently diminishing another.

Think of the forces we encounter on Earth—pushing, pulling, gravity, air resistance, that sort of thing. When opposing forces are in equal measure, balanced like a tug of war between two teams of identical strength, there shall be constancy, equilibrium. When forces are unbalanced, there shall be anarchy. So it is when cosmic forces are unbalanced. There is movement. You can see the chaos of the elements all around you. The Eternal Forces are unbalanced.

Open your mind. Mars and Venus are the twin powers from whom everything flows. They cannot be reduced to the depressingly mortal labels 'love' and 'anger'. Mere semantics! Look to the concepts behind them, to everything which makes up this world. It is the masculine and the feminine, opposite yet compatible. It is the physical and the cerebral—what is one without the other? Together in excellence they create something much greater than the sum of its parts. When out of balance, monstrous deformity. It is Yin and Yang, angst and calm, hot and cold, red and green, predator and prey, black and white. It is head versus heart, logic versus passion. Air fans fire. Earth fuels and smothers fire. Water drowns fire. Where is your fire? You as a human have lost that internal flame that is your core, your essence, your humanness!

Dr J. Sykes BACP (accred.)
Psychotherapist

Private Room
36 Harley Street
London W1G 9PG

Date:	Time:	Patient Initials:	Attendance:
Tuesday 24 November 2015	5pm	MEC	DNA

Notes:

Called MC and sent email. If no response, call next of kin.

-Looking at Anthony Storr, Art of Psychotherapy, wondered about this:
'Schizoid people are probably better able to stand solitary confinement than normal people because their relationships with others have been so tenuous that to be deprived of them is no great loss. What schizoid persons do is to develop a world of phantasy to compensate for their lack of fulfilment in the real world. Since schizoid persons have failed to obtain or to achieve relationships on equal terms with anyone else, their phantasy is one in which they themselves play a superior role. If one cannot be loved, one can at least be envied, or regarded with awe.' (p. 135)

-And also by Storr in a later work, Feet of Clay: A Study of Gurus, 1996:
'Can people be regarded as psychotic merely because they hold eccentric beliefs about the universe and their own significance as prophets or teachers? What are the boundaries between sanity and madness? What does labelling someone psychotic really mean? Are our current psychiatric classifications adequate? [...] The sane are madder than we think; the mad are saner.' (p. 152)

But Storr then quotes Ralph Waldo Emerson ('To believe your own thought, to believe what is true for you in your private heart is true for all men — that is genius.') Cf: 'My own view is that this is not genius but narcissism; self-absorption hovering on the brink of madness. In the case of gurus, it seems to be the consequence of isolation. Gurus go through a period of intense stress or mental illness, and come out on the other side with what generally amounts to a delusional system which, because of their lack of friends with whom ideas could be discussed on equal terms, is elaborated in solitude.' (p. 208)

XII

Matty becomes aware of a foot digging into his neck. Warily, he opens his eyes. The foot belongs to Fix who has an arm around Sylvie, both asleep. Jesus, is nothing sacred? Is it any wonder he prefers nameless one-nighters, girls on the internet, girls in brothels? All women are whores in the end.

Where are you? No caves here. Lude's house, an envelope would have it.

He stands up blearily and regrets it. But he must write. Hangover adrenaline dictates it.

Discipline, screams Hemingway or someone who looks a little like him and is very clearly propping up a Cuban bar, *is the cornerstone of writing.*

Work, work, work, you useless piece of shit!

Nobody else is awake. Thoughts of a shower are allayed when he discovers Gingko asleep in it. He stumbles out into the sun. The decrepit old sun. He notices it as if for the first time and hears the sounds of a thunderous new dawn beating on its doors. Maybe it will all be all right. Maybe this hellish reality isn't all there is.

The next age will deface your golden chariot, old sun.

He is somewhere near King's Cross. He'll walk to Marylebone and look in on Ben, and write there for a bit. Sylvie is suddenly by his side as he jaywalks across the road.

'Hey, wait a minute. Where are you going in such a hurry?'

'Not that it's any of your business but I've got to see my brother.'

'I thought that's what you said last night. And I said I'd come with you, didn't I? Is that still okay?'

'Whatever.'

She slips a hand in his. 'No need to be so cold. There's nothing wrong is there?'

'Depends on whether you consider fucking my best friend to be wrong or not, I guess.'

'What on earth are you talking about?'

'You and Fix, obviously. Don't insult me further by denying it.'

'Matty, nothing happened! You passed out pretty early on, by the way. Then we all sort of slept where we dropped and I was right by you.'

Amnesiac remorse takes over, momentarily, and he's grateful she's there. He puts his arm around her. 'Sorry,' he says. 'I would like you to come with me if you could bear it. Be good to have company.'

'Sure—then maybe I could see your real flat. Or you could come to mine. I share a house with four others so there's always something going on. I'm not working for the moment—you'll remember why.'

Matty sees his day suddenly all planned out by others and feels a frantic need for solitude.

'Come to the hospital by all means but I'm pretty busy today, not sure if I have time to do anything after.'

They walk in the daylight, two vampires. On the short journey they pass three political protests, one bus bomb scare, seven charity muggers and four people who are on their way home from the night before, eyes still loopy on E or similar. Matty regrets Katya's confiscation of his barred sunglasses.

'You can pick them up for nothing in Chinatown,' says Sylvie helpfully.

'I try to avoid that place. Too realistic a model.'

Before long, they reach the hospital. Matty ignores the respective scowls and smiles of the staff and heads straight for his brother's room.

'Ta-da,' he says inappropriately and regrets it.

'God,' she says. 'Not a well boy.'

'They say he's got severe brain damage. It's kind of a miracle he's alive at all.'

'But he's not really, is he? There's a machine doing the living.'

'Be careful what you say though, won't you? This might sound odd but I know he can hear us. He's in there, Ben is, listening, thinking, feeling inside the prison of his body. All we can see are the bars but the prisoner's very much there, hidden for the moment.'

'You seem very sure.'

'He's found ways of communicating with me, telepathically. He tells me what it's like in his jail.'

'Ri-i-ght.' As she looks at him he can see tears of pity forming in her eyes. 'Must be so hard to lose your brother. Of course, you find ways of coping. Whatever helps.'

'No, he really does—it's his punishment, this coma, for sleeping with my girlfriend.'

'Matty, um, do you think you should talk to someone about all of this? It's a lot to deal with on your own.'

Dr Psychosis zooms into his mind. She leans towards him displaying her uplifted cleavage, twining her long, golden hair around a pencil. He feels bad about not turning up to yesterday's session. Sykes clearly misses him; she's called and sent an email to prove it. He'll reschedule later, send her some writing to take the edge off her disappointment.

'No, I'm fine. Talking's overrated anyway,' he replies.

They sit by the bed, looking at Ben, and Matty thinks it's very just that Ben's condemned to stay in this dimension without any tools for living. But then he realises that he, Matty, is also trapped in this dimension with no tools for living. Maybe he is Ben, just a brain in a vat. He thinks about Feracor's last words. He thinks about his first ones. There must be a reason for all of this. He swallows.

'I mean,' Sylvie is saying, 'do you think people get stuck at some point in their lives, at some stage in their emotional development? The psychological equivalent of what's physically happened to Ben.'

'Is this directed at me?'

'No! It's just something to think about.'

'I think you think too much, sweetheart.'

Matty knows this is rich coming from him. Gratuitous thinking at the expense of action is his speciality. The only actions Matty ever takes are designed to crush the thinking.

'Come home with me. I'll cook us some lunch. Come on, you're so thin. Let me look after you.'

But Ben is trying to talk to him. He needs to be alone with his brother.

'I'm going to stay here and write a bit, okay?' he tells Sylvie.

'But you don't have your laptop or anything.'

'I'm going to type it on my phone. Really, I'll feel a lot better if I can knock off another chapter or two. My publisher's breathing down my neck, you know, and I can email it straight to her.'

Lies are so handy for the aspiring hermit.

When she's gone, Ben starts as Matty knew he would. But he's ready.

'At least I'm alive,' he retorts.

You're more dead than I am, man. You stopped living a while ago. You said it yourself—you got stuck.

'I didn't say anything of the sort. That was Sylvie's psycho-babble.'

Yes, well we both know it's true.

'Shhh. I need to concentrate.'

PRIVATE AND CONFIDENTIAL
DR J. SYKES

CONTENTS: THIRD LIFE-WRITING CHAPTER FROM MEC, WITH MY NOTES.

From: Matty Corani <matzcorani@gmail.com>
Subject: RE: Where are you?
Date: 25 November 2015 15:06:24
To: Julia Sykes <juliasykes@mail.com>

Julia, I'm so sorry! Completely forgot. See you at 5 next Tuesday? Here's the next chapter.

Matty

```
          LOOKING UP AT THE STARS


                 Chapter 4
```

In the summer of 2008 my plane left Heathrow, not to Beijing, which I was just beginning to explore and marvel at with teenage curiosity, but to Moscow. That was a summer of dead time and anguished nostalgia for something intangible, probably just a flood of coming-of-age hormones.

Autumn brought a new academic year and a couple of magical discoveries: girls and parties. Britain in the noughties throbbed with excitement. The music sang of youth, riots, the smell of sex and beer and promise.

My face was beginning to repulse me less. For all the downsides of a few pimples here and there, I started to look like a man, my face falling into the proportions of a grown-up, the bones more prominent, the skin less dewily pink and childish. My body grew rangier, longer, leaner and stronger, in spite of my refusal to exercise it except under serious duress. A light down of hair blossomed like mould on my upper lip and, to my intense fascination, darker ones sprouted wirily in all manner of places. Ruben, though nearly two years younger, had developed these things much earlier than me. He reminded me so much of Leya in his Cuban features (not in his prolific bodily hair). His smooth tan skin and dancing eyes stood out a million miles in Moscow, and from the pallid British faces lining up for the school assembly heralding the first exeat.

No exeats for me, just vast stretches of exiled[1] term time. Not once had my term been divided into the neat segments enjoyed by the other boys. Flights home would have taken more time than the breaks allowed. All term I remained in camp under the charge of 'Matron Briony', an Australian, a fitful and erratic creature with a fondness for gin.

There were other boys from diplomatic families at the school and from time to time, one might spend a weekend in the house. It was more usual, however, for the boys to go home with friends. The system worked well, as those who lived abroad were able to offer much in return when the longer holidays came around. No boy from Rockwell had ever been invited to Beijing or Moscow. I vastly preferred the stretches in the house when it was just me and Matron. Briony would get pissed; I'd be free to do as I pleased.[2]

In November, Ben was invited to stay with a new boy, Alec Foster, and he asked if I could come

---

[1]   ASK M. ABOUT THIS CHOICE OF WORD.

[2]   YET ANOTHER FEMALE CAREGIVER THAT LET M. DOWN.

too. Ben, you were always looking out for me, weren't you.[3] Alec lived beyond the usual home counties habitat in the wilds of Herefordshire with two older sisters, twins, Maya and Olmeca, who were having a party that weekend. Alec's real name, it transpired on the way down, was Aztec.

We arrived in Herefordshire late into Saturday afternoon, the delay of the train sending me into tangles of dread. I would have to talk to them. Endless talking. A whole evening. About what? I could not imagine, there, then, that I would have a single word of interest to say to any of them. And the sheer energy required to drag myself out of the deep, dark inner pit where I could exist unbothered... I could not imagine ever summoning that energy.

Spring was creeping in but the nights were not yet long. It seemed dusky when me, Ruben and Alec arrived at the Festers' house, a totem pole indicating a driveway lined with miniature Mayan pyramids. Though Alec blushed at their presence, his gaze fixed straight through the windscreen of his mother's battered Beetle, I felt an odd sense of familiarity, surrounded as I had been by the grand constructions of Muscovite decor.

We three boys were directed to one side of the house, blocked off from intrusion by a heavy oak door, the sort of door that might bar a fortress. It did not sound as if there was anything going on beyond it, but within seconds a rapid sequence of events had unfolded. Mrs Fester had knocked; the door had been opened; the mother had been despatched with scowls; the doorway, portal to another world, had been resealed with me on the

---

[3] DIRECT ADDRESS. ASK IF 'TELEPATHY' CONTINUES...

other side of it; a glass bottle of something blue, bubblegum flavoured and alcoholic had been thrust into my hand.

As my eyes grew accustomed to the smoky fug, I saw teenagers standing, drinking, talking, smoking, a boy of about my age strumming a guitar. On the far side of the room, a laptop, unmanned, was playing Amy Winehouse out of some huge speakers. Next to it was a record player and some boxes of records. I sidled up to them and started flicking through the vinyl, all the time willing invisibility upon myself.

—Do you want a drink? said a cloud of smoke on my right, watching me replace a Bowie LP in its sleeve. That's Mum's, from the seventies.

—Um, I've actually got one, I said, agitating it and causing a small foam fountain to overspill the glass top. But, er, you can never have too many, right?

I hugged my elbow across my stomach to hide the wet patch.

—Right, agreed Smoky. I'm going to get off my face. Want a fag?

Holding a blue WKD bottle in each hand, I decided with a novel thrill of depravity that I probably did. Her smoky halo had cleared to reveal a pretty blonde girl with an insolent pink pout and a glint in her strangely clear, pale eyes. She looked like a possessed china doll.

—What's your name? I stalled for time while wondering why the cigarette I kept thrusting into her flame wouldn't light.

—I'm Nik, she held my gaze. This is my party. Well, I'm sharing it with my sister, Nak, over there.

You know, simply changing the names does not a novel make. What would you know? All life stories are fiction.[4]

I looked and saw a replica of the girl before me. Same blonde curls, same blue eyes, different demons. Across the room flourished disordered eating, panic and shyness. Before me was boredom, rebellion, escapism.

—Here, let me. Nik took the unlit cigarette from me and placed it in her mouth, expertly sucking in a plume of smoke and causing the angry red to flash and glint. As I, impressed, placed it in my mouth, I marvelled at this subtle contact between her lips and mine. It was practically a kiss.

—Where do you go to school? I asked.

—Oh come on. Let's not talk about that dump. It's some shithole not so far away from here. I tried to run away last term but they found me pretty quickly up in London.

It had never occurred to me to do anything so proactive, no matter how much I might hate Rockwell. The world for me was too small. Even if I made it to Outer Mongolia, my father would have the diplomatic forces waiting for me at the first yurt I rocked up at.

It suddenly dawned on me that all situations have a way out. This was a new and comforting idea, as new and comforting as the blue bubblegum

---

[4] WHAT IS THIS? IS HE TALKING TO HIMSELF? ARE THESE THE VOICES? ASK M.

sparkles surging through my bloodstream and the heady rush of nicotine to the brain.

I really, really liked this girl. She was fit. She understood me. She didn't seem to see what the boys at school saw. In fact, she was acting like I was pretty damn cool. Maybe I was pretty damn cool, just of the variety that appealed to girls more than boys.[5] That was all right though. That was just fine. I knew some of the boys in my form at Rockwell would give their Xbox 360s to get this close to a real life girl.

She was getting closer to me, which made me feel a bit panicky. Was some action perhaps required on my part? There were few body parts left not engaged in balancing the social essentials of WKD and a Marlboro Light, though mercifully the latter was almost at the sticky end of its lifespan. I had never snogged a girl before. Actually, I'd never really met any girls before. I settled on stubbing out the cigarette with my right hand with one ferocious manoeuvre and gently brushing her shoulder with that same liberated paw as it returned to base camp.

Nik needed no further encouragement. Turning to face me squarely, she slid her own hand, heavy with silver rings and several layers of blue nail varnish, around my straight hips. Swinging in to meet me, she pressed her curvy mouth upon mine.

It was as if a Catherine Wheel had been ignited in my solar plexus.

She slid her pink tongue between my teeth.

---

[5] STANDS IN FOR FEELINGS OF COMFORT FROM MOTHER?

It was as if a Roman Candle had been ignited somewhere further down.

She drew back but I wanted more and pulled her into my arms as she squeaked coquettishly. This time I knew what to do. Slithering back into place, I returned the wet pressure of tongue upon tongue, feeling the first flush of breast swell against my chest, gratifyingly hard by contrast. The thrill aches and intensifies and I am transported. I must possess this girl; I want to climb inside her very being and set her alight.[6]

I could barely see, the brink of euphoria tightening, taunting deeply, dizzily as she led me through the door at the far end of the room, a door previously obscured by people who have now disappeared... where? How long had I been here? Time had failed in its duty as a measuring stick, an insignificant gauge in contrast to the stirring lust in my loins, the ever encroaching urgency.

The bed I anticipated materialised, but it was covered in other party guests delightedly invading each other's space and half-watching Superbad. Not for the first time, I reflected how little I had in common with my male peers. Girls were so much gentler, softer, interested.

Nik and I took our position as an item in a corner of the cramped bedroom, on a furry pink rug. I, strong and manly, sat with my back against the wall and my legs and arms enfolding Nik, bundled between me, legs crossed, ensconced. Though desire continued to blaze within me, another new sensation was coming to the fore. Fitting In. I stopped my whirling thoughts,

---

[6] OBSESSIVE. OR IS HE SAYING THIS FOR MY BENEFIT?

129

jumbled disconnected voices and acknowledged this moment. I had come here anonymously, unknown and unknowing and now I was pulling the hostess, sitting like a kitten in my lap. I'd done really, quite seriously, well. I wanted to turf her off me and punch the air in triumph.

One of the boys on the bed extended his body across a girl lying foetally around him to pass me a hand-rolled cone-shaped something which smelt of herbal tea and illicitness.[7] I was part of the gang now and did not hesitate to accept, particularly when Nika took it from me and performed some strange smoke and snog exchange.

-It's called a blowback, she said. Now you do me.

The sun rose upon the debris. Elusive sleep crept over us, artfully slotted together, my jacket creating a cover for wandering hands.

***

Matty read this last part aloud to Ben.

'I'm getting better at this writing thing, don't you think?'

Ben, for once, is silent.

---

[7] Is he trying to tell me something? Said never took drugs.

Transcription: EXTRACT FROM CONVERSATION BETWEEN DR J. SYKES, BACP (ACCRED.) AND MATTHEW CORANI

MC: YES, I WAS IN A CAVE — YOU KNOW THE CAVES? AND I GUESS THE MUSIC, OR SOMETHING, ALLOWED ME TO GET BACK TO THE VISION. BUT THAT WAS IN A DIFFERENT CAVE.

JS: AND HOW DID THIS CAVE MAKE YOU FEEL?

MC: SAFE, CARED FOR. LIKE I BELONGED THERE.

JS: A RETURN TO THE WOMB.

MC: THAT'S HOW I FELT WITH TERA.

JS: DO YOU THINK, MATTY, THAT IN A WAY TERA TOOK ON THE ROLE OF YOUR MOTHER? DO YOU FEEL LIKE YOU'RE BEING PUNISHED FOR HER DEATH?

MC: UM, NO. I DON'T THINK I EVER WANTED TO FUCK MY MOTHER.

JS: NO, BUT THERE WAS MORE TO YOUR RELATIONSHIP WITH TERA THAN SEX FROM WHAT YOU'VE TOLD ME. AND THERE ARE SEXUAL ELEMENTS IN A MOTHER'S RELATIONSHIP WITH HER SON — A RELATIONSHIP THAT WAS CRUELLY CUT SHORT FOR YOU.

MC: WELL, ANYWAY I DO FEEL LIKE I'M BEING PUNISHED — AND LIKE I SHOULD BE PUNISHED. I AM GUILTY. IF IT WASN'T FOR ME, TERA WOULD STILL BE ALIVE. I SOMEHOW PUSHED HER AWAY INTO MY BROTHER'S ARMS AND THAT LED DIRECTLY TO HER DEATH.

JS: MAYBE YOU WERE ANGRY WITH HER, PROJECTING YOUR MOTHER'S ABANDONMENT ON TO HER. AND I THINK THIS SENSE OF GUILT GOES BACK TO YOUR SHOCK AS A BABY BEING BORN; THAT THERE'S A PART OF YOU THAT'S STUCK THERE, PERMANENTLY FEELING THE SHOCK AND FEAR OF WATCHING YOUR MOTHER DYING. SHE SHOULD HAVE BEEN MAKING YOU FEEL SAFE.

MC: Yeah, well, she didn't have much choice in the matter, did she?

JS: The mature Matty can see that — but does the tiny helpless baby Matty see it in the same way?

MC: Mmmm. So anyway, I was in this cave, and Feracor was there with me.

JS: This is the 'god' you dreamed about last time?

MC: Yes. And I keep dreaming about him. He was talking about forces. How we need all the things he represents in the world as much as we need the opposites. It's a balance.

JS: What does he represent?

MC: Wine, women and song. He's a hedonist. Animal instinct.

JS: Like your father?

MC: Like Dionysus.

XIII

*Appear to our sight as a bull
or a many-headed snake
or a fire-blazing lion to look upon.
Come, O Bacchus, as a wild beast,
With smiling face throw your deadly noose...*[†]

A few days later, Matty is trudging home from another meeting with Squales with none of the levity of the hangover with which he had awoken. Time has revealed that this was, in fact, merely the terrible hangover-precursor, the faux-bonhomie of residual alcohol warming his soul. As the light fades so does that evasive cheer that comes independently at Matty rather than from him, depending on the chemical state he's brewed inside himself. It's never an exact science, more like experimental cookery.

As he turns into the Soho web, past the teatime Friday punters, he recognises a sort of human solidarity in the drinker's solitude. There are many men alone with their pints and thoughts. He does not want to talk to them, have their words adding to the many within his own head, but he appreciates their silent presence. He disappears into an unoccupied corner of The Coach and Horses on Greek Street, one of the few bastions of old Soho that keep defiantly buggering on. Matty orders a pint of Guinness. It's full of iron and his strength needs building up.

He's able to deflect the steady drone of chatter around him but the murmuring buzz seems to calm him too. He doesn't want the relentless silence of his room. He doesn't want the

---

[†] Euripides, *Bacchae*, lines 1016-1021.

voice of his father or his brother or any of the mental theatre he's created. He doesn't even want to lose himself in the past. Beer tethers him to the present and here he is, just a young man in a pub having a drink on a Friday afternoon. No big deal.

And must he think of the future? The success or failure of his memoirs, the life or death of his brother, the outcome of the trial. The invariable piling of mischief upon mischief, guilt accrued upon guilt. His shortcomings as a son, brother, lover, friend. God help the world if he ever had his own children to pass the pollution down to. The Greeks were right, guilt is hereditary. Why not instead treat oneself as a sort of pleasure-seeking tourist on Earth, just visiting, just enjoying the best of what Earthland has to offer while the trip lasts? As one would, if one only had a month, say, in Nigeria or Laos or Sri Lanka or... Belgium. You'd cut yourself some slack, wouldn't you? You'd say, yes it's expensive but I'm only here for a month, I'm never going to be in this position again so I might as well make the most of it. I will go to that place, or eat here or see this modern wonder of the world.

What you wouldn't do is put down any roots there, because you don't plan to be there for very long, and you know it's other people that cause all the problems. You can live with yourself and your misdemeanours and your misery as long as you're not constantly paranoid about upsetting more people. Better for all concerned just to cruise through life encapsulated safely within yourself. The people one meets are just fellow travellers, just passing through. Transience is key.

Stay in the shallows where other people are concerned. Particularly girls.

Maybe his father had the same hang-ups after his mother died. Wrap yourself in cotton wool by not going in too deep. Luisa, mother of his father's second child, was stranded passportless in Cuba without a backward glance. And as for Katya, for all her matriarchal stance and financial ball-crunching, it was common knowledge in diplomatic circles that Daniel Corani was more sexually ambivalent by that stage. Blind eyes were turned to Muscovite rent boys.

He can feel the beer trundling through his gut, a flood of acid forcing the muscles to relax. A little spark of energy and well-being unravels from some warm kernel in his heart. He could do with a little company, all of a sudden.

He calls Fix. He's a little put out to discover he's with Sylvie. They're both on their way.

Now all he wants is to be alone. He buys another pint, resentfully, and goes outside to smoke, thinking with some wist of the days when smoke must have saturated the Coach's bars and everyone looked prettier through the haze. Days he is too young to remember.

'Matty!' says someone smoking.

No, it can't be. It's bloody Niknak Fester.

'Yes, it's me, Meca, Meca Foster!'

In the days before social media replaced a social existence, they'd never have recognised each other, he thinks. He must look different from his fourteen-year-old self. Then again, she looks remarkably similar, not just to her profile picture on Facebook but to the little girl who was so sexually aggressive at that party almost a decade ago. She's hotter, if anything.

'Do you know,' says Matty, 'it's the strangest thing. I was just thinking about you earlier today.'

'I'm flattered.' She winks at him.

'Because you never replied to my letters.' He smiles. 'I mean, I know I was a spotty teenage dick,' he says. 'Fuck it, right?' But he feels sudden fury surge up inside him. He has to close this chapter the right way round this time.

Slowly, slowly. She must leave this encounter thinking well of him, thinking how stupid she'd been to let him slip through the cobweb.

'Sorry,' he says more softly. 'It was a long time ago. Listen, I'm getting a round—what're you drinking?'

She looks wistfully at her near empty glass, then at him and relents. 'Yeah, a vodka and orange'd be nice.'

'Sure,' he says, off to the bar with nonchalance he does not feel. Once there, he muses in wonder. It's as if he has conjured her up! A small chance to change history. This time, she'll be coming home with him.

By the time he re-emerges, Fix, Sylvie, Sasha and the Earthman have arrived. Three of them seem a little stoned and unsteady; Sylvie looks soberly upset. The talk is all of nuts, pizza, curry.

'We've got the munchies really badly,' giggles Sasha by way of introduction when Matty says: 'This is an old school friend of mine, Olmeca Foster.'

'I thought you were at an all-boys school,' says Sylvie.

'Yeah, I was. Alec, Meca's brother, was with me at Rockwell.'

'Ec, ec, ec,' says Sasha.

'How is Alec?' asks Matty.

'He's fine. He's working in Hong Kong. I don't see him very much, to be honest. Now look I must go… but keep in touch yeah?' She's downed her drink and angled away from him. 'If you want to join me round The Corner, my sister Maya's name's on the door, okay?'

He remembers, as she trips off, the many unrequited letters he'd written to Meca at school. He is aware that, though he'd dreamed them into some sort of coupledom, he'd only ever seen her one more time after that first party, that Alec had in fact asked him not to keep pestering his sister, after a while. He remembers her phone call after so many months of silence, the invitation to some shitty ball, his agonising over what to say and do, who to be. The queue, long, pointless, undrunken… and her absolute contempt upon seeing him there, as arranged, as promised. He remembers fucking someone nameless by way of compensation, having seen enough of Meca being passed around the saliva train. The girl, whoever she was, had no idea it was his first time and she certainly didn't act as if it were hers. He can't picture a face. It was satisfying leaving with her on his arm though, passing Meca.

It was satisfying until he got back to school anyway, and then the sickness and the worries began to sting. It hadn't occurred to him to think of anything but that moment in time, up against the wall. But picture after picture of diseases and babies sought him out from biology textbooks, plays about abortion, books about AIDS, an oversized poster in the surgery that yelled *It Only Takes That One Time* and most bizarrely this slogan engraved by compass point on the desk of his maths class: '*Before you attack 'er, wrap yer whacker.*' On and on came signals of mortal worry until the voices leapt off the pages and into his head, a terrible personal radio station of birth and death. He began to suspect he had a temperature.

If only he had a name or a number for the girl. He could call her up and turn this whole panicked fuck-up into something resembling a civilised exchange between two people. 'So,' he might say over waffles and hot chocolate, 'you're not pregnant, by any chance, are you?'

'No of course not, silly,' she'd reply. 'I'm on the pill. Oh and in case you were wondering, that was my first time, so you don't need to worry about any dirty diseases or anything.'

And that would be that.

As it is, he's condemned to imagine her fucking her way through the backstreets of Basingstoke, laden with some grotesque miniature version of himself inside her, voyeuristic passenger to every sick act he has her perform in his head.

He dreamed of Meca too. She, without any real resemblance to her actual personality, had been canonised in his head. Elusive, untouchable, immortal. Beautiful, funny soul-mate. He escaped to her, mothering angel, when his thoughts of Nameless became too much.

And now he's actively missing his chance with her! Someone who might genuinely heal the horrors of losing Tera. Smoky Niknak, Meca, whoever she is, has gone.

'We should check out The Corner,' he says to Fix. 'I've heard it's really good and kind of hard to get into. If her sister's got a guest list there, well. Come on, we'll all go.'

'We've only just got here,' says Sylvie.

'Well I don't mean right this second, on the double, pasodoble, do the quickstep there. Just, in due course, that's all. Well I'm going to anyway. We're not all surgically attached, are we?'

'Calm down, mate,' says Fix. 'We'll check it out.'

There doesn't seem to be much more to say after that. Drinks are finished.

'The night's yours, Matty,' says Fix. 'Lead on.'

But when they arrive at the bar, the suspicious-looking female on the door says there's nobody by that name, 'and no, there's no Maya, Meca, nor Olmeca, nor Alec, not any Fosters whatsoever inside this bar, except for the Australian beer that comes in cans and actually I very much doubt that that is in there either as this is a smart establishment.' She pauses to inspect Matty's distressed jeans. 'Can you stand aside please?'

When she sees Fix, however, it's a different story. The coy girl comes out of her hardwoman's attire and nothing is too much trouble. Matty's seen it all before, the way they crumble. Fix is heroic. In they go.

The place, once a shady, shifty Soho Shangri-La, is nothing much to shout about now. As promised by the Door Whore, no Fosters in person or in cans. Matty is deflated.

'Shots?' he suggests.

Sasha's keen. She's developed beyond the breeze blocks of word formation to fledgling sentences now. 'Crackbabies,' she says.

'No,' says Fix. 'No crack, baby. You had the last of it in the flat. Besides, it's not very good for you in quantity. Crack in moderation. That's the rule.'

It transpires that the Crackbaby in question is neither the drug nor Sasha herself but a drink, short and powerful, deceptively reminiscent of summer picnics.

It's only when Matty is enjoyably knocking back his third that he realises where they are. Amazing how the human mind can draw the veil over events and places it cannot bear to remember. Of course it wasn't called The Corner when Tera had asked to meet him there. It had been called Sick or Sack or Sock or something. Meet me at Suck, she'd said or some such. The great establishment whose cachet and address all subsequent owners traded upon had been the victim of an extremely convenient arson a few months back; this was the crap phoenix that had risen from the ashes—and it hadn't survived for long.

It's definitely the same place. He can see the alcove where she was sitting, waiting for him, quite clearly. There's another girl sitting there now, in the dimness, waiting for her boy-friend to return from the bar where Matty is also standing. As he looks at her, he sees Tera's shadow, or perhaps her ghost, waiting for him, a memory buried and blocked. Tera had been waiting for him. When was it? Not that long after his father's death, he remembers that.

She was sketching something on a napkin, or just fidgeting. She seemed nervous. Why? She wasn't nervous about anything to do with Matty any more. He didn't mean enough to her.

Tera had her glittering artist's future. She didn't seem to care about much else.

When Matty caught her eye, Tera's shimmered a little, cat-like in recognition. She arched her back and waited for him to approach. When he moved to kiss her, she drew back, then hugged him.

Something was up.

'And it's not in my trousers,' he remembers adding. 'What is it?'

She smiled sadly and shook her head. 'Let me get you a drink. They do cocktails here.'

'Tera, you're frightening me. What's the matter? Please tell me.'

'Matty…' She paused, rearranged her hands, picked up her glass of wine. A waiter was pouring nuts like brimstone and she was saying, 'You know what I'm going to say.' And suddenly he did, but he was saying very calmly and repetitively *no I don't know what's up, something wrong?*

Tera was looking grim, serious, and he knew it had to do with the many mistakes that had, over the years, been made by him.

'Matty…' she exhaled his name, charity hand on knee. 'We're done, darling.'

Matty's not sure where he is now. He doesn't recognise these streets. The streetlamps gutter and choke and wires hang down from them, as if some electrical storm has occurred while he's been in the bar. His friends are nowhere to be seen. No humans anywhere at all in fact. He narrowly avoids stepping on to the pavement when he sees that it's not an upwards step but a downwards drop into a trench. He peers down the side of it. Something rusty and red is seeping through it, thicker than water.

Out of the bleakness, he sees a preacher on the corner. 'It's the end of the world as we know it,' he is singing. As Matty draws closer, the man takes up a theatrical jig, hopping along with an umbrella and throwing up sprays of the red liquid with his heels. Pools of the stuff lie everywhere.

The man stops. He scampers off. Matty picks his way home through the blood.

When he goes inside, Feracor, having taken on the form of a fire-blazing lion, is already there, waiting for him with tonight's bedtime story. He holds out a spoon of ketamine for Matty, who sniffs it into his sinuses with gratitude. He shivers on the borders of the two worlds until Feracor starts to speak, and then he is entirely his...

Consider the humble microbe. Tiny, one dimensional, it has a simple purpose in life—to be the most microbial microbe it can be. Its essence is its function, and to exist it must perform that function. Never, never, never, Mandrax, would it develop some complex Ten Commandment moral code which ignored a whole side of its character and being. No, Mandrax, Survival of the Fittest is what it's all about. In perfecting its essence, the microbe joins with others like itself, all being the strongest at what they do; namely, exist as microbes. One joins with another, another with another and power creeps into this army of microbes, all doing their own thing in conjunction with others like them, none disturbing the natural order. Before too long, one has a microbial force that none can resist, a superbug if you will, powerful enough to attack any other species, no matter how great in size.

There is a planet, in a different galaxy to be sure, but not dissimilar to this one, where just such a humble microbe, purely by virtue of being the most microbial it could be, reached such heights of power that it wiped out all other species, humans notwithstanding. The humans had lost sight of their own essence, their function. They were incapable of resisting the onslaught of this little microbe, a virulent strain of syphilis, which crept in silently and wiped them out to a man. Do not you be as these humans. Do you as the microbe.

XIV

Matty is confused. He thinks he has had a truly appalling dream, the kind that makes you very happy indeed when you realise it's not reality. But when he crawls out on to the window ledge for the first drag of the day, London looks the same as it did in his nightmare. Red liquid everywhere, chasms where once were pavements. No people. It's like London's been hit by a meteor or something. And the microbe thing… is Feracor warning him about antibiotic resistance? Is that how the world will be wiped out? Or is it advice?

He dives back inside, calls Fix. No answer. He calls Sylvie. No answer. He tries to turn on his laptop but there's no sign of power. He looks out; someone's strolling down the pock-marked street below and he rushes back to the window.

'Hey you!' he calls, but the person just carries on gingerly sidestepping the pits.

This is boring, he thinks, but not necessarily the end of the world. A bit of quiet time. He fetches a beer from the miniature fridge and lies back down again on his bed, folding a pillow behind his head. He reaches for his laptop, to carry on writing his story. This is who he is now, a writer doing his writing thing. That's the thing which must define him. His function. His essence. Yes, his thing. This seems to be what Feracor is trying to tell Matty, or Mandrax as he becomes in that parallel world. Be true to himself, look after number one and he will yet get through what is to come.

He writes, and he feels Mandrax is writing within him, giving him the courage of his convictions. Feracor asks: *Who do you want to be? Only write it and you shall be. If you don't like what happened, change it! And don't think about Tera. She never split up with you; it's just your mind playing tricks.*

Now he is writing for Feracor. Dr Psycho will have to wait.

***

LOOKING UP AT THE STARS

Chapter 5

Niknak Fester. She just could not get it into her head that nothing was going to happen with me. Barely a day went by without another musk-scented delivery, studded with pagan signs and fluorescent doodles. At first I tried to be discreet. I felt bad for her; but when my classmates found one of them, it was all too funny. She was just so desperate.

The crowning chapter of Niknak's epistolary campaign arrived in a featureless, colourless envelope. It was a disappointing effort. Fortunately, it contained female hysteria of definitive proportions. Niknak had illustrated the grievous afflictions she hoped might befall me in gruesome detail. The structure of her voodoo curses resembled the love poetry, angst-saturated which had tumbled forth over the winter and spring... an avalanche of sentiment which now, photocopied and annotated, graced the inner desk lids of a large proportion of the school.

I could never have envisioned that I would feel such glee at being the object of uninhibited venom, nor that I might laugh until I cried at the suggestion that 'your knob might sprout pustulous (sic), weeping, incurable sores'.

144

Boys who had never considered me worthy of their time now saw that breaking through to my inner core might be a valid investment of that time. The words 'dark horse' were mentioned in the same breath as my name. The seeds of my reputation, germinated that weekend, took root at the school one heady evening towards the end of June 2009.

The dawning of my first disco with live girls imported from surrounding schools was met with incremental excitement. Having shared the secret of my raw sexual magnetism with my peers, delivering a step-by-step account of how to snog with tongues, confidence wavered inwardly on the night itself. It need not have. I was the boy the girls saw first, the one who sparked the whispers, the one who unwittingly roused sensations they had previously only read about. Courage was screwed to the sticking point by a joint shared with my new best friends, and a small bottle of vodka.

Gathering in a sports hall decked out with gaudy flashing lights and balls, both sexes eyeing each other surreptitiously from opposite corners, I assessed the situation. Long tables had been placed in the middle of the room: a bowl of punch, some crisps, some lurid attempt at confectionary. Such bait would summon the greedy, the brave and the stupid. Clearly the most cunning plan would be to proceed towards this dazzling assortment of Venus flytraps in battle formation. Safety in numbers. Forward as one.

Then my eyes locked with one of them. An electric shock of recognition flashed between us. I found it difficult afterwards to relate how this had happened exactly, but suddenly we were in the garden, the two of us alone, kissing with a ferocity I had not dared with Niknak. Time, the vodka, the cigarettes, the friends all fell from my mind as I allowed my hands to trace the curves of her body, the blossom just budding. I marvelled at how wildly girls' bodies varied, this one so lithe and feline compared to the muscular bulk of Niknak.

Trailing a finger across her open lips and feeling my own thud of blood as she gasped, I knew we could play a more grown-up game this time. She did not object as, overcome with lust, I pressed my full weight up against her, her back up against the garden wall, my hands, my mouth everywhere, until suddenly it was not my hands and it was not my mouth, it was me in my entirety sliding into her. She stopped short, catching her breath but I continued to move inside her, gently, slowly, my hands stroking her hips, holding her risen skirt in place, and the fluidity and the rhythm and the deep welling of fluttering warmth began to mount again.

I felt an almost painful sense of loss when, in what seemed like a matter of seconds, my conquest was rounded up by the Matron General of St Edmunds and removed from her place in my arms, a place she had fitted so perfectly, like a detachable appendage measured to fit my frame. A hastily scribbled note did nothing to curb my frustration, but did reveal her name. Ella.

All the girls stared transfixed through the coach windows as I retired to my dorm.

After that night, my love letters — this time of a more sophisticated ilk — were met not with communal derision but with a certain respect. The herd could sense a previously undetected element of power throw the hierarchy into disarray. Virginity was always a thorny issue.

A rough Russian summer, however, yet yawned ahead for me. Surprises lay in store, when the predicted flight details to Moscow did not present themselves.

Furthermore, I received a letter which was not coruscated with fine art or addressed in girlish squirl. I received my first letter from my father. It was written on British Embassy paper and dated two weeks previously. It was memorable for its brevity, but life-changing in its content.

June 23rd 2009

Dear Maxi, Queen Ekaterina and I have decided that it would be better for your education if you and Ruben were to remain in the UK during holidays. Mrs Stalina will meet you at the end of term and she will act as your guardian in London.

I remain etc.

King Darius, Tyrant.

For the first time in almost a year, I returned to my underground den of solitude to absorb this. When I emerged, it was with a smile on my face. I threw the postcard into the hole and returned to school to seek out my little brother.

Ruben was inconsolable. Further letters followed from our queen which did something to explain this new twist in our fate. The King was, in fact, no longer in his esteemed new position in

Moscow. He had been sent back to Havana, 'no place for the royal princes to hang about in the holidays'.

-But we grew up there, Ruben protested. My mother is there!

Queen K. was going with him, she said, and we wondered how Darius, who had managed thus far to dump a woman in every port, had failed so badly to do so with this one. She must, we said as we had said before, have some strange hold over him.

The end of term came swiftly. With one parent dead and the other spying on communists in the farthest reaches of the Earth, or so it felt, I had almost achieved the orphan status I craved.

I found I was not able to dismiss Ella's erotic eloquence quite as easily as Niknak's.

I wrote back. Such was the shock of male reciprocation that Ella's letters ceased for a couple of weeks. When she wrote back, the tone was different, less calculated perhaps. It became apparent that she too would be in London over the summer.

Ruben, adaptable and chameleonic, swiftly recovered from his devastation at leaving his friends. His disappointment at a summer without Russian, Chinese or Cuban travels, without his father, without his latest pseudo-mother, Katya, was transposed by gleeful excitement as the black car with the dark windows sped us out of the long school drive and into who knew what.

The flat was situated on the first floor of a block not far from Marble Arch. It was airy and white. A clean slate. To me it represented freedom.

Anonymity, solitude when I sought it. Company when I did not. The chance to exist away from school as my own person, not a victim of my loathsome family. There were three bedrooms, arranged in such a way as to place a desirable distance of living space between us and our grim new guard, Mrs Stalina. I was not concerned about her presence. I imagined Ruben would charm her as he had Matron.

It took me a week to figure out my escape route. The drop from my window was not significant but the climb back in was uncomfortable, even with Ruben's assistance. Mrs Stalina's hearing impairment had been much mocked in Russia and was used to good effect now; Ruben distracted whilst I slipped out of the window with her keys. Scenting liberty like a hound, I reluctantly sacrificed it for the greater good and searched for a key cutter.

Ruben's help in re-entering the flat began a summer of glorious collusion between us; the creation of a life in London. It was the kind of hectic fun I had assumed was not on offer to me until I met Ella. Suddenly I was able to come to every party. Suddenly it felt like I was the life and soul of them.

Dr J. Sykes BACP (accred.)
Psychotherapist

Private Room
36 Harley Street
London W1G 9PG

Date:	Time:	Patient Initials:	Attendance:
Tuesday 8 December 2015	5pm	MEC	Y

Notes:

-No chapter written this time. M. said he was working on it.

-We talked about 'conquest' of women, M.'s self-perception as lady-killer. He seemed to think I was flattering him, even that I was 'interested'.

-I explained archetypal idea of puer aeternus to M. He seemed elated – narcissistic reaction? Said it explained everything. Joining dots I can't see? He talked about Charles II bringing the party back after puritanical Cromwell, Dionysus doing the same after Christ. Pendulums swinging. Two essential sides of human nature.

-Tried to bring conversation back to significance of over-identification with this archetype for him. Answer, acc. to Jung, is work.

-M. said he is keen to work creatively (life-writing makes him feel better and he has another project on the go) and additionally to look for a more reliable, income-paying job.

-M. seems torn between idea of real life not yet having begun/real life being already over. Says he's missed the party. Soho 'over'. The world is 'over'.

-More dreams of 'Feracor' or Dionysus ('shape-shifting'). M. asked if I'd read the Bacchae yet. Quite condescending. Answer yes – but struggling to see the correlation.

-We realised that dreams are linked to recent memories, conversations, anxieties (sexual health in this case). Message about microbes this time... We were able to draw something positive from dream by examining its significance to M.

-Guilt over sexual promiscuity. Worries he may have STD but continues to fixate on women and sex. Does he wish to 'colonise' people like microbe?

-Considered possibility that dream was a message to his conscious self from an unconscious aspect of himself, namely that strength to be found in fulfilling all your potential. Talked about how we might follow this advice — back-to-work suggestion.

-M. described blood in the streets (apologised for not wiping feet/getting blood on my carpet). Worries about global warming, desertification, meteor strikes. These anxieties seem to be linked to Feracor visions — the one supporting the other and vice versa.

-We are going to have a break from therapy due to my holiday. M. going to France to stay with stepmother for his birthday on 18/12, Christmas, New Year etc. and meet again Tuesday 5 January. He's back on 3 Jan. Gave him mobile number if in trouble and he has my email.

AFTERTHOUGHTS:

-Something addictive about visions? Falling in love substitute?

-See Storr, Feet of Clay: 'It will be recalled that on one occasion (Ignatius) saw "the plan of divine wisdom in the creation of the world". These consolations are an example of an irrational spiritual experience, usually felt and remembered as deeply impressive. Neither psychotic delusions nor religious faith nor being in love can be shaken by argument. Nor can spiritual experience. A person either had such an experience or he has not. Mystical states may be short-lived, but they leave an indelible imprint. Even when dissociated from any religious faith, they are remembered and treasured, and their return is longed for.' (pp. 184-5)

And:

'Yet they had nothing to live by; no religious faith, no myth, not even a delusional system. Jung described these people as 'stuck', in that they had lost any sense of progress towards a goal.' (p. 94)

XV

As Matty looks out of his window at clear signs of cosmic demise, he thinks, as ever, back. As the unnatural December heat increases, the rays of the swollen sun burn his body through the glass and he thinks if he just turned round, Tera would be there in his bed, making everything okay, not so very, very hard.

When he met Tera, every single atom in his life took on colour, exuded strangeness, newness, hope. They were a complete entity created from two halves, undentable by dimension, space, time, life, death, fate. Nothing could ever, Matty believed, tear it apart. The two distinct hemispheres had become chemically fused. An irreversible change; the two had become one new thing.

He just can't imagine a happier time than when he'd shared the flat with Ben and his bed with Tera, his father back in Havana where international communications were gravely inadequate. Much as he would have loved a summer in Cuba, he could feel life opening up in London. Time to put away childish things. The London sky unfolded each morning as a lover unfolds from his beloved, each movement revealing chance, fortune, opportunity.

Tera was as integral to his sense of peace, his sense of home as the consistency of the flat itself and of his brother, the one constant of his conscious life. He would never have confessed aloud his appreciation for Ben's soulful understanding, reliable guidance. But some things do not need to be spoken. Ben seemed to him infinitely more mature than many of his peers and none the worse for it; he displayed a disarming wisdom in the rare junctures that

Matty admitted to problems but more often than not, he was simply a figure of permanence, just there. Ben and Tera were the pillars on which his existence rested, rocks which tethered his flighty mind. Ben was undemanding, non-judgemental and endlessly entertaining. If he required a role model in his older brother, this was a pressure Matty had never felt. In fact, he frequently felt as if he had been cast the role of the younger, free from the restraints and responsibility burdens of the path-finding elder.

***

Looking Up At The Stars on and on. I have forgotten the chapter. My memory of the timings of this period have vanished… where school ends and university begins. Thea was my timeline and time still does not exist for me outside her.

She had transformed my life into something wonderful. Since that first fateful meeting, apocalyptic raving, she had claimed my heart and my bed, spending such extended tracts of time in the latter that it was only a matter of weeks before I announced my need for her to live with me. It was not so much a question of Thea moving in as simply not moving out.

After that glorious first summer of 2012 we were both adamant that we must live together in my father's flat. Mrs Stalina had found a new job as a maternity nurse and was currently terrorising a lovely young couple in North Yorkshire; Ruben was still at Rockwell House during term time. Darius didn't give a shit what his son did. Thea's parents, though, were not overjoyed about this idea. I suppose we were quite young to make such serious decisions. But we felt like we'd spent all our lives being young, having decisions, often the wrong ones, made for us by those who knew only what they wanted us to be.

We went to Thea's parents' house to pick up the rest of her stuff. The place was suffocatingly dull, Mum and Dad dullingly suffocating. I wore a tie and the only trousers I had that weren't jeans. Thea took off her bandanna and paint-spattered white T-shirt and morphed into a girl I did not know. She looked like Alice in Wonderland with a daisy-strewn Sunday Best dress, each hair held immaculately in place by a blue velvet hairband.

We walked hand in hand from Putney Tube but she ripped hers out of mine as we approached Suburban Heights.

-Don't you love me anymore? I asked.

-Can you put that cigarette out?

I wondered what I'd done wrong.

-Darling! The door opened and an identikit version of Thea's new attire appeared in the frame. I suppressed the urge to say 'honey, you baked'.

-And you must be Maxi, she added. Her nose wrinkled unfavourably.

-Yes, Mum, said Thea. This is my new boyfriend.

-Enchanté, Mrs Martial, I said, strangely, and then tried to cover the strangeness by Gallicly kissing her hand.

-Do call me Angelica.

I followed the two of them, the mother wearing white tights I could see now, into the kitchen where Thea's father was fiddling with a radio. He smiled awkwardly and some alarming dentistry was revealed.

-Timmy Martial, he said, offering a hand.

-Pleased to meet you, I answered with a healthier Anglo lilt.

-And who are you?

-Ah, right, yeah. I'm Maxi Qurani, your daughter's lover.

Thea turned pale.

There had clearly been some arguments in this house. Thea was their only child and they fully intended to keep her as one. The spectre of tension hung between the three of them. Angelica cut through the silence by grabbing the radio from Timmy's hand and setting it out of reach behind the sink.

-Let's have some lunch, shall we? We can talk about this, Thea, like civilised people, can't we.

Not a question.

-Do you like shepherd's pie, Maxi?

-I'm actually a vegetarian. Sorry, I should have said.

-Actually, I am too now, Mum, said Thea.

-What? Why? You used to love your steak.

Thea looked at me.

-My body is a temple, I said, bowing my head earnestly.

Nobody seemed to see the irony in my smirk. Truth was I just didn't much like meat, having had congealed corpses forced down my throat for years at Rockwell. Again, no personal choice. Now I had choice, I was exercising it everywhere just for the hell of it. And if you've chosen to do something, it's because you want it in some way, or you want the consequences of it. So there's nothing to rail against.

-Well fine, said Angelica, determined to keep up the 'we are sensible, reasonable people' facade. Garlic bread and salad for you two then. For God's sake, Timmy, I already moved that bloody radio: leave it alone!

Timmy relinquished it, abandoning the hope that the cricket might magically come on and drown out contemplation of his daughter's sex life.

-Do you paint as well? He turned to me.

-Um, no. No sadly not. I can't draw a thing, though my ceramic image of Death bearing down upon a newborn baby was hailed as groundbreaking at school.

Once again, I watched the parents of my beloved recoil and decided against humour as a conversational tactic. The aim, after all, was to remove Thea from their clutches and if we could accomplish that with no bad blood, so much the better.

We sat down at a smartly laid table and Thea said, Maxi's just started at UCL.

-Great, said Timmy. What are you reading?

-Fear and Loathing in Las Vegas.

-Of course, Timmy sighed.

-Oh, I see what you mean. Philosophy and Greek. I live very close to UCL.

-Yes, well we did rather have closeness in mind when we suggested Putney School of Art and Design rather than Camberwell. So let's cut to the chase. We gather you two are thinking of moving in together. We don't think that's a very good idea. Thea, will you please continue to live at home until you're a little better prepared for the world?

-Dad, Thea protested, no other student lives with their parents. Living in halls with other young people is an important part of the process of growing up.

-Thea, we're not talking about halls, are we? We're talking about the extremely unsavoury prospect to any parent of you moving in with your boyfriend, a boy - forgive me, Maxi - who has no more experience of life than you do. And whom you've only known for a couple of months.

My eye was caught by a peculiar painting on the wall. At first glance, a fairly innocuous river scene, but upon closer inspection filled with sexual undercurrents, all caves and trees and twisted deviant shapes.

Angelica saw me and I snapped my eyes guiltily away.

-It's a lovely one, isn't it? One of our favourites. She's a talented girl our Thea.

-Thea did that? It was so different from anything she'd showed me. Much much darker.

-Yes, it's so innocent, isn't it? There's a sort of purity there. We used to go on camping trips near that river.

Thea and I glanced at each other and tried not to laugh. These people didn't have the first clue about their own daughter. It was my duty to rescue her.

It dawned on me that I should probably start selling myself a little harder.

-Er, Timmy, Angelica. I looked sincerely at both ends of the table in turn. I love your daughter. I want to make her happy and look after her while she focuses on her talent and becomes the great artist we all know she can be. I know I'm not hugely adult yet, but I know Thea, I know what she needs and wants and together we can make that happen.

Thea smiled at me, then shyly began to nibble on some salad.

-You're a nice boy, Maxi, said Angelica patronisingly. When Thea's finished art school, she can do whatever she likes, frankly. But until then, we'd vastly prefer it if she lived with us and lived by our values.

Timmy was moving in on his third glass of red wine. I could see Thea's features in his bigger, manlier face.

-Look, I said, she's practically living with me already and no great calamity has occurred, has it? If anything we calm each other down, make each other think about the future, work harder. We look after each other.

Angelica interjected: I really have had enough of this conversation. I'd like to draw the line here for now. In fact I insist upon it BUT we will review the situation next year. If you're even still together. You're young, you know. Feelings change like the wind at your age. Now can we please talk about something else?

I found this facile take on our love insulting, to say the least. The temptation to tell each of them what I thought of them, of their bourgeois, safe existence and their parochial mindsets, was almost irresistible. Instead I sought out Thea's foot with my own beneath the table.

Angelica leapt back from it with a great grunting of chair.

-What the hell do you think you're playing at!

-Oh shit – sorry, didn't realise…

On the other hand, it was only a foot for Christ's sake. God these people were uptight. My own father's liberal attitude to such things put them to shame.

Unable to further endure the emotional content of this lunch, Timmy started talking about football. I've never been a man's man and found myself even more at sea than before. Meanwhile, Angelica concentrated on manoeuvring delicate forkfuls of shepherd's pie into her affronted person.

-It's true what they say, she said finally. You do meet, not make your children. I feel like I barely know you these days, Thea.

After some ice cream and excruciating silence, we came to the denouement.

-I am going home with Maxi. Mum, Dad. That is what's going to happen now. Back home, really. I'm already living there.

-Darling, it's not your decision to make. We'll have the police bring you back.

-Yes, because they've got nothing better to do.

-I don't recognise this brat of a daughter. We've spoilt you. It's our fault.

-I'm going now. Come on, Maxi. I'm just going to get my things.

-You can forget that too, said Timmy with fatal quietness. You go now, you mess up your life like some fallen woman but don't expect us to send you off with hugs and kisses and don't expect any cash from us to tide you through and certainly don't expect to just rape our house of the things you consider your belongings. The door will remain open to you, Thea, until such point as you see sense, a point I fear will inevitably come as you have chosen to ally yourself with a complete cretin.

Angelica was watching his puffed-up chest with welling pride.

-Shall we go then? I smiled at Thea. She was a curious mixture of trepidation and relief.

She got up from the table, put her hand in mine and we left with nothing and without looking back. I'd never been so proud in my life.

-You and me against the world then, baby, I said as we waited for the bus to Marylebone. First thing tomorrow, we buy you some new painting stuff, whatever you need.

-You're amazing, she said. I know we're doing the right thing.

XVI

From: Katya Corani <katyacorani@outlook.com>
Subject: Happy Birthday!
Date: 18 December 2015 11:19:58 GMT+01:00
To: Matty Corani <matzcorani@gmail.com>

Dearest Matty,

Hope you have lovely birthday plans and that's why you're not picking up your phone. I'll try you again later.

Take care. Thinking of you.

Much love,

Katya xxx

***

Matty switches off the Wi-Fi, then his phone. Feracor urges him to go out and find new women, to celebrate a bacchanalian birthday, but Matty does not fancy his chances out there; strange things are happening. He nods at Feracor and continues to write. He must make sense of this time with Tera; he can feel that he is close to the truth.

***

We went to some parties, it is true, throughout the course of that final year together. And at some point the joints turned into lines and the sweets into pills. But we did them together — explored new horizons and helped each other

162

break taboos. We worked in the daytime and we played by night. Our bodies were young and able to throw off the ravages of the night before with ease. We were in love; we were happy. The 'friends' I'd had at Rockwell dispersed across the globe on gap years. I was happy to stay where I was, a steady slipstream of moneys from our man in Havana keeping both Thea and I afloat.

The flat was a gift, freeing me from insalubrious university digs and the unappealing company therein. Thea and I had it to ourselves most of the time, happy to have Ruben for the odd day release from school and the holidays. Then Ruben became a more permanent fixture. Much as I thought I would dislike this intrusion into quasi-marital life, the truth was that I loved Ruben being there. He provided the kind of unconditional friendship that enabled me to be myself. And when I had an outlet for my true self, I was able to be my most charming self with Thea. That is not to say I ever felt compelled to act for her, but occasionally I deemed it necessary to spare her my inevitable ups and downs. With passion come storms and our relationship was less tempestuous when Ruben was living with us.

It was a balanced microcosm, a happy familial nucleus.

When I left school and its mildly uninspiring gang of pupils, I left guessing that, statistically, the chances of liking my peers would grow at UCL, if only due to the greater element of choice. However, I felt nothing more than a mild disdain for the uninspiring crowd I met through the painful social exercises of Freshers' Week. They were just too eager, too excited to be out in London, a freedom which I now took for granted. Such liberty was, by itself, insufficient for true entertainment. Its charm lay in its role as a foundation for ingenuity, deployment of a little creative experimentation. My fellow students had little to offer beyond their infinite capacity for cut-price pints. I required more from a companion and I felt as if I offered more in return, ever enterprising in the pursuit of fun and the expansion of consciousness.

I was more compulsively drawn to Thea's art school crowd with their endless energy, reverence for beauty and open-mindedness. Life was for them a glamorous whirl, a feeding of the senses, a sybaritic search for the finer things in life. The good times were sensational, the bad times so excruciating in shared intensity, the very recognition of this depth of feeling made me revel in my own existence. These people, and Thea most of all, made me feel alive.

Thea had the unusual distinction of being equally at ease at a street rave as in a castle. Her presence was desired by all for her unfailing ability to light up a room, a heart, an evening. I found I paid for my parties with an overwhelming need for solitude — the flat would host a hibernation of plaintive self-beratings, wasted days before the desire returned to wreck the accumulated well-being and accompanying smugness. For Thea, life did not stop and start like this: She remained as vital and vivacious everywhere, all the time, making my flat a home, making art, making love. If we rowed, it was an expression of my internal irritation, a desire for provocation on my part, never hers.

That's not quite true, Man.

But what would Feracor know about it? He was not there. Type on, young scribe!

In the most graceless of situations, she charmed me, any slip of humanness making her all the more angelic in my eyes as her vulnerability told me I was needed, valued, loved.

I told her I loved her that very first weekend, all thoughts of playing the game so irrelevant to this meeting of souls that I had no choice but to abandon my teenage rules. She had looked at me curiously with those big old cat eyes and replied, Yes.

-What do you mean 'yes'? It's not a question.

-Yes it is, she said. And I accept.

Thea's friends persuaded me of the notion that you are what you do. I liked to be associated with those who were producing things, new things, interesting things, enduring things. The students I met at my own university did not seem to agree with my virtue hierarchy. Most of them were gaining a degree simply to guarantee entry to the slickly-oiled machinery of the City.

It's not that I didn't value the freedom of studying in London, more that I was able to imagine the freedom of not studying in London. Passing my first year exams had been a close-run thing but ultimately succeeded in showing me that a degree might be gained with minimal work, if one was prepared to make a concerted effort for the last hundred hours pre-exam. Buzzing on coke, spewing out philosophical truths, I had impressed even myself with the depth of my arguments.

The problem, really, was that the subject, philosophy, bored me. I found the topics it tore apart genuinely interesting before they were hoovered into the grey vacuum of academia, dealt with, contained. Who are we? What are we here for? The great questions of life reduced to meaningless squiggles, signifiers of nothing. Well, to all apart from our esteemed professor, it is eminently clear that the reason we are here can be expressed as 'gh%fx@=jtc' where 'j' is a happy medium and blah blah blah…

I liked Greek though. There was a celebration of things of beauty which endured, which changed the way people thought and felt. Life is a Greek tragedy. Family is a Greek tragedy. What family is so free from melodrama they can't identify with at least one? The trouble with the philosophical texts I was asked to read was that they were only ever a small part of a long and meaningless academic chain, the main purpose of which was to prove wrong the theories which had come before it. I grew restless.

In that first year I devoted less and less time to a degree which seemed only to sap and frustrate me, and more to the thrills I felt were providing a real-life education.

Felix was essential in the latter.

He seemed to me a dashing, dangerous figure; everyone's dealer of choice. Of course, back then, he'd only really been selling a bit of sniff, perhaps some weed to take the edge off. He was everyone's favourite guest, invited to hundreds of parties every week. Yes, then, truly the sun had shone on Felix. There was no gathering too bohemian, none too scabrous, none too hooray for Felix to pass it over.

Felix and I got each other. Any tension in our friendship lay in us both liking Thea too much.

Yeah right, you keep telling yourself that. You're delusional, Man. You came on to him! You made a pass at him! That's where the 'tension' lay.

Matty's completely certain that this is not the case. Feracor has become increasingly odd.

When I met Felix, I was hungry for the mad ones, the truth seekers, anyone with a bit of passion and determination to *live* this life. I recognised their blend of creativity and self-destruction in myself and I sought out mirrors. I could only empathise with their aggressive pursuit of fun in all its dubious guises. Felix, eternal child, was both the master and the pawn of such people. He was the porn of such people: everyone's fantasy.

Despite her evident distrust of Felix, it was Thea who had introduced him to me. I would have been jealous of him, he looked so cool, had he not instantly put me at ease talking about his band's music. Felix was the single most charismatic person I'd ever met. With his strange purple eyes trained upon you it was impossible to look anywhere else, impossible to hear the words of anyone else. His appetite for life seemed boundless and I was mesmerised.

Felix had the rare ability to perceive a situation full of potential for chaotic fun where others would see only a dead end. A thin man, his presence extended far beyond his slight frame and dark hair and when he spoke, he seemed to say exactly what I felt. He had the right idea about just about everything and the world seemed suddenly more exciting, less one dimensional. I found a brother, a role model, someone to follow.

After that first encounter, just a few drinks at a record label launch, I felt uncontrollably euphoric, though I couldn't quite put my finger on why. I felt high, more myself and happier to be myself than ever before, as if Felix had touched something deep inside me. I couldn't stop talking about him.

So I was surprised when Thea's silence turned out to be contempt. As we took the Tube home, she turned on me.

—For fuck's sake baby he's a coke dealer. You're not really impressed by that are you? He's a total loser.

We were sharing earphones, listening to the Libertines on Thea's iPhone. The guitar riff escalating in one half of my head suddenly began to grate. I took out the earpiece and looked at Thea incredulously.

—What? I thought he was one of your best friends! Do you really not like the guy? He couldn't be nice enough about you. Yeah, sure I know he gets stuff for his friends upon occasion, but it's not like you're horrified by the odd joint, is it?

Thea's eyes widened.

—Maxi, it's not just a bit of weed we're talking about. I was at primary school with Felix. His parents, believe it or not, used to play golf with mine. We used to be friends, great friends. But I have nothing to say to him any more — he's gone so off the rails… He's in debt; he's mixing in dangerous circles — and he's doing shitty shift work in hospitals, stealing pills from the pharmacy and dealing to fund his own considerable gak habit. It's like watching a car crash in slow motion.

For the first time ever, I doubted Thea's character judgement. Felix didn't look troubled any more than he looked like the offspring of golf-playing parents. He was a picture of vitality. And a very useful guy to know.

A snake of a thought crept across my brow - had those two had some sort of thing going on? She was a little too worked up for my liking. Maybe some casual fling or maybe she'd been in love with him. Was she still? I was unable to stop the thought crystallising into voice.

-God, Maxi! No! No. What the hell is wrong with you? Why would you...

-Okay, okay, I'm sorry! I held up my hands in a 'don't shoot me' pose and laughed at her staring in fury at me until her face cracked and she too began laughing.

XVII

*The soil flows with milk, it flows with wine, it flows
with the nectar of bees.
The Bacchic god, holding on high
the blazing flame of the pine torch
like the smoke of Syrian frankincense,
lets it stream from his wand.*[†]

By Christmas Day, Matty wants to see other people even less than he usually does. His present to himself is a double wrap of K, purchased perhaps unwisely from someone who is not Fix, and a bottle of brandy, his father's favourite drink. But first he cuts the mould off some cheese that has been languishing in the miniature fridge, removes the lid of a beer with his teeth and clicks on the link to his favourite porn site. Mythological porn is a niche fantasy, to be sure, but what fetish isn't? A little stress relief before he faces up to the memory, one of them anyway, that he's been trying to avoid: the trip to Cuba two years ago.

***

It was December 2012 when King Darius summoned us to Cuba by letter, and of course we leapt at the idea of a bit of sun, of revisiting my childhood. Thea was keen to meet my father, having to all intents and purposes lost her own. Timmy had come round to our flat only once, under the pretence of delivering some birthday cards. The timing was not fortuitous and did little

---

[†] Euripides, *Bacchae*, lines 142-7.

to persuade him that his daughter was in good hands. We'd had a party for her the previous night. At some point, uninvited (though I may have hinted to him that it was going on), Felix had dropped by and the usual carnage had ensued. The flat was in disarray, we were in disarray and several people had pushed on through the drug fug into the next day. A sad coincidence. Timmy backed off pretty quickly.

Thea had various art projects going on and I should have been writing a paper on the role of the Furies in Aeschylus' *Eumenides*. It's a pretty cool story: boy (Orestes) has no choice but to kill mother; Furies (bit like crack whores) punish him by driving him mad; and then the poor fucker still has to stand trial for matricide because not even Apollo can save him from the ancient hell hags. Anyway, I figured I could finish my work in Cuba. What we needed was a holiday. Plane tickets arrived in the post, reminded me of my schooldays.

-What should I pack? asked Thea, determined to make a better impression on my father than I had on hers.

-Oh, well, whatever. Doesn't really matter. But the King likes to live it up occasionally. Bring some smart stuff.

-I've been living in smocks and jeans for the past few months. My only smart stuff is at home.

-I wish you wouldn't call it that. This is your home now.

-Okay. My parents' home. Doesn't change the fact.

-We'll buy some smart stuff then.

Darius was nothing if not generous with cash deliveries to his sons. But with us all feeding from the pot, it didn't go so far.

I was blazing with excitement when we set off together to the airport, taking my girl on holiday. I felt like an old hand at long-haul. Thea had only been to the usual destinations of the Putney parent vacation market - Sardinia, Val d'Isère, Rock… I'd bought a linen jacket, which made me feel like my father. Or at the very least, like someone of whom my father would approve. I took charge, handling tickets and passports and failing to get us upgraded.

We left on Friday, due to stay with Darius for the week and then spend some time together alone. Ruben would come out after the first weekend, so I'd assumed we'd all be there for my birthday on Tuesday.

-We are so grown-up, I said, about to turn nineteen. There's nothing we can't legally do.

-Well there are some things, she said.

-I know, I know. Still can't snort a line off a dead hooker's knockers.

-Sad that a man of your maturity should be denied such pleasures until he's twenty-one.

-Criminal.

We made good use of the free bar on the flight and touched down at Havana with the kind of hangover only aeroplane boozing can give you; something to do with the air-con and the altitude, no doubt. Thea was in a fairly ill humour by the time we'd made it through baggage reclaim and navigated endless visa queues.

-My bag always comes out last, I said. I'm afraid if you travel with me you'll be tainted by the same curse.

She laughed feebly as we finally made it through to the arrivals hall and spotted a man holding up a sign saying 'Qurani'. He was, it transpired, my father's driver, and he escorted us into gusts of sunshine where all my Spanish promptly disappeared. To my surprise, the Chevy took us not to His Excellency's palatial residence but to the Hotel Nacional. I'd been there perhaps once as a child but my memories of that time were so hazy, I wasn't sure if I was recognising the place or making false memories from things I'd been told about it, or from a postcard I'd been sent in my first term by Leya, which had taken pride of place in my bunk bed collage.

The hotel rose out of the seedy jazz club lined streets we'd passed, giant white fortress of civilisation, a fragment from another era. The beauty at reception showed us to room 225 ('Ava Gardner and Frank Sinatra stayed in this room') and informed us that the King would meet us in the bar at eight.

-I wonder what Ava and Frank got up to in a room like this, I said hopefully, raising my T-shirt suggestively and scratching my chest.

But Thea was not up for recreating Ratpack sex. She was not on good form, I seem to remember. Premenstrual or something. She bucked up a bit when we hit the courtyard bar, where a band was playing Guantanamera and waiters hovered discreetly awaiting our drinks decision. Of course they and we already knew that a couple of mojitos were the only answer. We took a seat on one of the elegant sofas in the galleries which lined the gardens. These, full of flowers and peacocks and palm trees, sloped towards the Bay of Havana beyond. We were several drinks down and entering the Cuban spirit by the time King Dad arrived, Queen K. in tow and a couple of young men I did not recognise.

-Maxi, he held out his arms and I rushed at him.

It's a funny thing, seeing the person that made you after a long time. You tend to forget your actual relationship or lack thereof. He felt frail as I slapped him in manly camaraderie round the back. As he drew away I could see he was older, greyer of hair and complexion despite the suntan, more wrinkled. Still a glamorous old bastard though. Ekat was a deep mahogany colour and largely hidden behind a massive pair of sunglasses. Sunset had long been and gone. I moved on to her, shaking her hand with cold candour. Thea was still lingering uncertainly and I remembered my 'taking charge' role.

-Dad, Ekat, this is my girlfriend, Thea.

-Pleased to meet you both. She held out her hand timidly.

-Delighted, said Ekat with grace.

-This, said Darius gesturing to one of the unknowns, is Luiz. And this is Juan. They both work for the Cuban National Ballet.

-How fascinating, I said, instead of 'how fucking weird'. Are you all staying here?

-No, no, said Darius. No rest for the wicked, I'm afraid. I thought you and Thea might appreciate the privacy of being here by yourselves. Queen Ekat and I have business abroad from Tuesday.

-Oh, well at least we have this weekend to catch up.

-Yes, dear boy, and how very nice it is to see you both.

-You'll miss Ruben, though. I think he gets in on the seventeenth, Monday.

I didn't mention the fact that they'd miss my birthday the following day.

-Yes, he's coming with us though.

-Where exactly are you going?

-It's an international relations thing in Haiti.

-Sounds cool.

-I do wish you wouldn't use that teenage vernacular, Maximilian. I assume you don't mean the opposite of warm.

Thea was bonding with Ekat on the plush wicker sofas.

-I used to paint, Ekat was saying wistfully in her husky Rusky accent. Never terribly well, I just loved it, you know? I do so envy those who have that gift.

I'd been kind of hoping Queen K. might have been displaced by Leya, now that Darius was back in the motherland.

-Have you seen Ruben's mother? I asked him pointedly when we were all sitting down with yet more mojitos.

-Yes, he said calmly, squeezing Ekat's hand. I bumped into her in Habana Vieja. She was trying to offer my colleague a girl for the night.

-What on earth does that mean?

-She's a prostitute, Maxi. He smiled. They're all the bloody same in this godforsaken country. Anything to get some foreign cash. Anything to get a visa.

-It's true, said Juan, sadly. You should see the queue of women outside the Italian Embassy.

-I don't believe you, I said. Leya would never, never do something so low. I turned to Thea. This woman was like my mother; she practically brought me up. She was wonderful, she really was. She was an amazing stepmother to me. No doubt even more amazing as Ruben's actual mother.

-Maxi, you're too innocent. Grow up, boy. My father was smoking irritably.

-Well I guess we've got the week to find out if that's true or not. We'll ask around for her tomorrow. It's your fault if she's been reduced to, to… I couldn't bring myself to say it… If you left her destitute with no options and no future. I'm sure Ruben would just love to know what you've abandoned his own mother to.

-Oh do get off your high horse, Maxi. It was just a bit of fun, what Leya and I had. Children happen, you know. Sometimes. It's an unfortunate thing and it can't make a silk purse out of a sow's ear of a relationship. You have to move on.

I was astounded. Turning red, I began, If you think for one second...

But he had started laughing. Maxi, Maxi. Just my little joke. Leya is fine and well and living in suburban bliss in Miramar. You can go and see her whenever you want.

Sick joke. I got over it.

-What kind of monster... Thea was beginning to mutter in my ear. I shut her up by pretending to kiss her and watched my father scowl his disapproval of public displays of affection.

-So, you busy these days, Dad?

-Same old, same old. Less keeping tabs on the commies though, more sorting out travelling idiots like you two.

-What have we done?

-I said *like* you, Maxi. Don't be so touchy. Had a Brit call us up just yesterday, in fact, in a bit of a state. Been a lodger in a house up in Vedado. Cheaper than the big hotels, you understand, and this chap was on his gap year. He'd been buying marijuana on the Malecon quite merrily, not realising he was being trailed by the neighbouring inhabitants of the street in which he'd been staying. They have this terrible thing here, completely the opposite of Brit public school loyalty, more like a Neighbourhood

177

Watch scheme of sneaks. They call it CDR. Campaign for the Defence of the Revolution for you non-Spanish speakers. Basically an excuse to inform the government of any wrongdoings of your neighbour. In this case, the family whose home it was took the shit for this lodger's error - the government chucked them out and reclaimed the house. They're homeless. Lodger wasn't punished of course, they need his dollar. He came to me, distraught obviously, to see if I could help his landlords get their house back. Nothing doing. It's the side of communism we don't talk about here, you never know who's going to whip it back to the Castros - the Castrati, as I call them. It's a police state. Nobody wants to speak.

-You should write a book about it, said one of the ballerinas. You've got all these amazing experiences, all from the diplomatic heart of Havana.

-Ah well now's the time. It's all changing, you see, with Obama and Raul in charge. Before long, it'll be unrecognisable. Full of bloody Americans!

I wondered how much my father was paying these obsequious toy boys. I wondered why Ekat tolerated them.

-Do you miss Moscow? Thea asked her.

-Not so much, my dear. Besides, every American car you see here's supported by a Russian engine. I don't feel so terribly removed. Have you ever been to Russia?

-I have actually. Not Moscow but St Petersburg. I went with my father; spent a lot of time

178

trailing round the Winter Palace and being plied with vodka in souvenir shops. And I got chilblains in my bottom sitting in the snow on the banks of the Neva.

-Ha ha, exclaimed Darius. Well then, you've experienced everything Mother Russia has to offer.

-With a few minor exceptions, said Ekat huffily. She moved slightly farther away from Thea on the sofa.

-Certainly wasn't up Maxi's street, Darius continued. But then, what is? He turned to Thea. How are you finding life with my son then, my dear? Is he being awfully troublesome?

-He's wonderful, she said with beautiful simplicity. My heart grew hot.

-Is he indeed. How the times change, eh Maxi? He was nothing but trouble when he was little. A most disobedient child. We packed him off to school as early as they'd take him but he was always coming home for the holidays. Like a bad penny.

-Thanks, Dad. Nice to feel wanted.

-Oh I'm only joking, Maxi. Let your old Dad have his little jokes.

-Some would call it bullying, said Thea quietly.

-What's that? She speaks! You'll have to forgive me, I'm very hard of hearing these days.

As Darius levered himself out of his chair, he leant on a walking stick I hadn't seen earlier.

Falling to pieces, he said, seeing me watching it.

-What's wrong? I asked.

-Nothing, nothing. Just getting old. You two going to drop some sprogs then? I have to say I don't relish the prospect of being a grandfather.

-Um, we're not even twenty yet.

-I forget these things. You've been around for so long now, I keep thinking you must be grown up, pushing thirty or something.

-Some way off that one.

-Anyway, said the King, no use us sitting around here getting sloshed all night. Who's hungry?

We followed him, moving slowly and it seemed to me painfully, through some corridors lined with black and white prints of famous guests. The Comedor reminded me slightly of the dining room in our palace, regally and resolutely stuck in the fifties. I'd been hoping to go out and see a little of Havana proper but I figured we were in Darius's pocket for the first weekend at least and should play by his rules. Plenty of time to explore the streets we'd driven through in the week to follow. For now though, pristine waiters and chandeliers.

The King suggested Thea sit next to him, which pleased me. It was important they get on. And I kind of hoped that I might be elevated in my father's eyes by association with such a spectacular fox. Player that he was, such things mattered deeply to him. I was put between Katya, my favourite person as he well knew, and one of the ballerinas. I settled in for a long night.

Sure enough, before long my neighbours gave up asking the usual insufferable small-talk questions I'd been fielding all my life at occasions like this. I found myself slowly losing the will to live as they pried into my academic qualifications, my plans for the future, my daily routine. My answers became shorter and more bored until they phased me out of the conversation altogether in favour of an actually interesting one about assassination attempts on Fidel Castro. I sat back, an observer, a slightly drunken observer on the fringes of the table, eating stuff. How the stuff came at us. An *amuse-bouche* of oyster beignet here, a giant hunk of cow there. I attacked it all manfully, all thoughts of vegetarianism cowed before my father's scrutiny. Though I noticed he wasn't eating much.

-Of course, Maxi was cross-dressing at the age of seven. The unlikely words drifted across a brief moment of silence in the international politics lecture. Darius had a strange glittering expression in his eyes and his hand outstretched resting gently on Thea's back. She looked unsettled and I recognised her little laugh as profoundly fake.

-Could have mistaken him for a girl anyway, tiniest little cock I ever did see. Isn't that right, Maxi?

-Right, Dad. You made me in your own image all right.

-You do look terribly alike, Katya broke in, shit-stirring a speciality. There's no doubt he's your son, at least!

I looked at His Highness's craggy frame, his green eyes and greying hair, the bitterness apparent in his expression. This is a very unhappy man, I found myself thinking with unprecedented sympathy. *I don't want to be like you.*

-So my son's managing to keep you satisfied, then? Darius persisted, his hand moving up and down her back, all of the pseudo-concern of a parent apparent. He winked at me. Thea was looking more and more uncomfortable.

Finally, she said, I don't think that's any of your business. My heart was in my mouth. Talking back to the King was never clever. But Darius leant back in his chair, satisfied, as if she'd confirmed his suspicions of my inadequacy.

-A spirited filly, he said. Good luck, Maxi my boy. I'm sure you'll both be very happy living in that rather grand pied-à-terre I pay for each month.

I thought that little episode might have exorcised whatever was eating him. We'll let it lie, I said to myself, hoping Thea wasn't too pissed off and intending to make it up to her in the coming week. I'd told her a little bit about my father's delight in emasculating his sons at every available opportunity. I hoped she could take him with a pinch of salt. Back to the politics.

Time droned on. A volley of puddings thudded on to the table. I sank into a cement state of saturation, practically asleep where I sat.

Suddenly there was a great commotion at the other end of the table. Thea flung back her chair, eyes shining with tears and stormed out of the dining room. I stood up, about to follow her.

—What have you done? What did you say? I demanded of Darius who was smiling a predatory, closed smile.

—Sit down, Maxi. I command it. Your silly little girl's a bit overly sensitive, I'd say. Time of the month, perhaps?

The ballerinas chuckled sycophantically.

—She's upset. I'm just going to check she's okay…

—Move an inch from that table and you'll regret it. She's just gone to sort out her make-up, that's all. She'll be back in a second and I shall not tolerate dinner being further disrupted.

I should have stood up to him then and there. But he had a hold over me. I was a small boy again with all the terrors that entailed. On some rational level, I knew that the days of me physically submitting to Darius were long gone. The man was weak. Ill. I noticed I was shaking.

When in doubt, do nowt.

The voice in my head was clear and soothing. A calm oasis in a jittery desert. Reader, I bathed in it.

Thea did not come back. When eventually release came and Darius receded into the night with his hateful entourage, I still did not seek her out. I persuaded myself that she'd be in bed, asleep by now, and that the best thing I could do for our relationship would be to recover from Kingly trauma through the medium of alcohol. Pathetic, I know now. I did not go out and on this I congratulated myself. But I did return to the bar and stay there in drunken meditation 'til they chucked me out at four.

Then I went to our room. She was still awake and sat up in bed as I came in, looking at me balefully.

-Are you okay? I slurred and crawled in beside her. She turned away from me and switched off the light.

We'll sort it out in the morning, I thought, and fell into the sleep of the unwell.

Breakfast was somewhat sombre. I hid behind dark glasses and tried to pretend the night before had not happened. We were meant to be meeting my father by the cathedral in the old part of town.

-I think I've seen enough of your father to last a lifetime, said Thea.

-What happened? I asked.

-Why do you care? You patently didn't last night.

-I'm sorry, baby. Did he offend you in some way?

-I… I actually can't bring myself to tell you what he said. Too fucking horrible. But honestly, I'm far more concerned by your response. You were like a shell of a man last night. I was ashamed to be with you. I mean, if you won't stick up for me, who on Earth will?

-God. I'm so sorry. I'll make it up to you, I promise. Let's just tough out one more day with Dad and then it'll just be us and we can do whatever we want on our own terms.

At that moment, the woman from reception came up to us with a message from the King. He regretted that he'd been called to Haiti sooner than expected and would be unable to make the Grand Tour planned for today.

-Well, I said with forced brightness, that solves that problem. Let's go and explore.

Thea was not herself, though, until Ruben joined us on the Monday. Even then, she was chippy with me, charming with him. Ruben left the day after, too early to wish me happy birthday; after that Thea and I began again to have something softer together, my father religiously removed from the conversation. What was left of our big trip consisted of a few frustrating days looking for Leya, without success, and drinking ourselves stupid on rum in the street bars. Frankly, I was relieved to go back to London.

***

Matty, crushing up ketamine with some E he found in his jacket, wonders if this is where it all started to go wrong for him and Tera. Either she saw in his father the man Matty would become, or he failed to be the man she'd thought he was, by not standing up to his father. And even though his writing has shown him yet again what a bastard his father was, he can't help but wish he was still around.

It doesn't take much to find the rabbit hole these days. Feracor is much closer to the surface of his mind, to consciousness. Matty closes his eyes and asks for an explanation. Why was it so hard to make it work with Tera? Feracor tries to console Mandrax with a Christmas story.

A man—let's call him Matthias—wants to paint his house in contrasting colours. He thinks the epitome of such a contrast would be black and white. By black, he means the darkest, blackest black within and without the realms of the imagination. By white, he means the starkest, blankest whiteness conceived or conceivable.

Matthias is proud of his home. He feels that by uniting the blackest black with the whitest white, the combination of two perfect essences will transcend the sum of their parts. It will be a black and white extravaganza! People will come from afar to admire the crystal clarity of juxtaposed opposites—a monochromatic masterpiece.

Well, I tell you that the perfect whole is not formed by two dodgy halves. It can only be present when two perfect wholes come together to form a new and different whole.

A flawed Yin and a misshapen Yang when brought together create an ugly, deformed shape. They do not fit. They do not create the harmonious circle, split by a serpentine line. Each half must be in itself complete.

You, Man, once thought that two damaged individuals could, when fused in love, become whole, somehow filling in each other's gaps and becoming greater entities together than they had been separately. You worry more and more that two insecure, flawed people who fall in love make each other less than they are. They chip away at each other; their attributes, their confidence. Each is not whole enough to repel the destructive tendencies of the other. Each asserts his confidence by parading the faults of the other. The two damaged wholes amount, when united, to less than a half and Time only serves to diminish them.

It was only after many years of hard work and hardship

that Matthias, born into an impoverished carpentry family, was able to disentangle himself from his filial duties. He was thirty-five and reduced to a life of caring for aged, senile and, in the case of his mother, incontinent parents. The basic joys normally bestowed on virile young men had bypassed him and by the time he was twenty-six, he was the only one of his generation, both male and female, left in the village of his birth. All the others had adapted (yes, like the humble microbe) and migrated to warmer climes, more lucrative times. An only child, the care of his parents fell solely to him and they made damn sure a colossal boulder of guilt kept him bound to them, their house, and their village, which was called, incidentally, Southern Hornet.

When Matthias's mother's body finally caved from the wasting disease which had long before stolen her soul, he felt a rebellious liberty descend. Abandoning his father to whatever fate might befall him, believing that at thirty-five he was entitled to a life of his own, Matthias fled Southern Hornet with his stock of wooden produce. It had been the way in his village that each artisan would create and barter his own wares for another's. He was aware that this left his father, Divitus, with no means of buying the medicinal herbs which kept him just on the right side of the brink of insanity, prevented the crippling stiffness paralysing him into a rigor mortis of the living. But as his entire life had been dominated by guilt anyway, on balance, it now seemed better to endure the emotion alone and free than under an unendurable paternal yoke.

What did I say about planes, dimensions? Everything of which we can possibly conceive exists on one plane or another. In an infinite cosmos of galaxies, universes, times and spaces, everything which enters our heads has happened, or will happen, or is happening, or all three of these tenses simultaneously in different worlds. How else would it come to be in our heads?

Matthias left his village, left his neighbouring town, left the county containing both and, gaining courage and confidence, made plans to leave the country itself, an island called Grand Smitten. He began to sell his wooden creations along the journey. As he drew farther and farther from South Hornet, the quality of his produce was met with increasing astonishment and demand. By the time he reached the jumping-off point for his new land, Matthias had shed his wood, accumulated some funds and met a girl who showed him such unimaginable happiness, he felt truly blessed. His girl was just as besotted with him. As they smelt the sea air at the end of the land, they thought, 'Why seek any further? We have all we require right here. We have each other.' So they settled. Matthias bought a plot of land from a local farmer with the money he had made and a promise to fulfil any carpentry needs which might arise on the farmer's estate. He built a house. That house was perfectly formed. It symbolised everything Matthias had fought for and achieved until this point in time.

Understandably, he wanted it to be painted in a manner befitting it, a culmination of extremes— perfect poverty and perfect wealth, perfect guilt and perfect self-honour, perfect hatred and perfect love.

But Matthias tried too hard. The black shell he chose to crush into paint form was blacker than black. So black it obscured the essence of black. The white stone he chose appeared white, but it too was flawed. But the very worst of it was that when he used the two to paint his house, far from being the most perfect fusion and contrast any artisan could envisage, the two interacted, corroding, melding, moulding and bubbling into a greenish-grey. A colour devoid of a name even. Nobody likes grey, Mandrax. Nobody.

Matthias's girl left him, his house collapsed and he himself died shortly afterwards of a wasting disease tinged with madness. It was believed to have been induced by the noxious fumes created by the fusion of the flawed black and white paint.

188

Dr J. Sykes BACP (accred.)
Psychotherapist

Private Room
36 Harley Street
London W1G 9PG

Date:	Time:	Patient Initials:	Attendance:
Tuesday 5 January 2016	5pm	MEC	DNA

Notes:

MC subsequently emailed me – apologies for non-attendance.

-He is still in France with stepmother.

-Has been writing more chapters of 'Looking up at the Stars' but wanted to keep those for himself.

-Instead attached a piece of writing that appeared to be a myth about himself (name Matthias) in a biblical column layout.

-Can't really make much sense of it but seems to be a cautionary tale suggesting that Tera and MC had not been so perfect together – both damaged individuals who caused more damage to each other.

-That's quite a sane message expressed in quite a mad way?

-Could it be a positive, mature revelation – dreams of puer aeternus leading to transcendence of puer aeternus, beginning of acceptance of maturity and reality?

-Fear not. Ending concerningly brutal – preoccupation with death and madness. And in email talked about keeping head down, avoiding radioactivity, Thames running red. Apocalyptic dreams becoming delusions?

-Wants to meet next Tues. to discuss all this – going to talk to him about seeing a psychiatrist too. Must be careful to be clear that I will continue to treat him at same time – must not inflame attachment/abandonment issues.

XVIII

There's a knock at the door.

A knock on the door at any time of day or night will most likely be Fix.

Matty draws back from the open window and crosses the arm-span length of the room. He opens the door. It is Sylvie.

Sylvie is apparently unconcerned by the ravages of the world outside his window.

'Where have you been? No one's seen you for ages. You haven't answered any of my texts, Facebook messages, my WhatsApp…'

Matty idly watches a comet flash past the panes.

She says, 'Look, there's something important I need to tell you.'

'Sure, sure,' he says. 'Yeah, yeah. Whatever you have to tell me is obviously more important than blood running through the streets of London.'

He stops.

'What the fuck are you talking about?' she says.

Matty looks at her curiously. He steps gingerly over to the window and peers down over the antique roads, criss-crossed and winding as they ever had been. But a film of radioactive filth sits upon them. Debris and detritus litter the streets where the scorching sun has burned up trees and cars. The bloody Thames, inflamed, has burst its banks and runs russet through the ghost town. He inspects Sylvie's feet. They are dry.

Oh this is too much.

'Have you any drugs?'

'No. Sit down, Matty.'

If this is worse than the apocalypse, he will not listen to it sober.

'Let's go to the pub. If it's survived.'

'You're being really strange, you know. Even stranger than usual.'

Nevertheless, they walk through the atomic fug and at some point start to hold hands. The pub is shut but survivors, he finds, have gathered in a twenty-four hour coffee bar which sells liquor to the shocked. He remembers going there with Tera.

'Funny isn't it,' he says to Sylvie, 'that we're still doing the same old things. Never adapt, never move forward, though the human race is dying around you. Just carry on.'

'I know Soho's not what it was,' she replies, 'but I think you're being a little extreme.'

They sit only a few feet from a bunker, to their right a crater, yet still people meet for coffee. He supposes familiarity is the only thing they can find to cling to, a cork raft in a tidal wave.

'I think I might be pregnant.'

'Shit. Shit. How?'

'Um…'

'Right, yeah. Sorry. Whose is it?'

'It's yours, arsehole.'

'But you and Fix had a bit of a thing going on, right?'

'No! Not right. I—.' Short silence. 'Oh, what does it matter? I take it you're not overjoyed at the prospect of being a father, then?'

'Who'd be happy to bring a child into a world like this?' he asks, gesturing helplessly at a plague of wasps gathering in spiralling circles to their left.

'Well sure. I know we don't live entirely conventional lives but I'm ready to put all that partying and insecurity behind me. And I just thought you should know, you know? This is your child we're talking about. But I'm going to go it alone if you don't want to be involved.'

Matty is silent. He wonders if all the world is crashing, or it's just London bowing out of the rat race of existence. He wonders if he should go to Thailand and start a new life there. Chances of getting a flight out in a sky like this are pretty remote though.

'Do you know if any of the airports are still up and running?' he asks.

She stares at him blankly.

The good news is that whatever corrosive diseases may have passed between them, through the same channels as the foetal ingredients, they scarcely matter now the end is nigh. The soaring mercury, the plastic-choked bloody waters, the scourges and infestations… it is all in place, ushering in the destruction of everything. Feracor had warned him it was coming.

'Let's go and see Fix,' Matty suggests, unable to think of any alternative.

She sighs. 'Okay,' she says. 'Fix and I did sleep together once. We were really out of it and at the moment I don't know the exact dates but I think they couldn't possibly tally.'

Matty knows it. It's Ben and Tera all over again.

Tera had said the same thing sometime after their trip to Cuba, *I think I'm pregnant, I think it's yours.* He hadn't known what to do and he hadn't known how to make her feel as if he did know. Had it been before or after the first time she broke up with him? He cannot be sure. There definitely had been a break-up after Havana but it hadn't lasted long enough for her to move out. Again and again they split and reformed. Agonies of relief and agonies. *It's not me it's you, Matty. You're this, you're that. Unreliable. Mental. Delusional. Not what I want. Neeed. Now.* But she couldn't go home to her parents either.

Ben had been there, of course, to deal with the problem. He'd said *don't worry we'll do this we'll do that it'll all be fine*. And then she hadn't been pregnant, but apparently that had happened before Ben had acted.

At the time, Matty had been grateful, deeply grateful to his brother for stepping in, sorting things out.

Was probably Ben's child, he thinks now.

He wonders whether Ben's hospital has survived. He wouldn't be surprised if the machinery on which his life depends has gone haywire.

'Hey, you,' he summons one of the survivors in the coffee bar. 'Know if there are any flights out of here?'

Sylvie interrupts, 'Matty, you know you can't leave the country. It's in your bail conditions, Fix said.'

Bale, snail. 'What?' But a bell is ringing. 'Who've you been talking to?' But even as Matty's saying it, his mind is turning to more important things.

He has to see the full extent of the damage. 'Go and find Fix. He'll look after you,' he tells Sylvie. 'Maybe this'll all blow over. It's just a cosmic warning.'

He doesn't really believe that of course but it's his male duty to keep the females calm.

He sets off, leaving her in tears. To his immense relief, there's a wrap of something opiate in his breeches. It had been hiding in the seam. He's been feeling like the reluctant hero up to this point, a Frodo-style mission forced upon him but now, with energy and confidence within him, he can tackle this. The visions all begin to make sense. It is he, Matty, whom Feracor has chosen to warn about this, the end of humanity. *Chosen*. It feels good. He must have been chosen because he is special in some way, because there is a role for him to play in this transition of ages. Humans will self-destruct but some, a very few perhaps, maybe even him, will transcend the abyss and make the next era.

He can't self-pollinate though. He'll need a girl if he's to be the next Adam. Maybe Feracor will make one out of his rib. He's not sure he can face a world shared with Sylvie alone.

Though, of course, if she's having his baby, they wouldn't be all alone.

He stumbles as, lost in thought, he narrowly fails to avoid a pit in the street before him. The pavement seems to waver and dip as if the very plates beneath the earth are restless. He emerges from the caves of Soho blinking into the light of Piccadilly, the garish screens of consumerism. Only Matty is there, in the middle of the island, and all of the neon advertisements show Feracor, eyes flashing purple as he greets him. *The Fourth Age is dying, Man,* he says from seven different flashing boards high above Matty's head. *The Fifth Age is dawning.*

At the beginning of the Fourth Age, round about the time Jesus was knocking about Jerusalem preaching piety and telling you to love your neighbour, a young woman named Altera and a young man named Aramat were born in the territory near the Seranician seas. Aramat was born to a family of grand reputation, who counted royalty, great warriors and philosophers among its forefathers. Aramat had the bluest of blood, but had a brother too, Araben, the illegitimate son of one of his father's gallivants.

Altera, by contrast, was the fortuitous product of a fairly humble family. She was surpassingly beautiful but poor. Her father had worked in the fields all his life, ploughing and sowing, broad-backed son of the soil. He had married the eldest daughter of the family who owned the neighbouring (and considerably more fertile) plot of land and they set about a lifetime of drudgery and spawning children.

When Aramat and Altera were born, a wondrous constellation illuminated the sky, a new and marvellous configuration. One star burned more brightly than the others. This was the star which drew shepherds and wise men to Bethlehem. Their astronomical calculations were wrong. The other stars composing the picture linked Aramat and Altera like a celestial rainbow, the painting created depicting the union of Mars and Venus, the holiest union—the Great Creator.

Well, naturally this did not go unnoticed by the two families of the offspring, though it differed in effect. Altera's family had brought her up as the one who would break the family's parochial agricultural traditions, who would travel and seek great things. But they feared this omen, saw that Altera must be sheltered, protected from potential harm.

195

Fate had, as you, Mandrax, with your uncanny intuition have certainly guessed, intended these two to come together, the first man and woman of a new age whose offspring would create a new dawn for mankind. From love and anger come all things. Jesus distorted that balance; gave too much weight to love; denied Mars his right and his platform.

So it panned out that Aramat nearly fulfilled his destiny, leaving his father's palace and seeking his appointed bride. A perilous journey marred and highlighted to an equal extent by adventures, built up in him the spirit of Mars the warrior and eventually led him to the terrain of Altera.

But Araben had got there first. Innocent Altera had been unprepared for the onslaught of Aramat's younger brother, devoured by jealousy, made bitter and violent by the curses of his birthright. He had heard of the prophesied union and plotted to have Altera for himself and by impregnating her to create the line of noble heritage he had been denied.

By the time Aramat, swollen with the might of Mars, found her, the rape of Araben had so traumatised her, she had killed herself and her unborn baby. He had destroyed her feminine association with Venus and wrecked the natural order. That, my friend, was the real Original Sin. This subversion of what had been ordained.

What you need to grasp here, Mandrax, is that for the Embodiment of balanced eternal forces to be a perfect fusion, the two creators must contain the true essence of those forces. As we have discussed, Mars and Venus, the forces they represent, must in perfect totality enter the chosen mortals at the appointed time. The child shall embody the fusion of forces which are so entirely out of balance in this present age. I was ready to receive Mars. I felt those powers, those forces approaching me. But it was YOU who channelled them, you and Rhea Silvia.

Transcription: EXTRACT FROM CONVERSATION BETWEEN DR J. SYKES, BACP (ACCRED.)
AND MATTHEW CORANI

JS: ARAMAT IS YOU, MATTY, IS HE? AND ALTERA IS TERA? WHAT DOES THIS DREAM MEAN?

MC: THAT'S WHAT FERACOR SAID. BUT IT'S NOT A DREAM IT'S A PROPHECY. I DIDN'T
REALISE TERA WAS NOT THE CHOSEN ONE, BECAUSE BEN DEFILED HER CAUSING THE
REAL ORIGINAL SIN. IT'S ACTUALLY SYLVIE.

JS: WHO'S SYLVIE?

MC: SHE'S MY GIRLFRIEND. SHE'S HAVING MY CHILD, ACTUALLY.

JS: YOU'RE GOING TO BE A FATHER?

MC: IT IS OF COSMIC SIGNIFICANCE: I HAVE A SERIOUS ROLE TO PLAY IN THE NEW AGE.

JS: MATTY, I HAVE A COLLEAGUE I'D LIKE YOU TO TALK TO WHO MIGHT BE ABLE TO HELP
YOU WITH THIS.

MC: YOU'VE HAD ENOUGH OF ME?

JS: ABSOLUTELY NOT. YOU AND I WILL CONTINUE OUR WORK TOGETHER AS WELL.

Notes:
-M. SEEMS TO HAVE CROSSED A LINE. PARANOID DELUSIONS/PSYCHOSIS – SUSPECT DRUG-INDUCED.
-LOST WEIGHT, EYE TWITCH, VERY PALE.
-NARCISSISTIC TENDING TOWARDS MESSIAH COMPLEX?
-PUER AETERNUS ARCHETYPE DISTORTED/USED AS CENTRAL TO APOCALYPTIC FANTASY.
-THINKS DEATH OF DAVID BOWIE 2 DAYS AGO IS END OF AN ERA, AN OMEN OF 'THE FIFTH
AGE' BEGINNING.
-TALKED ABOUT PSYCHIATRIST REFERRAL. M. HAPPY TO GO BUT REQUESTED NHS NOT PRIVATE
REFERRAL. MAY TAKE TIME.
-WISH HAD SET THIS IN MOTION LAST WEEK BUT DON'T FEEL HE IS DANGER TO SELF OR
OTHERS. HAVE GIVEN HIM CRISIS NUMBER.

XIX

Fatherhood eh? Matty's not really up to it. He's not that sure what's involved, to be honest, as his own father never really showed him. His hand moves unconsciously to the scar on his scalp. Matty had been horrified when his father had swapped Cuba for France. It was too close for comfort. The idea of Daniel retired was unsettling as well. Where, he wondered, would all that energy go now?

Matty, as with most people, had never known his father as a young man. He had therefore never been able to conceive of him as a person motivated by anything other than his career. Daniel's sense of identity seemed to depend solely upon men who fawned and women who adored. He collected them, miniature tribes of devotion, wherever his job placed him.

As a young man in London, Matty had imagined that Cuba would hold his father and Katya for good. They had, according to Ben, come to some arrangement whereby Katya spent Daniel's money on trips to Europe while he had sex with pretty young men. Presumably it had been Katya who'd insisted on the Provence move—but why had his father agreed to leave? The return to Havana had given him what he needed, the freedom of being on the fringes of his countrymen, unobserved. Matty had a new family. He had Tera to love, Fix to father, Ben to hold it all together, a holy trinity. Tera, love of his life, the single most important thing ever to have happened to him. After that one disastrous trip to see Daniel in Havana he had vowed never to subject Tera to the bile of his father again. If he had been financially independent, this would have been very easy indeed.

He was, actually, constantly in need of money, despite his best efforts to juggle part-time work with his degree. Life in London, particularly the life he insisted upon he and Tera living, was expensive. He tended to ignore the implications of spending continuously until it was too late to try anything but stay afloat. The flat in Marble Arch, provided by the Foreign Office to his father, was the safe haven which saved them time and time again. If he had had to pay rent on that, he would never have survived.

Matty has returned to Piccadilly Circus, looking for more messages from Feracor on the big advertising screens. Feracor's gone, but now the screen flashes a TV soap episode of his life. He recognises the theme music, the old flat, the stock scene; the canned laughter grates on his nerves—is this some terrible sitcom? Everyone is laughing at him.

He watches a more youthful, screen-bound Fix saying, 'You're a spoilt brat, dude'. He has come round with a small delivery for Matty and is now awaiting a lentil stew that Tera has made, padding it out with something of indeterminate yet evil odour.

Matty can smell it. Its fumes seem to waft out of the screen set high above him. The sight of Tera up there too makes him grind inside himself.

'Sixty pence for all of this,' she is saying proudly, lovingly smacking out dollops of the brown slop on to four plates.

Matty, clearer of eye, cleaner of skin, holds out his hand as she goes past his chair, stroking the back of her smooth calves. 'Sixty pence, huh? You're amazing.' *Laughter.*

She sweeps past him, batting his hand away from her legs and goes to sit by Ben.

Is this before or after the first break-up? Pre- or post-baby disaster? The Cuba trip? As if to answer his questions a date appears at the bottom of the screen: Sunday 24 November 2013. Ben had just turned eighteen then.

'Yes, Matty,' she says coldly. 'Sixty pence. Think about that, will you, when you're smoking that dope that Fix has so kindly brought round for you.'

'For us, baby. For us.' *Laughter.*

'Discount, of course,' Fix jumps in. *Laughter.*

'It's economic, when you think about it. If we're chilling out in here, we're not running around London chucking away cash.' *Titter.*

'Fine but for fuck's sake, Matty—it's got to stop somewhere. It's Sunday night and I'm not a student any more. I have to work.'

'What?' Matty sees his eyes widen—a puppy watching its mother take a beating. It is true that Tera has completed her year's course at Camberwell and is now renting a studio in Peckham. Matty, at least nominally, is paying for it.

'Oh nothing,' says Tera. 'Let's not talk about it now, eh? Come on, eat your Michelin-starred stew.' *Laughter.*

'Fucking delicious,' cries Fix, scooping up what he can of the liquid and slamming it into his mouth as it slips through the grooves of the fork.

'I've got to go,' says Ben suddenly. He looks white.

'I don't blame you,' replies Tera. 'This is disgusting.' *Laughter.*

'Where?' asks Matty.

'Anywhere,' he says desperately. Then, with careful deliberation, 'Actually, I said I'd meet a friend—'

'A man about a dog—' *Laughter.*

'God, Matty do you ever shut up? It's like living with a hyperactive child.' *Laughter.*

'I said I'd meet a friend and I'm already late. But this was great, Tera. Thanks,' he finishes lamely, trying not to look at the abundant brown remaining on the plate.

'Why don't we all go out?' says Matty. 'Come on, it's Sunday night. What else are we going to do? Sit around and slit our wrists? I'm still a student. This is the one time in our lives when it *is* acceptable to piss about on a Sunday.' *Laughter.*

'Okay fuck it. Let's go.'

'That's my girl.' Matty springs up and goes to put his arm around Tera, but she ducks aside, her eyes full of contempt.

'What? What have I done?' he asks, hurt, but she just shakes her head as they leave the flat.

It's always about money, he figures.

'So make some,' says Fix's voice from within a cubicle as the scene changes and Matty sees himself staring into the mirror of a public toilet. It's his birthday, a few weeks later.

He can hear Fix racking up lines on the cistern. Fix pauses to snort one noisily, then continues, 'There's some to be made, you know? You could help me for a start.'

'In the band? But I can't play anything, mate. And I'm shit at singing. Ask anyone. Ask Ben, he used to—'

'Not with the band. With this.' He opens the door and gestures to the white caterpillar awaiting Matty.

'Hmmm,' says Matty, feeling the cocaine hit the back of his throat and the dizzy surge crawl up the back of his neck, fly through the top of his head. 'Food for thought, Fix. Food for thought.'

The scene changes again and on all screens where Feracor has sputtered out, cradling a child in a comet, his father now stands erect, looking down from great heights.

Whenever Matty thinks about the last time he saw his father, during a solo trip to France in April 2014, he is not convinced that he handled the situation as best he could.

'I'll go alone,' he had told Ben and Tera, memories of the unhappy reunion in Havana still sore. If it was just him, there would be no hiding behind Ben's peacemaking charm. Nor could he brandish Tera like a shield, as if to say 'but look, look what I won'. No, this had been about him, Matty, Daniel's eldest son and in fact his only son by the woman he claimed was the love of his life. The air needed to be cleared. The idea of his father sitting just the other side of the channel, a stranger, was ridiculous.

There were important things to discuss. Matty's life had reached a turning point. And if his father was retiring in Provence, presumably his life had as well. The way things were going, Matty was going to need that inheritance more than ever. He just could not risk that particular back-up plan screwing up. Supporting Tera on his allowance was not easy. It was also not happening without considerable supplementation that came from dealing for Fix. But he was going to marry her. Matty saw a new incarnation of himself as a husband emerging, the adult version. He had played around for long enough, Tera had convinced him. He agreed; all the right things were in place for his future happiness. He needed to cement them.

'You do realise,' said Daniel sitting at the head of the table in their new Provencal garden, 'that it's not really my permission you're supposed to seek. I am not, after all, the father of the bride-to-be.' He looked distinctly grey, almost waxy, and there was the same walking stick he'd had in Cuba leaning against the chair where he sat.

'Ha, ha,' Matty grinned through a jangling hangover. 'Good one. Yes, of course I know that. I just thought you might like to know what's going on. You've met her. You know how special she is.'

Daniel frowned.

'More salad, darling?' Katya thrust the wooden bowl between the two men. Daniel waved it away, reaching instead for the bottle and replenishing both his own and then Matty's glass. Katya's hand hovered over the top of her own.

'You're awfully young to be getting hitched, Matthew. Don't you think you should be thinking about finishing your degree first? You've nearly finished your second year, haven't you? Then only another year to go and you're free!'

'Well, actually, Dad, that's the other thing I need to talk to you about.'

All three watched in silence as a bud of apple blossom floated at leisure from the tree shading the table.

'Why do I get the feeling I'm not going to like what's coming?' Daniel sighed.

'No, don't worry, it's nothing bad. It's actually quite a good thing.'

'What is?'

Katya removed the salad bowl and plates from the table and took them into the old farmhouse they had just bought. She re-emerged with a new bottle of unlabelled wine—'from that very vineyard,' Daniel had boasted earlier—which she placed on the table, and some SPF 50 suncream which she removed to its default position by her recliner at the side of the pool.

'Well, the thing is…'

'Come on, come on. What is the "thing"?'

'The thing, Dad, is that it wasn't really going anywhere. The course, that is.'

'I don't believe it's supposed to go anywhere just yet, is it? Surely the traditional idea is that you get the degree and then you use it to go somewhere else. Clearly I am mistaken. Please do go on.'

Bluster was not something to be feared in the Corani household. Quiet, calculated sarcasm on the other hand was as likely to lead to pain as a wasp in a Coke can.

Treading carefully, Matty said, 'I think I've gained everything I've got to gain from it—'

'Everything apart from the qualification.'

'I think I could get a decent job without that, and I'm ready for that. I'm ready to grow up and take some responsibility for myself.' He was quoting Tera now but she had made a pretty good case. She'd persuaded him after all. 'I want to marry this girl and I don't know if she'll hang around if I'm a student for another year and a half. I want children and a house and all that stuff and that can't be got on a student loan.'

'Ah yes, your student loan… I'd been meaning to ask—'

Matty heard his brain yelling *Abort! Abort!* and swiftly changed the subject. 'I think it's time I got a foothold on my career.'

'Right. What's that then?'

'Well, I think its high time I figured that out. I want to try my hand at a few—'

'Do you have any idea how many times you've used the words "I" and "want" in this conversation?'

'Sorry. I *would like* to do some work that I'm actually paid for, unlike writing essays and going to lectures. And if I like it, I'll stay in that industry and, um, *climb* that ladder.'

'I think what you're so inarticulately getting at, Matthew, is a stint of paid work experience in a field of potential interest. Which is precisely what I think you should be doing. *Around* your studies.'

'That could be a problem.'

'Oh? It can't be money that's the problem, surely? You've got a considerable allowance from me, your student loan, rent's not an issue.'

'I don't quite know how to say this, except just hear me out because it's not as bad as it sounds and—'

'WHAT?'

Matty took a deep breath and said, 'I can't finish my degree. I've been asked to leave UCL.'

Editing the truth as skilfully as he was able, Matty explained how word had got around that he'd been selling drugs to students.

'Nothing heavy, just a bit of weed, and the whole thing was made up anyway. But they said they couldn't ignore something like this and said that it would be in my interests to leave. So I thought, maybe this is a blessing in disguise and, you know, the universe asking me what I really want out of life. And if I ask myself that, then ultimately it's not the chance to do another year studying philosophy, it's the chance to get on with the rest of my life, get a job, get married, get—'

'You fool.'

'It wasn't really anything to do with me, Dad. They just needed someone to make an example of, I think, and I was an easy scapegoat because someone, I don't know who yet, but when I find out, I'll—anyway, someone was saying stuff about me so it all kind of fitted together.'

'There's no smoke without fire, Matthew.'

His father did not even sound angry, just weary. Matty almost wished he would give him something to fight against, to defend himself.

'Well, it sounds like you know what you're doing. I wish you well with it.' What was this? A dismissal? Ask him, then. Ask him now.

'Thank you. I think my first step should be, as I said, making Tera my wife.'

'Go for it.' Curt, polite, removed.

'But to do that I need to buy a ring.'

'Matthew, are you honestly going to try and tap me for cash now?'

'Not cash so much as a very small loan... which I'd pay back as soon as I've got this job I'm planning on getting.'

'Enough, Matthew. I've clearly done you no favours so far in life by handing everything to you on a plate. But I'm going to do you a bloody big one now. No more money from me. Not now and not ever. You're on your own.'

'Come on, darling,' said Katya remotely from the pool-side. 'Don't upset yourself.'

'Shit, Dad! Can't you just help me out, just get me started?'

'Don't you have any dignity? Yes, I will help you out. I won't kick you out of that flat you share with your brother until you've got income of some sort. In fact, I'll set up a meeting with Teddy Hanson and see if he can't get you an internship at his office.'

'Oh come on—I don't want to work in insurance for fuck's sake.'

'What you want and don't want is of little consequence. This is my offer and you can take it or leave it. And I'd put all thoughts of marriage out of your head until you've proved you can stand on your own two feet.'

Daniel was so relentlessly fair. He was so self-righteous, fumed Matty, blowing off some steam in a bar in Paris with an old girlfriend he'd looked up for the occasion, a sometime partner in crime in the early days of London living. He had planned to go home on the ferry. Then again he had planned to spend the whole weekend chez Daniel, but as Saturday drew into the evening, the urge to run had become irresistible.

'So get a job,' said the girl. It sounded more aggressive than she intended over the thumping house music.

Matty sees himself sipping his fifth cocktail—effete in looks but hardcore in content—and slurring, 'That's not the point, beautiful. The point is he just wasn't surprised, not remotely surprised that I cocked it up. He's never had any faith in me.'

He remembers, barely, crawling home on Monday morning, reeling with self-hatred and smelling of that girl. He had barely entered the flat when he found himself turned 180 degrees by Ben and back on the ferry to France. Daniel had shot himself in the early hours of Sunday morning.

XX

The images fade. The theatre curtain comes up and London is unscarred. Matty has no idea what has just happened. Piccadilly zooms around him. The neon boards advertise Pepsi, a play, a computer. Tourists and businessmen shove past him. It dawns on him that the world has not ended, nor is it in the process of doing so. Life goes on.

He feels a little odd. He moves off in the direction of Fix's flat. If anyone can make sense of this, it's Fix.

Soho is conspicuously not soaked in blood.

Fix opens the door with a sheepish smile. 'Sylvie said she'd seen you and told you—ah.'

'Forget it,' says Matty. 'We've got bigger fish to fry.'

'Sounds serious,' says Fix mildly.

Matty remembers Fix's wisdom when he'd come to him, not to Tera, after his father's suicide. 'Everyone,' Fix had said then, 'exchanges one family for another in this lifetime. It is the natural order. A child is born into one family, then begins a family of his own.'

But Daniel's suicide screwed you up. You were left with very little option but to blame yourself.

That's so typically self-centred. It's nothing to do with you.

Ben said it. Tera said it too. Did not mean much. Obviously the timing was unfortunate.

I was the last person he saw. I told him I'd dropped out. I disappointed him again.

'He had a lot on his mind that you know nothing about.' That's what Katya said. 'I'll tell you one day when it's not such a betrayal to fill you in.'

Oh but Ben clearly knew about it. Ben the confidante. Ben, it transpired, was also the heir to a significant amount of money, which was to be passed to him via Katya on his twenty-first birthday. Matty received the flat, apparently bought from the government by his father at some stage while the boys were still living there. On the plus side, Daniel's decision to end it all had been swift enough for him not to have amended his will to prevent Matty inheriting anything at all.

Matty had been unprepared for his emotional response to his father's suicide, a betrayal of the self he thought he knew. Remorse, regret, ever encroaching.

Did I give him so little to live for?

Matty could see Daniel finally for what he was: a bereaved man who had tried his utmost to do the right thing. A father who had kept his son at a distance as he knew he was no good.

And now I am an orphan.

It had taken Matty a while to come to terms with Daniel's death, that much was true.

He wonders now if it wasn't his constant mewlings of guilt that drove Tera into his brother's arms. He's never been brilliant at finding silver linings, but with those safety nets whipped from under him, he had been forced to take responsibility for himself.

It was a queer summer. In August, Isis beheaded an American journalist. Carnage and crucifixions followed, and Matty could sense the unleashing of ancient, long-suppressed forces of savagery, the invocation of arcane, ignored deities and the emotions they champion. Gods abhor a vacuum.

Matty is a very different person now, stripped piece by piece and rebuilt accordingly.

He likes who he is now, sitting in Fix's kitchen getting high with his old friend.

'You need to finish your book, man. That's all this is. Your imagination's running away with you.'

Yes, the writing. That's something Daniel would have been proud of, surely. There's no part of his old life that he has not replaced with a newer, shinier version. But some things remain the same; Fix is the one constant. His best friend. The only one who has always been there for him.

'I love you, man,' Matty feels compelled to say as Fix's chemicals fondle the nostalgia bone inside him. Things are on the up once more.

'That's great,' says Fix. 'Now I know you don't like doing this, ever since your old man—well, you know—'

Matty closes his eyes and lets his head hang back dreamily over the top of the chair as he makes an enquiring sound.

'Well, you owe me money again, you know. And you probably could do with some income yourself, no?'

Could he? That is almost certainly the case, but it doesn't do to dwell on these things. Daniel's legacy (other than a bad temper and an addictive personality) has been pretty meagre now the flat's been sold, debts paid, Ben kept alive. He figures he's down to about two month's rent. Provided he keeps his nose clean.

'And there's all your legal costs,' says Fix.

'Katya's dealing with them,' says Matty.

Of course, a little bitter thought surfs in on the tide of serotonin, it would help if his inheritance wasn't sitting in a paraplegic little goldmine on life support. When could he expect it to start supporting his life? Or was it all doomed to sustain Ben in a vegetative state until one of them died? Katya has him by the balls on this.

'Well,' says Fix gently. 'Well maybe it's time for you to do a couple of jobs for me again. Think about it—you'll get your own supply cheap *and* make some cash. And it's great experience as a writer—think of all the people you'll meet…

in weirdly intimate situations sometimes. Maybe you'll make some publishing contacts. See how I get invited to all the big media parties?'

Matty is assailed by memories of his last stint as Fix's delivery boy. One of the most embarrassing had been dropping off forty pills and ten grams of coke at what he supposed to be a random house party. Tera had been standing in the corridor, drink in hand, when her friend had opened the door to him, which had been a shock. Turned out to be the birthday of a guy she'd met on her art course. She had said she was meeting an old friend of the family in Islington. So they were *both* guilty of deception, he had countered in the ensuing row.

He still marvels at the idea that you can live in such close proximity to someone, day in, day out, but never quite know what's going on with them.

'I don't know,' Matty says finally, 'whether I want to get back into all that. Courts won't be impressed, that's for sure. Squealer thinks he can get me off the charges by playing up my spotless character.'

Fix snorts.

'Prison's losing its appeal, man. I don't want to take those kind of risks anymore.'

There's something else for Matty too though. With the recession of the terrifying nightscape of Soho, for the first time in a long while he's feeling the chronic panic lift and a possible future open up. It's got something to do with Sylvie and something to do with Feracor's insistence that there's something bigger than all of them, something which values Matty's existence. A chink is opening up in his nothing-to-lose outlook.

'Well that's a pity, Matty, because this can't go on forever. You're going to need to get your shit together and pay me pretty soon. You and Sylvie put away a fair bit before she got knocked up and you went AWOL.'

'Chill. It's under control.' The warmth curls around him, mutates into the fleshy cushioning of the womb.

He hangs on to the positive things emanating from him and turns their vision in on himself. He sees his mind from the outside, the seething mass of hateful voices tangible as snakes poisoning his head. Things are not that bad. He has this loyal friend. He has, potentially, a family of his own with Sylvie. He has the spiritual guidance of the bizarre experiences which seem to have found him, to have saved him. He can work with these things and set himself back the right way up.

'Okay, mate,' he tells Fix. 'I'm going to do some work now. If you see Sylvie, tell her I was just caught off guard, yeah, and I'll be in touch.'

You really have to grow up.

What the fuck do you think I'm trying to do, Dad?

Matty whistles as he walks back to his flat, only so recently fraught with terror, now benevolent and reassuring.

***

LOOKING UP AT THE STARS

What is a chapter, what is it not? A chapter is the shadow of a dream.

Very poetic.

Maybe you are not as lucid as you thought, eh? Maybe crystal meth is not the path to clarity, eh?

Matty pulls himself together. Lights a cigarette. It occurs to him that if you try to rewrite history, the repressed truth might break out to bite you in one way or another. He vows to write more honestly.

The night of the French king's suicide was
electric. Comets were exploding, fevers
convulsing, fireworks cascading as forward went
the killers, forward as one. Chants were pulsing
through the city, glittering livewires, the
human spirit was rising again. The mania was
building, frenzy kicking in as they marched
upon his palace, all those demons.

Matty sighs the satisfied grunt of the satisfied creative and
snoozes into the abyss. Behind his closed eyes, Mandrax
wakes with a girl in his arms to see the great emperor, Divitus,
fallen, and his concubines—he spies his own mother, and
her replacements, first Lucy, then K.—tearing at their clothes
and hair in mourning. Feracor stands triumphant over them
all, the new tyrant.

'Your father, Mandrax, did a terrible thing,' says Feracor. 'Your brother, Benzo, was a wicked man. But in doing what he did, he saved you from perverting the fate of the world once more. Tera was never fit for Venus. She was just a girl from Putney. You know that. It is Silvia who is the fertile furrow now.'

Mandrax stands behind Silvia, arms encompassing the female fortitude with pride. Entrusted with such secrets, arcane, eternal. Though he has been feeling a little flat of late, a little put upon, a little out of sorts, now he feels powerful. He is important. He will do whatever it takes to keep his place in what is destined to be.

'And Benzo? What is to become of him?'

'He has played his part. He is already in the fourth dimension, though his body may remain here for some time.'

'What next then?'

Feracor sits on the bed where Benzo lies, wrapped in wires and fifty pound notes and pulls Silvia, malleable and drowsy on to his lap. She moulds into him. Convex against concave. Softness into hardness. Curves into straightness.

213

Transcription: extract from conversation between Dr J. Sykes, BACP (accred.) and Matthew Corani

JS: How are you feeling now, Matty?

MC: Oh fine, fine. Getting ready to be a father.

JS: What do you think makes a good father?

MC: Probably not being an eternal youth. Taking some responsibility.

JS: Yes, I think that's a good start. How's your job search going?

MC: Well, I've been looking, but there's no point committing to anything until after the trial.

JS: What trial is this?

MC: Ah yes, I should have told you. It's next month.

JS: Is this connected to Feracor in some way?

MC: Yes it is. He's on trial for usurping Christ and I'm on trial for being associated with him — helping him break free of prison. I'm his prophet. And also I have to attend a trial for stealing a bike. But none of this really matters because Silvia and I are having a baby and that baby's going to lead us into a new age, The Fifth Age, with Feracor in charge. Everything's going to change.

XXI

It seemed so clear when he said it to Dr Psycho but now, by himself, Matty is confused by all this cosmic baby stuff, bemused by his latest memoir entry. He tries to steady his jittery mind, to avoid thinking about this week's various mistakes and escape into writing. He closes his eyes and tracks the aftermath of dropping out of university and his father's subsequent demise. He remembers that an existence entirely free of structure was thrilling at first. The blank canvas of a life undrawn offered infinite possibilities, dizzying prospects. Each route he mentally embarked upon took him swiftly from lowly beginnings to heights of success and acclaim. Back in his younger psyche, he sees the roots tangle before him in different directions. He tries to be honest. He writes.

***

I toyed with the idea of drama school, for example, but was unable to content myself with this rung of the imaginative ladder for long; before I knew it, I was mentally flicking V-signs at the paparazzi clamouring for a quote from the Great Qurani, the actor who had defined a new cinematic age. Of course, with such fame would come problems. These invariably of such disastrous magnitude that I would panic and retreat, overwhelmed, from the initial idea. I was incapable of thinking small.

-If I were you, said Thea, I wouldn't worry too much about the long-term just yet. I think you just need to get into some kind of day-to-day routine that brings in some cash.

-That's a totally blinkered way of looking at things, baby. You've got to see the bigger picture. It makes far more sense I think, I paused in sage reflection, to figure out what I really want to do while I've got all this time, than to rush blindly into a job just for the sake of working, only to find myself trapped in forty years of thankless servitude.

I sank back into my rocking chair, a perch most conducive to this kind of speculation, as Thea left the flat, muttering something about melodrama.

I genuinely knew I was right about my own career. About the need for consideration, that is. My father would surely have agreed that much had he had a few more living hours to come to terms with my decision.

Ha! You think so, do you?

This did not stop me feeling a creeping envy for Thea's success. She was spending more and more time meeting backers, buyers, sponsors. She had already sold one of her pieces out of her studio to a passer-by. It had not been for sale, but the man had offered her so much money she had been unable to refuse. Her sketch — the back view of a woman sitting on a bar stool in a blues bar — paid for the next few months' studio rent.

There had even been a small piece in *The Sunday Times* supplement about upcoming talent, which had featured Thea looking elegant and quirky sitting before a portrait of Ruben.

Well that says it all, doesn't it.

I hadn't taken that too well. There were, after all, enough studies of my own anatomy to fuel a class of med. students.

-Is that all you can say? Thea had been close to tears. Aren't you proud of me?

-Oh God, Thea, I relented, feeling like a bastard. Of course I am. So, so proud, it goes without saying.

And I was. Her talent was undeniable. I couldn't help but feel she'd had it easy. To be born with such a clear-cut path in life. She'd barely had a choice. It would have been a criminal waste for her not to paint and draw. She'd had the full support of all humanity since the day she had produced a precociously detailed depiction of a pony in the 'Make and Draw' class aged four. And her parents off her back, thanks to me.

It was not an easy world to enter, the art world, but suddenly real opportunities were opening up for Thea. I had always taken it for granted that we would be in the same dreamy, creative boat for some time. She was displaying business acumen I had never seen before. She was growing up, I guess. There was now a website, designed by Ruben, which displayed my girlfriend's endeavours to the world.

At school, Ruben came up with hundreds of different inventions which, he thought, might enable him to make his fortune. Highlights included a pen/ torch which attached, ski-boot like, to the index finger for unprecedented dexterity. He had been runner up in a national competition with his masterly self-writing calendar, and had worked on a solar-powered food blender, 'for greener smoothies'.

I had little doubt that Our Father *(which art in heaven)* would have left Ruben, his blessed son, the flat as well as all that money if he'd had time to amend his will. Luckily, his wits had been so addled that suicide had come first. Still no light shed on why, though Queen K. continued to mutter surreptitiously.

Our father's death, and subsequent riches, had cut across all this with a new clarity.

-It's time to grow up, Ruben had told me, and to stop dicking around.

-Hmmm.

-How would you feel about me using this money to support Thea?

-Well that's very generous of you but I don't see why…

-Nothing generous about it, Matz. It's a business proposition. She's got the talent. I've got the business sense. And now I've got the money to invest as well.

-Well that's a wonderful idea! I'll talk to her about it tonight.

-Actually, I've already spoken to her about it…

It was round about this time that I came up with an ingenious business proposition of my own, to start charging Ruben rent.

Meanwhile, life was good for me in happy ignorance of what was going on behind my back. I capitalised on the ease with which I could spend long hours in bars and started doing Felix's PR. Being his publicist took up a lot of my time and opened more doors than it shut. I don't regret it.

More often than not, I found myself publicising the drugs Felix sold too. I told myself it would all be worth it when the money came rolling in and I told Thea nothing. Her contempt grew.

I'd imagined life on tour, the point of contact between the adoring public and their idols. If truth be told, I had spent much of my life thus far regretting my lack of musical talent. It was a cruel truth, for as a career sphere, the lifestyle would have suited me perfectly. This was a compromise, sure, but a happy one.

Felix had just formed The Cracks then — they had mutated out of an electro-folk trio with the Earthman and a crackhead called Rong. Rong's descent was swift and scary and by Christmas he was dead. The Cracks sprung up out of him, the cycle of life insistently moving forwards.

-And cracks in humans are good things, said Felix. They're how the light gets in.

Though I later realised Felix had sourced this wisdom from a high street greetings card, I appreciated the sentiment and thought there was something noble about new musicians rising out of the ashes of old ones.

Members of The Cracks came and went and the band rolled on in ramshackle fashion. All of them were quiet in real life, noisy on stage. Only Felix had star quality on and off stage. I was proud to know him, proud that I'd been trusted with his livelihood. And I was good at it too, the publicity thing.

It got me out of the house and fitted with my nocturnal preferences. It did not, however, do much to improve my relationship with Thea. I tried to encourage her and my brother to come to the gigs I arranged. Ruben showed me how to use a computer to design flyers, but after that, he just let me get on with it.

I see it with a gnawing clarity now that I stand ahead in time. So many disasters behind me, still so young. My feelings for Thea had been so all-consuming they had terrified me. I had been forced to act against them or otherwise I would have smothered her. Always I'd had it playing in my mind *you're young, you've got to give each other freedom to grow or you'll stunt each other. You'll end up seeing the other as the person who stole your youth, stopped you fulfilling your dreams.*

Clearly Thea had not sensed that danger.

It's unbearable to me now. Whatever she did to me, I realise I pushed her into it. I wish I could tell her. I wish she could know that she was always loved. That she always will be.

You'll never have that again.

It's odd to me to think that there was once a time when anxiety had not sat parasitic within me. Thea's love had bound me safe. But now I felt her disentangling herself, extricating the binds in which she had so tightly, exquisitely trapped me. Like an octopus stuck in a mucky clump of stagnant seaweed, tentacle after tentacle frees itself then waves triumphantly in the deep.

I dealt with this in the only way I knew how. I too pulled away, withdrew, in the instinctive belief that if I took two steps back, she would take two steps forward. I knew that if I were to follow her retreat, she would draw further away. She was, at least, spending time with Ruben still and what was he if not an extension of me?

Everything I did annoyed her. I'd come into the flat, catch her eye and see the irritation just floating there beneath the surface, waiting for its activation code.

The best thing, I thought, would be to stay out of the way. I'd keep a low profile, bury myself in working for Felix and bring in the cash until she remembered whatever it was she had loved so much about me. And I do think she did, once.

We slept in the same bed but we had not slept together for a while now. The first break-up had taken the edge from whatever skill I may have had in this department. The make-up sex was a bit of a flop.

-If you didn't take so many drugs... she'd started bitterly.

Part of me thought my incapacity was a relief to her, though. Even before she announced our split, she'd had an unfathomable amount of headaches. She must have been exhausted, of course, what with all the art and all the shagging of my brother. It brings me some satisfaction now that he'd be little use in the sack as he is.

Unless you had some freakish necrophilia proclivity of course.

We got back together before anything drastic had happened, like her moving out. Again, I was powerless. Her decision. And of course I

221

went along with it. I was in love with her. But paranoia crept in. When next might she decide to leave?

I saw myself as a silent psychiatrist, gathering evidence from her actions for her state of mind. You can't trust what people *say*, clearly, as she'd said nothing at all to me before The Dumping. No, to really see what's going on in there, you need to scrutinise the actions.

But when the actions made my hackles rise, I stopped hanging back, giving space and distance and started addressing the issues.

I'd notice, say, an uncalled for criticism of my life, friends, clothes, turn of phrase, and I'd bite my lip and absorb it. Then some hours later, when the ache behind my eyes was becoming insufferable, I'd bring it up in a heavily casual manner.

She'd say, What? Oh, sorry, I didn't mean anything by it.

But because of the incubation time, the comment would have already festered into a pre break-up statement and I'd be on hyperalert for another 'we need to chat and I will ruin your life' type conversation.

I'd catch myself digging for confirmation of it. At least I could have the satisfaction of being right, even though the last thing I wanted was what I was right about.

It was worse than that, actually.

God, what is this? Confession?

222

Yes, I would pick up on her fears, things she was usually able to dismiss as unfounded, and announce them as accepted fact. Undisturbed by her worry and upset, I would then embark on a psychological interrogation, hunting for motives, feelings, confusions. I knew exactly which buttons to press, which triggers would evoke tears, always so close to the surface these days. I was always horrified when I did push her over the edge, of course. But there was a small part of me that felt that she couldn't expect *every* part of her charmed life to be perfect.

She needled away at my own insecurities too. She made me feel needy.

And you don't think, do you, that you might have been responsible for any of this change in her demeanour and happiness? Are you so blind that you can't see what you did to the girl? How you ran away when she was pregnant with your child? How you were always away in some doped-up state? Silvia is your second chance. Don't fuck it up, boy.

XXII

Matty is growing tired of his 'novel'. It does not seem to be performing the task he assigned it. He is unable to distance himself from the characters. He is unable to alter the way they behave, as if by deviating from their actions in life, he is somehow lying. The process of writing is futile enough without charting meaningless falsities that have no relevance to anyone or anything.

He is beginning to realise that this is not a position of power either. Yes, he gives life to his characters; technically he should be able to control what happens to them. He wants to have them all at his beck and call, jumping when he says jump—exactly, in fact, as they never did in life. But he can't make them behave in ways that make no sense, which are out of character. In that sense, he is a slave to his own creation. He can't reduce Tera to a puppet, forced to do his bidding, by writing about the behaviour of a fictional girl with a similar name. He is gaining no psychological insight into any of it, except perhaps a hideous realisation that it might have been his own behaviour that pushed Ben and Tera together. And what use is that knowledge? It's too late to change now. If anything, he has become more firmly himself as time and tragedy have progressed.

Writing upsets him. That's the truth. It leeches too much self.

And what more is there to write? How will it help him to imagine Ben and Tera conspiring behind his back, to drag up from his terrible unconscious the precise unfoldings of that time, that climax. He can't do it.

But the scenes spill into his head. It is impossible to tell what is real and what is imagined. He must put them down in some kind of order, outside of himself where they can't hurt him anymore, and unify the disparate voices that bark at him.

PRIVATE AND CONFIDENTIAL
DR J. SYKES

CONTENTS: FOURTH EMAIL AND LIFE-WRITING CHAPTER FROM MEC, WITH MY NOTES.

From: Matty Corani <matzcorani@gmail.com>
Subject: Life-writing
Date: 25 January 2016 12:03:42GMT
To: Julia Sykes <juliasykes@mail.com>

Hi J, More thrilling insight into the life of Matthew Corani. Maybe we could discuss it over a drink?[1]

M

LOOKING UP AT THE STARS[2]

I developed a sort of obsession with my biological mother after the king died.

I remember asking Ruben about his own mother, Leya. He found it exasperating, I think. Or maybe embarrassing; perhaps she really had become a hooker. But the more things went wrong with Thea, the more I buried myself in my unknown past, trying to unravel it, work out why I was so worried all the time, why I kept taking it out on her.

She told me once that she understood it came not from malice but from some undeveloped, child-like unawareness of the capacity to hurt others and invade their boundaries.

This smacked of Dr Psychosis[3] to me. Eternal child! I was a fucking child.

---

[1]   ?
[2]   WHAT HAPPENED TO CHAPTER NUMBERS? INCONSISTENCY/DISORGANISED THINKING?
[3]   IS THIS ME? OR DOES IT SUGGEST HE SOMEHOW FINDS COMFORT IN DELUSIONS.

King Darius had never had much time for me. He seemed to recognise only Ruben as his son.

I knew that my father blamed me for my mother's death,[4] knew that he hated the reminder of her face in mine. But that wasn't fair. I would readily have died in my mother's place just to experience one ounce of recognition from him. I would probably have agreed to not being born at all.

I could not understand why Ruben seemed so unaffected by his comparative situation; he too had grown up without his mother when Darius swept off to Beijing leaving Leya with nothing. Half-brothers, why did we not feel an equal sense of loss? It is true that I do feel that my situation was more difficult; the absolute finality of the death of my mother, the cruelty of having no memory at all to pin on her. But if I were Ruben, I'd at least wonder where my mother went and why she was no longer with my father.

I never tired of asking him about it. It must have been annoying. I felt that if Ruben were only honest, he might reveal to me some sort of genetic pattern, allow me to understand myself a little better.

-To be honest, I can't really remember Mum that clearly, Ruben answered as he always answered, staring into the watery coffee — rationing — before him. London had realised, what with the advance of gross acts of Isis brutality in humanity, and tsunamis, floods and earthquakes in nature,[5] that Armageddon was indeed, as had been

---

[4] WE NEED TO FOCUS NOW ON FREEING M. FROM THIS MISTAKEN SENSE OF GUILT — IT'S EXTENDING ACROSS HIS WHOLE LIFE.

[5] M. JOINING DOTS THAT AREN'T THERE.

clearly indicated by the Blood Moon Prophecy,[6] on its way. The Survivalists were mobilising. Insect recipes and how-to-build-your-own-house-after-the-apocalypse diagrams started to appear in the newspapers.

I was unconvinced by Ruben's maternal apathy. Admittedly I had been older than Ruben when we'd lived in Havana; obviously, than when Leya gave birth to him, but she was so vibrant, so bright, I was certain she must have made some irresistible impression on her own son.

-But don't you wonder where she is, whether she's safe? Whether you've got any more half-brothers kicking about? Wouldn't you like to see her again?

—Maxi… Thea warned.

But Ruben did not seem particularly bothered.[7]

-Look Maxi, he said, I know you find this hard to believe but I'm not that different from you. For all the infant time I spent with Leya, I might as well have been put with a wet nurse like you.[8] My memory just doesn't stretch that far back. My maternal upbringing was just like yours—a string of interchangeable women.[9]

Not to mention the boys! Tee-hee.[10]

---

6   But we have passed September 2015, date for this apocalyptic/second-coming prophecy. Is this connected to Feracor visions?
7   Avoidant attachment patterns in brother.
8   So he was breastfed – claimed not to know. But not by mother, so same lack of cortisol-diminishing hormones.
9   Like M.'s sex life – ever replacing mother, girl found wanting.
10 A joke? Another fragment of M.'s personality?

But my upbringing wasn't just like that. I had known real love, even if it had come from Ruben's mother.[11] I was able to transfer that kindness, that closeness to the images I had created of my biological mother. Or at least to animate the photograph I had of her.

All this is by the by. I'm just trying to work out the characters and the plot line, as if it were a story written by someone else. I'm delaying the event. I was at a party, or maybe the after-party in the flat — I think that's where the police called. The point is I wasn't there at the accident. I didn't see what was going on. And I hadn't known there was anything going on between those two before the accident. Though it seems likely, doesn't it, given the compromising position in which they were found, that they were pretty familiar with each other's bodies by this point. I was called up by Felix, I think. Either that, or Felix was there when I went to the police station. Or he was just there after, like a little father,[12] looking after me.

Police said it looked like Thea'd 'distracted' Ruben; she was bent over his lap.[13] He'd driven off the road. God knows where they were going. They seemed to be heading north, crashed somewhere near Hatfield Tunnel. Thea was dead, no question, Ruben pretty mangled.

Felix took me to his flat in Soho and nursed me back to life. It was a strange time, full of blanks, full of nothingness. He protected me from responsibility and truth. To be honest, he

---

[11] Should be possible to find Leya/Luisa in this day and age.

[12] M. has distorted views of role of father. Have strong impression Fix is like M.'s father — both suffering puer aeternus complex. Identification with the aggressor.

[13] Does this definitely mean they were having an affair?

was under no obligation. I mean, who is? But he went beyond the call.

Felix even sorted me out for money, got someone to buy the flat I'd been left by Darius (to the horror of Queen K.). It meant I could rent near him in Soho and sort out my debts: I paid him back for everything he imagined I might have owed him from my lost period.

There was no one left for me. Felix was guardian and angel.[14] And when the polar icecaps are melting and the day is very nearly done,[15] you need someone like that.

***

So that's that. He can move on with his life. He's sent it to Dr Psycho.

Ben's betrayal is easier to deal with, now that he has revealed his true nature in *Looking Up At The Stars*. There's no remorse there, Matty can see that now. The most difficult part had always been trying to reconcile the image he had of his brother—easy-going, loyal friend—with what evidence suggested was his actual personality. Now he can see a coherent picture of a character, previously unknown to him, always waiting in the shadows, biding his time. A jealous character. A ruthless one. Of course Ben would have gone to every available length to disguise his essence and purpose from Matty. For he was (and Matty had assumed

---

[14] DEIFYING MEN TOO. MAKING FIX ATTACHMENT FIGURE? SEXUAL? SEE MARIE-LOUISE VON FRANZ, THE PROBLEM OF THE PUER AETERNUS: 'THE TWO TYPICAL DISTURBANCES OF A MAN WHO HAS AN OUTSTANDING MOTHER COMPLEX ARE, AS JUNG POINTS OUT, HOMOSEXUALITY AND DON JUANISM. IN THE CASE OF THE FORMER, THE HETEROSEXUAL LIBIDO IS STILL TIED UP WITH THE MOTHER, WHO IS REALLY THE ONLY BELOVED OBJECT, WITH THE RESULT THAT SEX CANNOT BE EXPERIENCED WITH ANOTHER WOMAN. THAT WOULD MAKE HER A RIVAL OF THE MOTHER, AND THEREFORE SEXUAL NEEDS ARE SATISFIED ONLY WITH A MEMBER OF THE SAME SEX.' (P. 7)
[15] SUICIDAL IDEATION?

until this point that he had the monopoly on this one), he was *clever*.

Growing up, Matty had been the thinker, withdrawn to the point of sociopathic. Ben, he realises now, had facilitated those immature characteristics. Ben, by his relentless over-compensation, his chattiness, his happy-go-lucky exterior, had ensured that Matty never had to grow, take responsibility for himself.

He had thought they were closer than they were. These things happen.

But as his senses fill with Ben and Tera, his eyes well with tears—why, still? It just sometimes overwhelms him, the desire to talk to one or both, the people he knew them as before he learned the horrible truth. It is in these instances that Matty truly feels what it is to be alone in this world, even when the streets around you are saturated with people.

He decides to see Ben in person, to say goodbye to him in reality as well as in writing. Then he will see Fix, his true brother. Then he will see Sylvie and the child within her and perhaps he will propose to her now too. His life is in order.

He's in the hospital in what feels like seconds, quick calls made en route arranging meetings with Fix and Sylvie. This is the first day of the rest of his life. Relief becomes euphoria.

'It's farewell to all that, Ben,' he says triumphantly. 'It's time to cut you loose. It's the NHS for you, m' boy.'

He studies Ben's passive, uncreased face. No sign of any tremendous rue in there. Perhaps some people are just born bad. Or bitter. Or jealous.

Matty assembles a thin white line on the white, dead hand of his brother and, in what he determines will be a final farewell gesture, sniffs the cocaine. He feels his nose in contact with the needle sticking into Ben's hand, feeding him drip by drip. He wants to pull it out. But he realises that would cut short Ben's punishment, the half-life, caught between dimensions like a moth in amber.

He walks out of the hospital with a spring in his step. Enough now. He is ready to let go of the past.

The hospital is next to busy Marylebone Road. He crosses it and, spying green ahead, decides to walk around Regent's Park before returning to Soho, where he is due to meet Sylvie and Fix in the evening. Within ten minutes he is surrounded by an expanse of flat, tailored grass and the traffic is a distant hum. His spirits slow and lift as he congratulates himself on a good decision.

He walks for twenty minutes, pathless, undisturbed by disorientation. But suddenly he feels a strange nagging to look behind him, just to check there's no one tagging him. Don't be stupid, he tells himself, and is able to dismiss the circular thoughts for a couple of minutes. He snaps his head round and, as in some deep part of himself he had suspected he would, sees Ben duck back behind a flower bed, obscured from view by a bonfire of many colours.

His mind must be playing tricks on him. He walks forward with more speed towards the nearest path where there are people to tether him to reality. For a brief and terrifying moment, he sees Ben's face superimposed upon man, woman and child on the path. But then the boundaries shift and regroup and normality is restored.

Nevertheless, he is a little shaken. Nature, while considered a calming influence on most people, is clearly a disruptive force upon him. He gets out of the park as quickly as he can and jumps on the open back of a passing bus, sweating lightly and uniformly.

When Matty arrives home, his boot leaves a footprint on the addressee side of a letter that's lying on the mat behind the front door and—great joy—it does not look like a bill.

Ripping it open, he notes the address with interest—isn't that where Fix works? Mile End Hospital? Ah yes, it's the mental health unit, long-dreaded, prison-like, summoning him for appraisal. But he remembers what Fix said about the tremendous range of mind-bending substances they feed you. Does his friend even still take shifts there? Matty realises he very rarely asks Fix about himself. He scans the letter, sees that it is attached to some sort of questionnaire and requests his attendance on Monday 15 February. Just after Valentine's Day; how romantic. Well that's a long way off—and after the trial on the 2nd. He's had enough of therapy, to be honest. That's not doing what it said on the tin either. Sykes can't cope with him so she's palming him off on others. At the last session she'd recommended group therapy, 'to encourage him to look outside himself and connect with others'. He does not want to explain himself to others from the beginning again. He can cope with the scrutiny of one person. Can keep track of what he's said and what he has not.

He's feeling terrible; the Jitterer assails him with sporadic waves of panic and nausea. Sleep or another line are the only ways out. Ideally both, but more coke would rule out sleep before Silvia's arrival and he really needs to be on good form when he sees her. And he really needs to keep up with Fix, should they go out and make a night of it, which they obviously will. Fix has a stamina that makes Matty feel old. Sylvie has a pregnancy that makes him feel old. Either way, sleep, so unnecessary in the past, is now essential.

He's had the last of the cocaine, he realises, but his ketamine stash is ever replenished by what Fix gives him to sell, and he still has some crystal meth left over too. Meth has been a revelation; gets him higher than God, and a single hit can last for hours. It can't be too harmful either because they prescribe it to children with ADHD, Fix claimed. The Earthman confirmed it, presenting a stolen packet of his little brother's Desoxyn. And if Matty can't trust them, who can he trust? Besides, he only snorts and smokes it. No needles. He has always prided himself on avoiding the street stuff, the seedier side of it all. Dirty drugs like heroin emphatically *are not* for him. Fix has told him how dealers store the little bags of brown in their arses, how they're transferred from mouth to mouth. Not for me, he decided. You absolutely must have boundaries.

Sleep first, fly later. He takes four little yellow Xanax pills—his metabolism is so fast these days that normal doses just glance off his surface—swallowing them with water from a glass left on the bookshelf. He is half-expecting it to be dregs of vodka or gin or some other clear spirit, but it is not, sadly. He mentally scolds himself for thinking in such terms. If he wants a drink, he can go and have one like a normal human being, in a nice clean glass, in a nice clean flat, into a nice clean body.

Ten minutes later, the shakiness is starting to dissipate, his body loosens, and his thoughts solidify. Matty lies down on the bed with what remains of his beleaguered *Bacchae* and reads of Feracor's earlier reception. 'If I catch him within the boundaries of this land,' says Pentheus the King, 'I shall stop him making his thyrsus ring and tossing back his hair—by cutting his head from his body.'

It's never been easy being a new god on the block.

Dr J. Sykes BACP (accred.)
Psychotherapist

Private Room
36 Harley Street
London W1G 9PG

Date:	Time:	Patient Initials:	Attendance:
Tuesday 26 January 2016	5pm	MEC	DNA

Notes:

M. referred as outpatient to The Tower Hamlets Centre for Mental Health, Mile End Hospital, Bancroft Road, London E1 4DG

-Anthony Storr, The Art of Psychotherapy, really seems to be the master on this one:

'Esoteric beliefs and phantasised superiority go hand in hand. The alienated and the isolated are attracted to strange sects because the systems of beliefs which such sects promulgate hold out the promise of understanding their own difficulties in life, and partly because being a member of such a sect carries with it the implication of possessing more insight into life than the average person.' (p. 143)

And in the later Feet of Clay, Storr writes:

'Because he is the subject of so much unwelcome attention [ie voices, visions (J.S.)], it follows that he must really be a person of consequence. Perhaps he is of royal descent, or a reincarnation of an Old Testament prophet. Prophets with a new message are usually rejected by the establishment – consider what happened to Jesus. He must certainly be someone very unusual indeed; is it even possible that he is the Messiah?

Grandiosity and isolation march hand in hand.' (p. 158)

'The important point is that paranoid delusions have a positive function. They make sense out of chaos within, and also preserve the subject's self-esteem. They are a creative solution to the subject's problems, albeit a creative solution which does not stand up to critical examination.' (p. 161)

ORESTES (*in sudden terror*): A-a-ah!
These grim women here—like Gorgons with their
dark clothing and snakes twined thickly in their hair!
I can't stay here longer!

CHORUS: *What fancies are swirling you round,*
you dearest of men to your father? Hold on,
do not be afraid; your victory is great.

ORESTES: *They are not fancies to me, the torments*
I have here: these are my mother's rancorous fury-hounds.

CHORUS: *That is because the blood is still fresh on your*
hands; this is the source of the agitation now invading
your mind.[†]

†   Aeschylus, *Choephori*, trans. Christopher Collard, lines 1048-56.

XXIII

'Who's there?'

The voice has been veering in and out of earshot, like a mosquito whining near one's eardrum. Matty tries to slap it; it vanishes. The noise ceases for just long enough to allow him to imagine it has finally given up, saturated with its bloody dinner, perhaps struck down by blood poisoning. Or perhaps his hand did actually reach its target; it's just too dark to tell. Soothed by such thoughts, and another bump of K, he begins to drift away to a different dimension. And then the high-pitched whine starts up once more with all the malice, all the volume of a hive of hornets.

So it is with the voice assailing him. It clashes with his own internal rattle. It speaks of Mars, of Venus, of children and ages, of an epic journey, of a prophecy, an oracle and a messiah, of Dionysus, of Feracor breaking out of prison and the future of mankind, greatness and immortality.

You've been writing the wrong book, Man. Ignoring your calling.

The voice presents itself endlessly, relentlessly. This is not his father, not his brother and it's certainly not Feracor.

Maybe, says the voice which he cannot place, *it's not Feracor that the world is crying out for. Maybe it's you. You, the chosen one to show the people a new religion. A philosophy for the twenty-first century. It's all in your head. Feracor doesn't exist except as an element of you.*

The voice has more authority in it than Feracor's ever did.

You're on the verge of making the biggest mistake in history since Jesus Christ was allowed to usurp the appointed leader of the Fourth Race. Feracor is merely your internal antenna. He's your conscience—your messenger, your prophet, the guy who's put you in touch with yourself. It is you who accepted Mars and impregnated Rhea Silvia. It is you who's the descendant of Aramat. The time is over for Aramat and Altera. A scar in your past which needed to be inflicted, simply to clear the way. The deadwood is cut away now and the time is right to create. Don't fuck up another generation by abandoning your Silvia to that tuneless junkie, Fix.

Mandrax is panicking, hands clammy as his mouth is dry.

You were not ready back then.

The voice reads his questions.

The Feracorian element of your brain had the confidence and presence, wizard and charlatan, to convince the other voices of your head to back down. You needed that ferocity to intimidate those in mental power, to overthrow the established order of your messed-up head and show you that you don't have to live the rest of your life consumed by guilt. Feracor's purpose was to clear the way for you, Mandrax, to assume your rightful position. Feracor was to lead by example. He has done so. The way is clear for you. But Feracor has become too bloated inside your head. He has taken over all your thoughts and almost taken over you. You have come to believe his voice. But this was never meant to be. The yarn for your fairy tale, the creation of your own mythology, lies before your feet. Will you let an imposter spin the tale? Do so, you lose your love, you lose your place in destiny. You lose the human race. There are no second chances.
There is only a genesis.

Matty falls, spinning, into the scriptures. He turns over and writes…

BOOK I
CHAPTER I
VERSE I

Night had fallen but colours of exceptional beauty carved up the purple sky, shards of gold, of blue, of green like the trails of shooting stars forming a kaleidoscope of angles, weaving a frame for the constellation within. The Fourth Age is dying, the Fifth Age is dawning. All the dual forces from which spring all things are at their peak; all elements at their most harmonious, yet in their harmony at their most destructive with their conjoined strength. Raindrops flood the deep and thunder shatters the firmament; fire from the sun blazes and swoops, illuminating the moon in a savage halo. Every star, every single star in the sky, shifts, leaves rank. Like cavalry performing a drill, they realign themselves into troops and patterns, streaming inside the angular shape, a gargantuan star delineated by luminous rods of colour.

Outside this glowing frame, a purple emptiness of space reigns, devoid of stars now, devoid of life. Only Earth. A microcosm, it mirrors the universal pattern occurring in the expanse. Above, each little spark takes its place in the greater order, forming a pattern ever more recognisable, as if a greater, unseen artist was tweaking them into place. Were there a mortal left on Earth, looking up he would have died to witness such exquisite, such powerful, unutterable beauty. The larger stars encapsulate the muscular might of Mars, clusters of them forming swathes of blonde hair the size of seas as he shakes his head, roars wrath and war. The smaller stars, more silvery in aspect, draw a perfect female form, a soft curve for every smooth, hard counterpart of the male. Mars and Venus, emblazoned by the starry pawns of the universe, dance triumphant. They fit together, two halves of a whole, Yin and Yang, the very elements of the cosmos their dance floor.

239

On Earth, an instant of infinity, Feracor and Rhea Silvia prepare to channel the contrary forces. Their role is pre-ordained, inscribed in the annals of time. They must allow themselves to be ciphers for the powers of the universe, to create something greater than themselves from which a new race of man must spring.

But they have been writing their own script. They forget the higher power that spins their fate. Even Mars and Venus are subject to governing laws of time and space. Even Jupiter is subject to Fate.

Where is Mandrax? He is writing. He is spinning.

Where is Benzo? He is written. He is spun.

The stars above are shuffling, reshuffling. Mars is diminishing, stars dispersing from his outline like molecules of water evaporating from a boiling pot. The gas condenses. Another outline forms, male once more, grows larger and harder as the former male image fades. Venus smiles. She moves forward to her new lover.

Feracor crumples, the blade firmly embedded between his shoulder blades. Silvia sees Mandrax, recognises her true love. In him she sees the past, present and future. In him she sees infinity. The power of Venus fills her as she receives the new deity. The firmament flashes approval, a sonorous dance thundering above them as the waves crescendo.

Silvia, lost in ecstasy, conceives that night of the rightful heir of the human race, the Embodiment of universal forces. He will be called Iacchus, the Eternal Child.

Mandrax wakes up. Something inside him has shifted. Matty feels intensely calm and can see the world, all worlds with clarity. The pair stand above space and time, perspective not from a tethered point in either but above that whole maelstrom. They look down upon it like a bird circling a worm. They are higher than they have ever been in their lives.

Matty walks to meet Sylvie with a preternatural slowness. He will not make concessions to the fake chains of watches and clocks which humans treat with such reverence. He is beyond it, rattling through galaxies and aeons, or perfectly still, static, not even his atoms vibrating. Matty Corani is all and he is nothing, the new Jesus Christ and yet, so much more than that. And then it occurs to him. He's writing a new sacred text: it needs a name! Something catchy like Qur'an, Bible, Torah. It comes to him: The Word—that sounds holy. But also a touch urban. Better in Spanish: PALABRA. Sounds a bit like parable too. The word of Feracor: THE PALABRA FERACORI.

Intrusive scrutiny of his own self makes him realise the calm consists of the retreat of any and all of the voices which have comprised his self all these years and, most loudly recently, of Feracor. There is silence except for the single track of his own thoughts, uninterrupted. Mandrax is used to flitting between the voices, the ball flying from racket to racket over an expansive green tennis court.

Now it is just him playing. Now it is just Mandrax in there, Matty on the outside.

He notices that the comets have started up again. A shooting star thuds down in front of him. He observes it with contempt. Impudent rock.

Sylvie is waiting for him outside Bar Italia. He smiles with pride at her swollen shape. She does not smile back.

'I didn't handle your news very well, Silvia, last time we met. I've had a bit of a revelation since then and I'm ready to be a father to our child,' he says, amazed at the obviousness of this decision.

She looks less than delighted.

'Great, Matty,' she says. 'I appreciate your bluntness.'

'What's wrong?'

'The baby, I—'

'The baby you… what—'

'Well either I was never pregnant… or I'm now not.'

Mandrax howls. 'How the fuck can that be?' cries Matty.

'It happens, you know. Early days. I'm feeling okay about it, you know? I'm too young to have a child. I can barely look after myself.'

'It doesn't happen. Not to this child. You have no idea, do you? The whole world will know who you are and what you've done when they're throwing themselves from the windows of their houses rather than face judgement.'

'Matty, you scare me. I think you need some help.'

'What was it, did you get high with Fix and poison our child? The future of the human race snuffed out by a joint?'

'Matty, I'm going to leave now. And when I have, it will be goodbye between us, okay? I really can't take any more of this. I just thought you had a right to know about the baby.'

'But we've got to make another one. You can't go. Everything's in alignment—the elements, the planets. It's now or never.'

Sylvie runs.

It does not befit Matty's new status to run through the streets of Soho after her. He will wait. She will return. So it is written.

He goes instead to Fix's flat.

When Fix opens the door, Mandrax can hear that Sylvie is already there. He summons the might of the ages and makes Matty hit Fix hard in the face.

Fix reels backwards, one hand to his bloody jaw.

'What the fuck was that for?'

'That, my friend, is for fucking my girlfriend. And this,' he swings wildly in on him again, 'is for fucking humanity. I know you had something to do with her losing the baby. And you can't even begin to consider the consequences which shall befall you.'

'Matty, you're nuts. You're psychotic. Too many drugs, man.'

He shuts the door and Mandrax can hear him muttering 'too many drugs' over and over again.

'And you can shove your PR job,' Mandrax yells through the keyhole. 'Because you're shit and no amount of publicity can disguise that.'

Mandrax walks Matty back to Piccadilly Circus to survey the ads, announcement boards for those in the cosmic know. A spring in his step.

XXIV

Losing Fix is a bit of a blow. There is no one left for Matty now. It is only when a man is stripped of his loves that he can truly understand the point of everything else. Everything, that is, which is aimed at stirring, at soothing the troubled human soul: it is the human condition to suffer loss as much as it is the human solace to try to appease the loss of others. Matty looks through his window down into Soho, the tops of heads revealing nothing about the minds below. But Matty can hear beneath those scalps, pink tinged from the cold. He can feel the lonely, the worried, the desperate and the hopeful. He can pick out the woman crippled by apathy, the man fearful for his life, the man for whose life others fear, for he himself has no such concern as he pursues his own destruction. Matty can smell them all, mingling in the filth of their own corrupted, rotten dreams. These are the flayed spirits for whom art, music, philosophy and religion come alive.

Questions which had bounced off the young Matty, interested and intense as he had been, now prey on his mind, vultures pecking away at his brain, at his liver. Paintings which had left him cold though he had professed to admire the skill, the vision, now shake him to the bone as alien beauty assaults the darkness of his life. He sees the artist behind them and behind every artist he sees Tera, still. The human psyche cannot make sense of it, cannot endure such loss. Always it seeks a way out, a distraction in which to bury itself.

He is so tired.

This icy winter wind zooming through the Soho streets has robbed him of the many masks he has used formerly as hiding places. There is nothing left. He is used up, ugly, spent. He is an old man at the age of twenty-two. The wild swings of emotion, the determination to escape, to start again, to forget, even the voices have all ebbed to quiet. And this, *this*, is all there is left. Just a shell.

What is the fucking point?

It strikes him as odd now that there has been no gradual inner commentary as he has sunk lower and lower. Why has this internal voice of self-recognition only entered now, when he's finally slid to the bottom of the helter-skelter? Why so alone, now? All his life, he's been fighting the vocal cross-fire, deafening, infuriating. Now in this bleak, bleak chill, he misses the comforting drone. A thousand blurred radio channels tune into white noise now. That's all that is left of him. White noise.

If he didn't have PALABRA to write, he'd go mad. But Mandrax has a purpose: scribe and savage. The animal, primitive, fierce-hearted side of man shall be embodied by him alone.

Fix had in fact come round a couple of days ago, a livid bruise on his jaw. It would be laughable if it wasn't so bloody inconvenient: Fix, his friend, livelihood and bottomless drug pit, had dared to say he thought Matty could do with a 'bit of time' to sort himself out, that 'stuff' had got out of control. Well of course it had. Wasn't that the point of ingesting mind-altering substances, Fix, you wanker, Matty had asked. Rock and fucking roll. It transpired that Fix's band, newly renamed The Furies (at Matty's suggestion) had finally and against all the odds, been signed. This was no thanks to Matty's attempts to publicise them. But then that title had always been a disguise for Matty's real job—Fix's errand boy, dispensing drugs where Fix would not.

Fix and The Furies were about to embark on a national tour. Matty is not invited. This change in his old friend's fortune makes him want to weep.

Luckily, in addition to his helpful advice, Fix had also left the telephone number of an acquaintance who could help Matty out, *in extremis*.

So here he is all alone; he'd say that counts as *in ex-fuckin'-tremis*. Not even Sylvie to keep him company. She's played her part, or failed to. Matty can no longer see how he ever saw Tera in her; always a leap of faith, even with a squint. It became virtually impossible when she destroyed his child.

It is lucky Mandrax is so absorbed by THE PALABRA FERACORI.

It will be the book to define an era, a holy book, written by the new Messiah. He knows there are quite a few radical ideas in there, but he feels people are ready for that, what with the world caving in on itself. Christ, too, had entered an arena of shifting morality and given advice that fitted those times. It had no longer been viable to ruthlessly demand an eye for an eye. People had been ready for an altogether more forgiving philosophy and Christ recognised that. All he'd required to make people accept his guidelines was a little bit of magic, a few hints that there was more to it than met the eye.

Mandrax has been a little short on miracles, it's true. They tend to manifest themselves in his own inner consciousness. But he feels confident that his manner of self-publicity will be dramatic enough to secure his position in history. And not only history. Though he has, perhaps, failed in life, he would accomplish more by his death than any man before him. Unlike Christ, his was not a way of life for that time only, one that would grow old and out of place. This, for the first time in the history of *Homo sapiens*, was not a religion dumbed down for infantile human comprehension, but one in tune with the very essence of the universe.

The final chapter, then.

He has been thinking a lot about how he should go. Nobody ever said being the Messiah was an easy pathway.

In fact, it was the various hardships Jesus Christ had been through that made him so impressive, so memorable as a human representative of the religion. This keeps Matty going forward. It is His suffering and betrayal that will make people sit up and take note of what He has to say. The story of His life has a sort of 'I've been there' empathic kind of appeal. This much is evident in the comments on his Facebook posts. Not a day goes past when there won't be some cheering message from wannabe disciples 'SuperKev' in Arizona, or 'Bettyblue' in Cape Town telling him to 'Keep Smiling' (often illustrated by a host of yellow faces, grinning maniacally) or 'Keep on keeping on'. This is touching, but he can't help but feel that these people are missing the point of his message. They need to be shocked into acceptance of the new religion.

Matty snorts a little methamphetamine as he waits for his computer to wake up and his Facebook page—THE PALABRA FERACORI—to load. He has given a lot of thought to death since the clarity of his mission came to him. Feracor seemed to have receded from his mind as if recognising the need for brain space in contemplation of such a complex topic. Mandrax's thoughts are clear and pure, white upper ether, an uninterrupted stream of consciousness.

He will not, of course, be the first in his family to die by his own hand. His father would be proud of him for upholding a family tradition. But he will be the first to accomplish something great by doing so. That much is left to him. Not for him the grotesque lolling head of his father's brother, Uncle Edward, found hanging from a door hook in ultimate ignominy.

In a way, his own mother's death had been a form of suicide.

He can't shake the idea that she might have been so revolted by what had come out of her that her heart had just stopped of its own accord. Can you will your heart to stop?

He had tried, tried so hard when he'd found out about *them*, but it had just kept beating regardless. But the worst suicide was undoubtedly the failed one, where you have to live with the consequences of your actions and the removal of any implements which might enable you to try and get it right this time. This had, he'd heard, happened to an old school friend of Fix's who now resided in a high security asylum in Berkshire. Who'd have guessed it?

Mandrax does not fear death for two reasons. The first of these is that his life ceased to contain meaning to him or to anyone else some time ago, on that Day of Discovery. The second is that he is acting for the greater good of humanity. He is acting on behalf of Feracor, who will, he has absolute faith, look after him—for what could he possibly gain by not doing so? He is not sure exactly what Feracor has in mind for him, but he wouldn't be surprised if he had a grand resurrection up his sleeve à la J. C.—which you have to admit was pretty attention grabbing. But failing that, Mandrax had seen life after death, he'd touched it, surely, that lull between dimensions where all the worlds, all the people he'd ever encountered, mentally and physically, collided.

Or there is nothing.

Peace.

There are so many hours in the daytime. In all of these hours one is expected to do something. Or wait for those hours to pass. Matty views waking up as the beginning of a process of winding down. He waits for oblivion. He waits until he does not care. Life is too slow. He would rather have two hours in a day; one would be spent achieving some-thing—making something beautiful; one would be spent thrilling himself—high on achievement, high on life, high on whatever he could lay his hands on. And so to bed with Tera for the longest night of sex and sleep, dreams and desire.

Or Sylvie.

Or any two-bit whore dancing in the doorways of Walker's Court.

But when he walked through there yesterday, he saw that finally, as had long been threatened, that alley of illicit pleasures was all boarded up.

Katya rings to say she's on her way; he must meet her for lunch. The thought of food turns his stomach but not so significantly as the idea of sitting upright looking at his father's mistress.

The swift turning of the universe has slowed to a lithium dullness. He walks as if in molten iron, each painful shuffle jangling some part of his anatomy. He smokes a cigarette as he walks. An inadequate distraction.

The Soho grey hangs heavy as he turns down Dean Street, the pavement cafes brimming with braying unbohemians. He must move somewhere else. Where did all the drunken poets go? France probably. If he makes it through the trial he'll move to Paris and spread the good word there. A tramp considers asking him for cash, then thinks again and crosses the street. He must look as he feels then.

He reaches the rush and lights of Shaftesbury Avenue and navigates some buses and bikes to reach the Chinatown lanterns. The bustle and spit on the streets has him back in Beijing in an instant. No big black communist buildings, no mile-wide roads of traffic, no asbestos-filled building sites it is true, but the mentality is the same. People swerve or collide. It should give him great pleasure that the apocalypse has temporarily receded but actually he feels melancholic. The Day of Judgement will at least shake things up a bit. It's all so fucking staid here.

He forces his way past some tourists opposite stands full of foul smelling durian, jackfruit and papaya on Lisle Street and makes his way into The Golden Dong over a fake bridge riding a fake pond of fake Koi Carp. Anger rises in him. Where is truth?

Katya is sitting elegantly (prissily) at a table in the corner.

'Hello, Matty.' She stands up to hug him. 'This is rather a fun place, don't you think?'

'Hmm,' he says. 'Like a Chinese theme park.'

She preens then relents. 'I suppose it is a little bit.' A laugh of sorts.

'Not your usual sort of posho palace.'

'No, that's true. But your last day before the trial—I thought you might want to have a chat somewhere a bit more "you". Your father was always going on about how much you boys loved Beijing.'

'He was? That's funny because I actually and transparently fucking hated it.'

'Look, I know you must be nervous about tomorrow—'

'I've got bigger things on my mind, to be honest.'

'I find that hard to believe, Matty. Do you want to talk about it?'

'Let's have a drink, shall we?' The idea of trying to explain the truer reality of his visions to Katya is ludicrous.

She sighs. 'Why not? What would you like?'

'What have they got? Anything but Tsing Tao. It tastes like gnat's piss.'

'Your father thought so too.'

'Did he ever take you to China?'

'No. No he didn't, but he talked about it often. Seemed to much prefer it to Moscow, and Havana.'

'That's funny. He didn't strike me as terribly happy in Beijing. None of us were.'

'I think maybe he had problems with nostalgia. The last place was always superior to the new one. And the last mistress for that matter.'

'I thought he preferred boys.'

'God you really go for the jugular every time, don't you, darling?'

Matty sits in scowling silence until his triple gin and tonic arrives. Katya fiddles with her napkin, then her lipstick and finally with the menu, asking Matty if he wouldn't mind ordering for them both. She's not really an aficionado of Chinese food.

'Actually, this is all quite different from the food in China. It's Cantonese for tourists.' It's actually not but he can't resist a dig. Knowing that he won't be able to eat anything, he sources the most repulsive items on the list, starting with pig lung and ending with jellyfish.

'Now I'm glad you brought up your father,' she says when there is no option but to talk again.

'I didn't. You did.'

'Whatever, Matty. There's something I think you should know about him. We have to be prepared for the worst out-come of the trial, I mean I'm sure it won't come to—'

He can't understand why everyone's making such a fuss about it. Yes court's never fun but it's just a little possession charge. He's unlikely to go down for that, surely.

'What is it?'

'Well, you know he wasn't well. That's why we moved to France… He wanted to stop working so hard and be closer to you boys.'

'Why?'

'Because he loved you. I know he had a strange way of showing it, but you were everything to him. He was dam-aged, Matty. Never the same after he lost your mother.'

The guilt crashes in again. Your fault. Your birth.

She went on. 'You don't know how damaged, though. He was HIV positive when I met him, darling. I think Ben knew. He guessed in Cuba when Daniel was so vile to you. He'd been feeling so ill; he'd just had test results and found out it was full-blown AIDS. He was determined to hide it from you and not ruin your trip with Tera, whom, contrary to appearances, he thought was very good news.'

'God.' Matty, for once, is rocked on his heels. 'Poor bastard. Is that why my mother died? Could it be in me?'

'No, no that's not how it was. After your mother died, he was extraordinarily promiscuous. Women and men. I think he was always trying to lose himself in them, or to find your mother in them. I don't know. When he found he'd contracted the virus in Cuba, he decided to leave everything behind and move on.'

'What about Leya, I mean Luisa?'

'She didn't have it. He'd been horribly unfaithful to her though. A post came up in Moscow and he didn't think twice. I think he thought everyone would be better off without him, like he was doing her a favour by leaving her. And maybe by protecting you boys from himself as well, by keeping you away from his increasing bad temper and discomfort. You were looked after in London, at school, weren't you? He just couldn't trust himself to be a decent man around company. And he couldn't deal with the self-hatred that ensued when he was his usual self.'

'Hmm. That's a very charitable way of seeing it. But I mean, what about you?' For the first time in his life, Matty feels a pang of something he can't identify for Katya.

'I loved him as a mother loves a son. We looked after each other.'

There's not a lot Matty can say to that. Life seems bleaker than ever. The pig lung rocks up and introduces its tripe-like fragrance to his churning gut. Mutilated offal and putrid intestines follow, like the descent into hell. Katya is starting to look a little desperate.

'Some Last Supper, Matty.'

'We used to eat like this the whole time in Beijing,' he lies, swallowing rising bile. 'But I have to say, I've rather lost my appetite.'

'I just wanted you to know the truth. I thought about it a lot and concluded it was more deceptive to have you take your father's behaviour towards you at face value. Perhaps now you know what he was going through you can begin to understand why he was the way he was.'

'I need some time to digest it.' If this news is not an excuse to escape, he doesn't know what is. 'Big day tomorrow and all that. Thank you for telling me all this. Would you mind if we called time on lunch?'

'I completely understand,' she says, clearly much relieved to leave the steaming excrement before her. 'Is there anything I can do to help you prepare for tomorrow? Is your suit clean?'

'Of course. Cleanliness is next to godliness, innit?'

'Well then, I'll leave you to it. I'm staying at the Connaught if you need me and you have my mobile number.'

'You're a fucking saint, ma'am.'

'See you tomorrow then. Good luck. Get a good night's sleep and fingers crossed Squales can do his thing. He's the best there is, you know.'

'So I'm told, though I must say he's seemed a little vacuous in our interminable meetings.'

'And if it all turns out okay, you must come and stay in France. A little recovery time would do you good. You look inside out.'

'Thanks. Yeah. We'll see.'

'Bye then.'

Choice. It's not all it's cracked up to be. Even with the most trivial decision there is the threat of getting it wrong. Matty believes in the butterfly effect. Small variations have cataclysmic consequences. If his father had been called to his

253

aeroplane two minutes earlier, he would not have met his mother, who would not have died giving birth to Matty, who would not be alive, sitting here debating which drug might best suit the theme of this Monday evening. He doubts, as he considers this, that his mother, had she lived, would be proud of him at this particular moment. His father might though. They're clearly two of a kind. It gives Matty some satisfaction that Daniel had effectively already killed himself before he pulled the trigger. Not much though.

Once a drug has been experienced, Matty finds that the taboo is broken; the process dilutes to the same consistency as eating whatever's in the cupboard, shagging girls he's already had. Normality to euphoria. Me to empathy with you. Neutral to rocket fuel. The problem comes when the drugs don't do what they're supposed to do. Increasingly, and invariably as the sleepless nights accumulate, Matty can sense uppers and downers flying over his head, as shuttlecocks fly over a net. Even when they shuffle over the top of it, the impact is minimal.

He has slept a little. Just enough to make him feel like shit.

He's feeling really low now.

I'm feeling, he thinks, really low now.

He deals with this in the only way he knows how. He goes out.

He comes in.

A beautiful girl is watching him evenly. He takes a hit of the crack pipe and passes it to her, feeling the almost simultaneous rush of bliss through his veins. The girl leers at the happiness nestling inside it, draws on it greedily, then turns to him.

His breath's coming faster now. The girl's kneeling, grinding her back against the table leg, its thick rigidity expansive as a backdrop to her skeletal frame. Matty can see scars up and down her arms but they do not diminish her beauty. They are war wounds. He sucks her strength as she sucks him.

In a flat. His? Glass on the floor, be careful. Clothes thrown. He does not know her name. He likes it that way. Thinks:

Of Tera
Love love love
I love you
Still.
Silvia.

This close, she could be Tera. He draws her closer still. The falsest of gestures. But the searing sexual highs that had swept him up in his youth have shrivelled to a horrifying physical inertia. He thinks he's up there, his mind on the brink of coming but when he looks down, he's not even that close to the girl, and his cock's curled up like a sleeping puppy. The mighty warrior fallen. The mortification of the flesh.

She blurs in his distorted vision but Matty realises it is not just the two of them. Mandrax is on her other side. His face is buried in the girl's scrawny bosom, now they're nose to nose as the boy groans, grows stronger and faster upon her, within her and for a brief blinding moment the world disappears in a burst of exhilaration. It reappears all too soon, lying and leaking in a puddle as damp as his sullied soul.

'Oh, Man,' she is saying, 'Oh, Man, that was good.'

God he wants her out. Get out, get out he is screaming inside.

'That was great,' he says to her in an attempt to crush the guilt he knows will crush him once he is in a position to consider his actions. He offers her some of his K but she shakes her head.

'Have some of this, man,' she says and Matty realises that what she is doing in his kitchenette is cooking up a fix of smack. Her teeth are gone; she must be twice his age.

Why would you not want to try everything there is to try?

XXV

*ATHENA (to the FURIES): It is for you to speak—I now
bring this case to trial—because the plaintiff should
properly be first to tell the matter from the beginning,
and to explain it.*
*CHORUS: We are many, but we shall speak concisely.
(to ORESTES) Make answer, putting word against word
in turn. Say whether you are your mother's killer.*
ORESTES: I killed her; there's no denying it.[†]

When Matty comes to, he sees Katya staring worriedly into
his eyeballs. He is standing up unsteadily, like a tranquilised
horse, in the debris of his flat.

'How did you get in?' he asks, confused.

'We don't have time for this, Matthew. You know perfectly
well you just let me in. And you can leave now, please,' she
tells the evil-smelling woman next to him, who has conspicuously failed to leave, barely to dress.

Katya looks at Matty's glittering yellow eyes, the parapher-
nalia-strewn room. 'Christ, look at the state you're in. Look,
Matty, it's time to face the music now. Your attempts to kill
yourself with excess in time to avoid facing trial have not
succeeded. So given you have to face a jury, you could at least
turn up on time and look presentable.'

'I'll have a shower,' he says nobly.

'No time, no time. For God's sake, get a bloody move on.'

'Shit, man, you're a criminal!' His smacked-up wreck is
impressed, at least.

'Get out!' Katya is losing her cool.

[†]   Aeschylus, *Eumenides*, trans. Christopher Collard, lines 583-8.

The woman scarpers.

Matty looks down. His body seems somehow disconnected, unfamiliar. He recognises the feet, though of all extremities feet seem the most alien appendage. Ugly, ill-planned, malformed they protrude in a sinewy stew of knuckle and vein. Shudders. Continues upwards through his corporeal inventory. It's all there, as far as he can see, and most of it somehow clad in suit, less naked than his exposed feet.

Hands, white, dead but for a whispered suggestion of hae-moglobin trotting meekly into his palm. Fingers tingling. Why? Fear. Breathe. Hands reach searchingly around the places his eyes cannot: hair—check, mouth—check, liver—check check check. Palms kissing body like a French mime clawing his invisible wall, all evidence dictates Matty's actual physical presence here.

A hand enters his, squeezes it. Katya gestures to his shoes. 'There's a taxi waiting outside. We can make it on time if we go now.'

His shoelessness reminds him of those panic-inducing dreams he used to have where he realises, too late, that he is walking into the classroom naked. Or he smiles and finds himself toothless, like that girl. Or he's suddenly bald or impotent.

He's feeling pretty sick in the taxi. His mind is throbbing and the Jitterer's back in full throttle. Is this Judgement Day? Is he dead? As the car pulls up the hit of déjà vu flipping his veins intensifies as he recognises that ol' Crown Court and Squales waiting for him outside it with his solicitor, a red-head, whom he remembers, suddenly, he does not like, nor fancy.

Slowly something starts to come back to him. This is not the first time he's been to St Albans Crown Court, he knows that. But the details of Round One elude him. Squales told him to plead 'not guilty'. That's all. He'd get him off, he said. And he wasn't even asked to plead at the baby court just next door when Squales had secured his unlikely bail. Some odd conditions to it, moving house, not going to visit his brother, that sort of thing. He'd broken that last one and a few others many times in the months since the preliminary hearing.

He draws the veil. No point worrying about something so far beyond his control.

He can't understand the palaver. It was only a bit of blow he was carrying.

Squealer is talking about CPS rooms and 'disclosure'. Matty closes his mind and lets the words run over him, water off a duck's back. Katya's saying goodbye—she's crying, to his amazement. Now he's in the waiting area. He wonders if Fix is touring anywhere nearby. He could do with a friend right now. Squales says something else but he pays it no real attention. And then he's walking into the dock; a female security guard with a face like a bulldog awaits him and once he's in, she locks the door. It's slightly roomier than his bedsit at least, though he can't wholly prevent a wave of claustrophobia. The guard sits down to one side of it and Matty follows her example. The dock is at the back of the court and Squales sits in front of him, resplendent in his barristerial wig. Next to him, the prosecutor, the same bastard as last time. It is Ruben, a pearl of sweat glistening horribly on an otherwise serene forehead. Well, this is rich. To be prosecuted by his own fictional character, Ruben, beloved betrayer of all that was once pure and sacred, straight from the pages of *Looking Up At The Stars*. More of a spiv than ever Matty had imagined, with his peculiar style of dress and extreme Hollywood facial features, as if evolution has conspired to the perfect symmetry exhibited there but has come out the other side. A parody of high cheek-boned, straight-nosed, almond-eyed youth. And

Matty *had* imagined him. Surely this, he thinks with sudden misplaced fury, is taking quite serious liberties.

With an onslaught of head spin he sees Feracor, presiding over this Grand Court, the Judge. Feracor breathes authority. His serene and powerful face remains uncreased; his amethyst eyes flash eternity. Swathed in purple robes, he sits entrenched in gold, one hand casually wielding a sceptre from whose top a blue flame rises majestically.

Matty's thought processes are doing cartwheels.

He is, however, well-practised at suspending disbelief as he takes his mind to new worlds. The ubiquity of mind-expanding drugs in his own dimension has opened him up to the suggestion of travel to others. And Feracor does make a good judge, he has to admit. He is larger and more forbidding than even Matty had imagined. He reminds him of one of the giant guardians of heaven which mark the entry into Buddhist temples in China. Feracor is serving a similar purpose. Behind him spins a black vortex. Three Furies with snakes for hair and blood-dripping eyes join the jurors in their box.

He looks around the courtroom—it's like a leaving party. Everyone he's ever known seems to be there, dead, alive, somewhere in between. He catches sight of Angelica and Timmy Martial and, delighted, waves at them. Support from the most unexpected quarter. Where's the party photographer? But Timmy is standing up, his expression mutinous. Angelica is in tears. They've come to see him hang then.

Matty looks up and can see Mandrax above and behind him, in the front row of spectator benches. He is scribbling something. He turns it round and presents Matty with a pencil sketch of himself in the dock, frowning, wild of eye. Maxi is waiting to one side. Handcuffs swing down from his pocket. Matty's eyes swim through the sea of spectators, face after recognisable face smacking into his consciousness, each one more aggressive than the former. Here scowls King Darius; here the pugnacious face of Matron Briony crumples into folds of disapproval.

You silly silly boy, scolds the Jitterer, who, it becomes apparent, is also the clerk. The sentiment echoes through the hall, as if borne on a Mexican wave. He reads out a description of a case that makes no sense to Matty. Cocaine possession is not even mentioned, nor is selling skunk, nor stealing bicycles.

He reels with terror. He must be in the wrong courtroom. He's been set up. It's some cosmic conspiracy. 'Ummm, I think there's been a mistake,' he tries to tell the courtroom but finds himself unable to speak.

He sees his brother, Ben, lying in his prison of life support near the back of the courtroom, a ghost of the strutting advocate Ruben. Matty is starting to feel a little hysterical. Trapped.

His darting gaze is held by the purple lasers shining from Feracorian orbs.

Ruben speaks: 'Good morning, ladies and gentlemen of the jury. My name is Ruben Corani and I come here to prosecute this case. My learned friend—the man sitting to my right—is Mr Squales. He is here to defend Mr Matthew Corani. Mr Corani does not attend of his own volition. He has been brought to the court by the Crown and it is the Crown that must prove the case against him. He has to prove nothing.'

Matty tries desperately to zone out, to disappear, but the voice is not external; it is as if it is being delivered to him by his own mind. He is spellbound by Ruben, his own bloody character, transfixed by his words. He can only listen.

Ruben marches relentlessly on: 'So, what is it that the Crown say? Well, you will recall the words which the clerk just read out in open court. That is the indictment. And, the words on the indictment mean that the Crown alleges that Mr Matthew Corani is guilty of causing death by careless driving while under the influence of alcohol. So, ladies and gentlemen, what that means is that it is the Crown's case that the defendant, Mr Matthew Corani, drove his car, having consumed so much alcohol that his driving was sufficiently impaired and, unable to control the vehicle, he committed a series of dangerous actions: he drove through a red light at ninety miles per hour; he tried to overtake another vehicle on the inside; and finally, he swerved, albeit to avoid crashing into the car in front of him, but causing his vehicle and the occupants within it to drive off the road through a hedge. The car was out of control and it rolled several times before landing upside down in a ditch, the impact of which directly caused the death of his girlfriend, Tera Martial, and serious injury to his brother, Benedicto Corani.

'After this incident took place, a passing car alerted the emergency services to the accident. The defendant was found some metres from the car in a catatonic state. He was unintelligible and evidently intoxicated when placed under caution and arrested. He submitted to a breathalyser test and was found to have a blood-alcohol level three times the legal limit. When, after a full twenty-four hours, he was sober, he was interviewed by the police and had the benefit of legal advice during that time. The defendant said he had been drinking but claimed his brother, the man who has ever since been in a coma, had been driving the car.'

Matty is shaking his head in disbelief. It's not true. How could it possibly be true? Why is he being subjected to this monstrous put-up job?

'Now, the fact that Mr Matthew Corani is sitting here and you, members of the jury, have volunteered to give up your time to try this case, means that the defendant still denies any responsibility for the death of his girlfriend and serious injury to his brother. You will hear from the following witnesses who underpin the Crown's case that it was in fact Mr Matthew Corani who was driving the car. Ms Emily Smith, whose car the defendant so recklessly overtook, says in her statement that she witnessed him manoeuvre his brother's injured body into the front seat of the car, no doubt significantly worsening the damage caused by the crash. Mr Robert Hearst, a police expert who examined the forensic evidence of the car, states that his findings wholly support this account. You will hear in detail what the defendant said when interviewed by the police shortly after the accident. You may find that the account he gives is incredible and you may wonder how it is that Mr Corani's brother (who was shown to have no alcohol in his bloodstream) could have driven this car, borrowed from Mr Felix Hardy, so recklessly without leaving evidence of having touched any of its controls. You may also wonder how Matthew Corani's fingerprints are all over the steering wheel, stereo and gearstick.

'But more than anything, members of the jury, the Crown says that you will not fail to find persuasive and conclusive the evidence of the prosecution witnesses, Ms Smith and Mr Hearst. You may feel these witnesses have absolutely no reason to lie and no axe to grind... and if that is the case, members of the jury, and as long as you are sure that the Crown's case is the truth, then you will have to return a verdict of 'guilty' to the charge on this indictment. Now, would the clerk of the court please bring in the first witness, Ms Emily Smith. Your Honour, her statement appears at page twenty-three of the bundle you should have in front of you.'

A beautiful girl is watching him evenly. Is it Tera? Are all girls Tera? He catches his breath. Scarless now, peerless, she sits as if removed from another world, certainly as if removed from this one. As has always been so, the world and all its dross recede and only Matty and Tera remain, alone in time and space. All her actions irrelevant, all the hurt, the betrayal dissipated. She is no longer what she does, simply what she is. Matty breathes her like a man released from a stifling cavern into the open air; just a boy and a girl, the most basic, the most resolute union.

Tears collect unbidden as Matty stares and imagines he sees in those eyes what could have been. She is perfect. Every line and curve so familiar, every angle known, explored, marked. She seems only a few feet from him, yet the distance is unfathomable. His eyes anchor an intangible cord that connects his to hers as through a dream or a mirage. Fossilised, a split second of eternity lingers, holds two floating halves together.

She smiles, shatters into ash.

'Will the defendant please look forward.'

Matty wakes up.

Matty wakes up.

Matty wakes up.

And he knows now. He remembers. He sees Tera's mother looking at him with tears in her eyes and he knows it was all his fault. He took her only child and he brought her back dead.

He did it. The truth of it comes at him like a hurricane.

He, Matty, had been driving the car.

He had been wrecked, lost in some black alcoholic hole. Not drugs, for once. It had been a condition of him and Tera getting back together. He supposes that if he had been on crystal, she'd never have let him drive. As it was, he'd insisted on driving them both, Ben and Tera, his adored, his family. It had been a long night and the morning light had done nothing to sober him up but everything to make him want to make amends for being such a shitty boyfriend, such a burden of a brother.

He said, please let me drive you. He took Fix's car keys and left Fix in the flat, practically unconscious.

There was a meeting with a man whom Ben had met. He wanted to put on an exhibition of Tera's art. He lived near Hatfield. Monday morning meeting. Matty was jealous.

'Please slow down, please slow down,' Tera had been saying. He'd tried to but he had no control over his limbs, over the wheel. He was too far gone.

Matty drove faster and faster, music up and up and up because he did not want to think. Because it should have been him setting up a meeting for Tera, because he felt inadequate, because he was wrecked. He knew there was no affair going on between them, though. He sees the protective lies he spun for himself, the denial, as the horror rolls in. How could he have convinced himself it was their fault? That *they* had betrayed *him*. Too gutless, even to pay for the crime he'd committed, he'd dragged Ben into the driver's seat with the strength of the paralytic. He'd thought he was dead, that it was a sacrifice which would make no difference to Ben. But maybe, maybe if he'd left him where he was, he wouldn't be on life support with a broken body.

He is evil. Feracor can't save him now. He's going straight to hell.

He drove off the road. *He* killed his love. *He* crippled his brother. He knows now. The veil of his self-deception rolls up like a theatre curtain exposing the bleak proscenium of his mind. There is nowhere to hide now. He remembers the arrest, the breathalyser, the night in the cells to sober him up, the jibbering loneliness, the police's refusal to grant bail and being remanded in custody, Squales's arrival on the scene and the endless interviews, being picked up by the police van from his cell and travelling with the other dregs of the earth to the magistrate's court and Squales's brilliant and successful application for bail, his preliminary hearing at the Crown Court, the grace he'd been given even after that as both sides prepared their cases. God, he made the most of it. All over now. His freedom is gone and he is glad of it. He deserves to die.

Matty collapses in the dock as the sheer weight of guilt courses over him, a pack of hounds upon the fox.

'Your Honour, may I have a few moments to confer with my client?' asks Squales of the Judge in all his Feracorian splendour.

'Yes, I think that would be a very good idea indeed.'

Matty opens his eyes and the courtroom blurs before him, a tangle of hissing serpents. He follows the bulldog back into a secure area behind the court. Through the haze, resting his head on his hands and his hands on his knees, Matty drifts in and out of consciousness. He shuts his eyes tightly again and tries to drown out the unmistakable tones of Squales's attempted conversation.

In his head, the trial continues. There is no escape, no respite.

Mandrax raises his left hand as instructed and places it on a copy of THE PALABRA FERACORI. *He is enchanted to see it bound, regal in aspect, emanating power. He swears to tell the truth.*
Ruben speaks again:
'Furies of the jury, the Crown suggests that Mr Corani has mixed his myths and his meth. He thought he was Dionysus. He was not. He killed his own mother once, and now he has killed her again. For this double murder, we hand this loser, this woeful Orestes over to you. Do as you will.'

FURIES:
We convict him. We drag
Out of his body the price
Of the blood he has shed.
Night is our mother.[†]

Squales draws back from trying to shake Matty awake. His eyes have rolled back into his head as the Furies scratch at them, and his mouth is emitting a thin white stream of foam. 'He's not fit to stand trial,' Squales is telling someone, perhaps himself. Of the various characters housed in Matty's person, there is only Mandrax left to hear him. Matty has fled into the recesses of his own mind, a self-incarcerated prisoner of his own psyche. Delighted to have the floor, Mandrax settles into a long morning of enlightening the good Mr Squales. He begins with some gravitas.

'I am your god,' he whispers. 'Worship none but me.'

[†]   Aeschylus, *Eumenides*, trans. Ted Hughes, p. 167.

THE PALABRA FERACORI

This is the word of Feracor. Now the reason we're a little cross with you, Mandrax, is not so much that you've crossed our boundaries. It's more that you've transgressed your own. You have splintered your very self to evade the consequences of the terrible things you have done. The golden scales swing pensively as Feracor strokes them.

You thought you could escape reality by imagining a religion which champions what the real world considers a sin. You have, unbidden, unwitting, unprophesied, made yourself the scribe and usher of the religion of that which is. And yet you have falsely claimed yourself as its god too.

You made things up. In your power-crazed, self-appointed role of messiah, you made things up and it seems you came to believe your own press. You have denied a god, Mandrax. And that is a very dangerous thing to do.

Yes, you ushered him in—chaos and ecstasy— and then you usurped him. And all of it too soon anyway! The natural terrors which must herald Feracor's coming, the melting of glaciers, the blazing inferno of global heat... all of this is in its infancy! Religious truths do not fall upon full bellies and peaceful singsongs. They fall upon the desperate, the dispossessed, the disastrous.

Since you have meddled with the natural order, you must pay the appropriate penalty. You are the prophet of this mighty deity. You, with your meddling have made it so. Your duty now must be to amend this premature situation and prepare the way for Feracor. Your punishment shall be the sacrifice of yourself. This is the only way to realign the balance of the forces you have churned up cross-dimension. It is the only way to restore order.

It is the only way you can undo the mistaken beliefs of generations past and alert your world to the truth, the essence, what is. You must alert the people to the nature of the universe

268

with your writing. But you must go further than that. The action you take will give your writing dignity and credibility. You shall die by your own hand once THE PALABRA FERACORI is complete and the way laid. You shall die with it in your hand and release its devastating light upon your fellow man.

THE TOWER HAMLETS CENTRE FOR MENTAL HEALTH

MILE END HOSPITAL
BANCROFT ROAD
LONDON E1 4DG

DATE: TUESDAY 3 FEBRUARY 2016	**TIME OF ADMISSION:** 3.45PM

PATIENT:
MATTHEW EDWARD CORANI
WHITE BRITISH MALE, AGE UNKNOWN – ESTIMATED MID-THIRTIES

ADDRESS:
25F MEARD STREET, LONDON, W1F OEW

MODE/REASON OF REFERRAL:
BROUGHT IN BY AMBULANCE AND POLICE TO A&E/MHU UNDER SECTION 136. FOLLOWING MHA ASSESSMENT PLACED UNDER SECTION 2 OF THE MHA. ASKED TO ASSESS BY UNIT BED MANAGER.

PRESENTING COMPLAINT:
COLLAPSE AND CONFUSION, PROBABLE PSYCHOSIS.

HISTORY OF PRESENTING COLLAPSE:
PATIENT COLLAPSED IN COURT (ST ALBANS). LOSS OF CONSCIOUSNESS OCCURRED; SUSPECTED SEIZURE. SIGNS OF HEAD INJURY–SCAR ON CROWN (UPPER R) (<12MO).

FAMILY HISTORY:
PATIENT INCOHERENT, NOT KNOWN.

MEDICAL HISTORY:
PATIENT INCOHERENT, NOT KNOWN.

PSYCHIATRIC HISTORY:
PATIENT INCOHERENT, NOT KNOWN.

DRUG HISTORY:
SEDATIVE IN AMBULANCE, INDICATIONS OF HABITUAL ALCOHOL/DRUG USE (MALNOURISHED; BURN MARKS ON FINGERS & LIPS; DILATED PUPILS).

PERSONAL HISTORY:
PATIENT INCOHERENT, NOT KNOWN.

MENTAL STATE EXAMINATION:

APPEARANCE AND BEHAVIOUR EMACIATED, FAIRLY UNRESPONSIVE INITIALLY (SEDATED), DISTRACTED — HEARING A VOICE. BECOMING EXCITABLE/AGITATED AS SEDATIVE WEARS OFF.

SPEECH LOW, QUIETLY SPOKEN, SLOW SPEECH PATTERNS, LONG PAUSES (LISTENING TO/ RESPONDING TO VOICES?)

MOOD ELATED — GRINNING. OUT OF KEEPING WITH SPEECH PATTERNS. HAS APPEARANCE OF MANIA DESPITE SPEECH TONE.

THOUGHT SLOW TO RESPOND TO QUESTIONS (APPEARS TO BE WAITING FOR SOMEONE ELSE TO RESPOND ON HIS BEHALF).

- GRANDIOSE/PARANOID DELUSIONS — SAYS ALL MUST LISTEN TO HIM, SPEAKING AS PROPHET ('MANDRAKES'?)
- FORMAL THOUGHT DISORDER — LOOSENING OF ASSOCIATION
- DISCONNECTED IDEAS, USE OF OBSCURE (MADE UP?) WORDS — 'PARAMBOLA'?
- FIRST-RANK SYMPTOMS OF SCHIZOPHRENIA PRESENT

PERCEPTION AUDITORY/VISUAL HALLUCINATIONS: SINGLE VOICE TALKING TO/THROUGH HIM. CLAIMS VOICE IS NEW GOD — 'FRACKER'?

COGNITION PATIENT HIGHLY CONFUSED — COULD NOT COMPLETE ASSESSMENT. SEEMS NOT TO KNOW DATE/YEAR. KNOWS IS IN LONDON.

INSIGHT POOR, DOES NOT BELIEVE HE IS MENTALLY UNWELL OR REQUIRES TREATMENT HENCE DETAINED UNDER SEC. 2 MHA 1983.

INITIAL CONCLUSION:
LIKELY FIRST EPISODE PSYCHOSIS POSSIBLY SECONDARY TO DRUGS MISUSE.

INITIAL CARE PLAN:
1. ADMIT UNDER MHA SEC. 2 TO GENERAL WARD. CONSIDER PICU (IF BECOMES AGGRESSIVE OR HIGH RISK OF ABSCONDING).
2. 1:1 OBSERVATION TILL REVIEW BY TEAM TOMORROW.
3. PRN SEDATION WRITTEN UP (ORAL AND INTRAMUSCULAR LORAZEPAM AND HALOPERIDOL AND PROCYCLIDINE PRN WRITTEN UP) IF REQUIRING MORE SEDATION CALL PSYCHIATRIST.
4. BLOODS AND URINE DRUG SCREEN, MAY NEED CT SCAN.
5. COLLABORATIVE HISTORY FROM NEXT OF KIN.

XXVI

As Matty lies comatose within the shroud of his own body, Mandrax is wide awake. He can sense the straitjacket restraining him as he rattles down a corridor, bump, bump, bump on the trolley, watching the ceiling lights of the hospital trip into one another. But this is merely a physical restriction. His body is obsolete, unnecessary—Mandrax is a mind set free, Mind at Large; the body merely the vessel, a brain in a vat. In his mind he can fly. In his mind he waits for Feracor. He is full of joy, his purpose confirmed by Feracor's judgement. On Earth as it is in Heaven, he has been judged by man. By man he has been judged crazy, delusional, sentenced to psychiatric care while he is examined, deemed unfit for trial, unfit, perhaps, even for prison, but what are earthly judgements? He waits for his god and he is answerable only to him. What prophet, saint, martyr has not suffered at the hands of man for their faith?

'Answer me that!' he yells, the sudden noise causing the two nurses pushing his trolley to jump.

'Calm yourself, love,' says the one with peroxide hair. 'You don't want us to give you another injection in your botty, do you?'

'Sedative! Feed me! None so divine as sedative.'

The vision that confronted him under the influence of the last injection had been so uplifting, so phenomenally powerful. He had felt the presence of his god all around and through and in him. And he knows now that as the son of Feracor, he must suffer on Earth before he is united with his Father, with what is essentially himself. He is God. Yes, Feracor claims he is the scribe, the prophet, but if one looks at the *history* of these kinds of affairs, they always turn out to be one and the same—the messenger and the message, the divine portal and the divine, the Son and the Father.

All the great religions have some form of self-sacrifice. All the great religions, Feracor declares, are tapping into an element of what is, just not the whole perfect story. Feracor has claimed Mandrax as the scribe of what is. Feracor has said Mandrax must end his own life to bring his message to the people.

Mandrax is the Messiah so he must be the Son of God.

Like Christ, only better. An upgraded version.

He always knew he was different, in some way exempt from the mundane.

The secret knowledge of his mission, his privileged position within the new world religion, the burden he must carry like great prophets and martyrs before him; well, somehow it just puts it all in perspective. It makes sense of a life spent dodging dodgy voiceovers, makes sense of the trials and betrayals. He has been a pawn in the world order, exempt from blame, useful, nay essential, to those at the top.

Mandrax is very careful now to act as if he is not thinking about any of this. The success or failure of his duty to Feracor depends on gaining sufficient freedom to carry out his final task. His jubilance is masked in sober contrition.

The trolley has stopped. The ceiling is static. Someone is shining a light in his eyes.

He's always been partial to a bit of death, particularly in his grand depressions when the ravaged world is laid bare before him as the graveyard it is. But in all his dream-like encounters with Feracor, the issue of death has not, until now, arisen. It's always been his own speculative burden. It's good to have the divine go-ahead and, with that, the suggestion of messianic reward beyond the grave. He believes a resurrection

273

is traditional. No PALABRA has presented to him the possibility of life after death, nor considered the traditional roles of places of reward and punishment. In his heart of hearts, he has always felt that there is nothing beyond. He has even been cheered by this prospect; cuts down the options; means you have to put your all into this life. He also knows, however, that the promise of some sort of eternal bliss is the unspoken motivation for most believers. Takes the sting out of death; takes the edge off the insane inevitability of life. His Facebook friends will love it.

Never has he felt a greater sense of his own mortality than when he allows himself to look beyond the nurses to Feracor, standing at the foot of his bed and beyond him, a spinning abyss.

'Whatever you want me to do, I'll do it, no questions asked,' he addresses his god.

'Hold tight,' says the non-peroxide nurse. 'We're going in.' She ploughs a needle into his left buttock and Mandrax clenches with exquisite pain.

Drugs. They're just a portal to the divine, signposts to the destination—and he's arrived now. Yes, there had been a time when he had momentarily lost his gauge. A dustbin for whatever nameless hybrid of chemical was available; he, he sees with the benefit of hindsight, lost the ability to predict accurate doses for maximum enjoyment. In a blind spot, he mixed what he should not have; he took no precaution for the comedowns; he forgot where to stop. He forgot the need for anything to stop ever as the power of the drugs he shovelled into himself made him veer from manic to mellow to manic to panic.

But now there's a new voice of self-control in his head. Feracor, little Father.

Feracor approaches the side of the bed and touches his straitjacketed shoulder. It means so much that he's here, in touch with him, helping him through these last crucial days. He realises the true might of this wondrous, brutal deity. He worships him silently from the hospital bed and plans the final instalment of the book his unconscious intended him to write. The events of his past were just a way in to the PALABRA. Now they are fiction: Feracor is the only reality. Mandrax is not sad to let go of this shadowy twilight life. The human is always compelled to look upwards to the illuminations of the truth. What really is.

What he realises now, though, is that the martyrdom of messiahs, hindsight would suggest, has got to involve something pretty spectacular. Crucifixion, for example, is going to make people sit up and take notice, how much more so the impressive encore of the resurrection? Enamoured of the humble sedative as Mandrax is, he feels it's simply not significant enough to slide gently away in a veil of Valium. It must be an act which changes the world, which makes it ready, or even vulnerable, to the coming of the new religion. An act of self-destruction which creates.

Finally he is all alone.

Night dawns upon the mind of Mandrax. The hospital lights dim.

One final PALABRA to be written.

Why is his head taking so long to bring up the document? That's all that's in there; version after version of PALABRAS and prayers.

Calm down, calm down. I'm doing the best I can.

Who said that? There is no one here in this head except Mandrax.

Peering closer into the black static screen of his mind, he sees a small white figure in the corner. Further inspection reveals that this figure is Matty. Mandrax watches him and knows that this character is his other. It is not himself, for Mandrax is neither dressed in white nor little more than an inch tall. Crucially, unlike the diminutive impostor before him, he is without, not within, his own head.

What's the problem, Matty asks him, looking bored. *You know what it's like to be in two places at once, don't you? You've written a fictional self into books but carried on living another life. You know what it's like to be chatting to Fix here in your hospital bed, yet wander in your mind to a different dimension for a quick consultation with Feracor.*

I don't remember copying and pasting you into my brain.

It's all about you, isn't it?

Well, you being me, it's kind of hard to be objective here.

You wouldn't exist without me. I set you free.

You were my jailer long enough.

Matty, like the Microsoft paperclip of old, has been endowed with a range of impudent facial expressions not accessible to Mandrax, much to his irritation. He is a shapeshifter.

He is shifting even now.

Right Guv, I'll be straight with you, a newly spruced Matty prances across the screen in a mincing choreograph.

Straight is not the first adjective which springs to mind. Mandrax has never seen Matty as a miniature gay man with a cockney accent, more as the wanker that kept shutting him down, kicking him out.

I've been sent by Feracor—

Who else? Finally something makes sense.

—to help you with the final PALABRA. *He don't want it written like the others. He wants it enacted by you. You are the final* PALABRA. *And I am the illustration. Whatever you do, I'll play out in an identical scenario on your mental screen. You just need to set me up in the final pages of the on-brain version of* THE PALABRA FERACORI *and we're rolling.*

This is forethought indeed. Mandrax had hoped that the manner of his death and his internal blog will be sufficient to spread the word. But so much better to leave a little part of himself behind: a virus to burrow through the channels of the mind, a spokesman to deal with all the publicity.

He feels he is leaving things in good hands.

And so he sets up Matty in the final chapter, having shown him the list of mental chatrooms where he is registered, stored handily in a file 'Messiah Favourites'. Mandrax is free to complete his own story. Internally, he begins to write.

Three flies settle on the starched white bedclothes.

Some way in, he is interrupted. Blinding strip lights illuminate the ward. The nurses are doing their drug rounds and Mandrax finds he can move his arms and his body. The jacket has been removed. Feracor is standing majestically at the end of the bed.

'Fix! What are you doing here?'

'I work here, buddy. I'm a porter, remember?'

'But I thought you had The Furies tour?'

Fix has returned for him. Matty is more important than rock stardom.

'No, that never actually happened. Anyway, how're you doing now, man?'

'I'm not well, Fix. Not a well boy at all.'

'I know, I know. But you'll get better in here. That's why they brought you here.'

Mandrax, finally, is nothing but his essence. The core of his existence.

Have you heard the news? asks Feracor. There is ecstasy in his voice.

Fix sits by him, strokes his hair.

'It's okay, Matty. It's all going to be all right, you'll see. I'm sorry I left when you needed me. But look, these doctors are amazing. You'll be out of here in no time.'

Mandrax reaches a drowsy hand out to touch Fix.

'News,' says Fix. 'Ben's woken up.'

Can you get me out of here, Mandrax begs. *I need to do something important.*

'No mate. No, not for the moment. But I've got a little something for you. Should make it a little more bearable.' He hands him some Valium, blue pills removed from their packet and passes him the glass of water by the bed.

Mandrax swallows and flounders, falls back into the abyss as Fix's face distorts above him, glinting, gleaming, purple eyes searing into his soul. Just as suddenly, beauty and peace start to creep out of the malevolently twisted features; the blue of the sky pours through the window, iridescent waterfalls of truths which come hard and fast upon him. A thought is trying to get through, trying to fight it—something to do with Tera—Ben—and then Mandrax surrenders to the pillowy bliss, cradled in maternal arms, the soft straitjacket of the Earth itself. A light goes out.

So   Matty, out   by   an decomposed this: capri- ing the right
PALABRA- *all-power-* wreaths and cious woman thing. Again
bound, leaves ful   scribe, *sympathy*. always fucks and   again
his mind for reduced to a The   ground things   up. the   shov-
the last time stick man on has hardened Of course he el splits the
and goes be- a page, the beneath the would rather warm bleed-
yond the iron visual essence turf   veneer channel Fer- ing womb of
bars of the of a human. and   above acor to Earth the   Earth.
cemetery. As A   strength, the wooden as once he Down, sta-
he stands in- however, is casket where had, when mp, scoop.
side its con- required of Tera lies ina- bright suns Down, sta-
fines he feels him now that nimate, wai- had   shone mp, scoop.
a momentary he is more ting. Pulse upon   him, Down, sta-
fear. Fierce than human. beats. He can when Tera's mp, scoop...
indeed must Feracor is hear her wai- warm body stops against
one be to kn- with   him, ting. Digging had awaited hard wood.
owingly de- a   spiritual her out will, him witho- The moment
stroy one's hand on his he   knows, ut condition, is here. The
own essence. shoulder, a be by far the without rest- constellation
It is human muttering in hardest part raint, with- flashes pur-
nature to cre- his ear. Wit- of this mis- out fucking ple in the
ate, not ne- hout Ferac- sion, but he his brother on sky.   One
gate. Matty or's illumina- steels himself the side. An six-pointed
looks down tion, it would to think of internal mon- star gleams
at his world- have taken the greater ologue re- at the con-
weary flesh him longer to good as he assures him junction of
and reflects find Tera's sets to scrab- over   and the two de-
that the job resting place. ble into the over, with ities. Stellar
is half-done The   grave- core of the a Feracori- genitalia. It
already. Di- stone has Earth. An- an authori- is that same
minished, it sunk steadily ger gives him ty, that no star which
seems as if into the soil, strength. It matter what once guid-
he is steadily cemented in did not have doubts creep ed   mystics
being rubbed the decay of to be like in, he is do- and   seers

to the birth to a roasting invincible. ty. The side places   **THE**
of   Christ. tin.   Bone He   takes which turns **P A L A B R A**
The wrong juts out, bald her to the the   other **F E R A C O R I**
birth.   The and shocking Millennium cheek, which on the pave-
wrong child. as he takes Bridge, eu- *i g n o r e s* , ment.   He
He cannot her in his phoric now, which buries lifts Earth
not bear to arms to be- enjoying the the fierce hu- on to the
look at her, gin the spec- long, long man essence other side
can barely tral dance. walk.   The embodied by of the bal-
endure the Somewhere, hard part is Feracor, em- ustrade and
saturating somewhere done. What bodied by secures her
malodours in there is the is crucial is him, Matty, head in the
which   as- girl he loved. the   correct Son of Fera- loop of rope
sail him once 'I   forgive formation of cor. But the tied to the
the coffin you,' he says the star, the Star...   the railing near-
lid has been to her, bun- symbol by Star is the fu- est the book.
prized open. dling her into which   the sion of male As he lets
The damage the black people might and female, her hang
caused by bin liner he come to the universe loose, a bone
the car crash has brought know their whole, com- drops free
has been and retreat- new god. plete, singing of its fleshy
superficial- ing from the Christ's Cru- in harmo- confines and
ly patched *graveyard*, cifixion had ny. Arrang- plunges into
up, and this where it spelt out ing Tera the angry,
plastic re- seems as if symbolically as anything red Thames
construction a thousand all that was other than seething be-
is what re- grey shadows wrong with the straight neath them.
mains best cry out in his religion: line which You're do-
intact. The protest, rise a cross—one runs down ing the right
flesh falls up to stop side of the the centre of thing. You're
from it like him. But he deal. The the Star is a doing the
the sticky is doing the soft, fem- physical im- right thing.
black meat work of Fer- inine side possibility. You're do-
which clings acor. He is of humani- Carefully, he ing the right

thing.   He her on the top ing his eyes, he and Tera passing into
climbs   over rail, he places he   undoes would   live and through
the side and his feet on his trousers. and   love. him. He en-
stands   next the   support He thinks of It   was   the ters Tera. The
to her, sur- of the ledge, Feracor, of world   that stars   collide
veying   the forming the the   human had   been as the noose
wide   gulf four-point race, of his wrong. They sweeps   the
beneath him. star   across reward for would set it breath from
Eternity. Se- her. He slides services   to to   rights. his body: the
curing   his his head into m a n k i n d : Finally, he is portal opens.
hands on ei- the   second this   would close. He can The   stars
ther side of noose. Clos- all be over— feel Feracor slide aside.

ACKNOWLEDGEMENTS

My heartfelt thanks to Naim Attallah for his vision, instinct and generosity of spirit, and to James Pulford and the fantastic production team at Quartet Books. Many thanks to Mandi Gomez for her insight and inspired editing, and to Nicholas Monson, a most excellent mentor. I'm extremely grateful to Sally Stubbs, Madeleine Inkin and Dr. Kam Harvey for their psychological wisdom, Verity Buchanan for her legal expertise and Isadora Welby for sharing her experience of bubblegum alcopops. Zinnia Welby, Felicity Gibbs, Josie Stapleton and Dan Holloway all gave invaluable help and guidance when it was most needed, and I have seriously appreciated the comments of everyone who read the manuscript. Thanks to Chris Dawes for his photographic skills and Tony Lyons for his haunting designs. Above all, huge thanks to Charles and Suzanna Welby for their eternal encouragement and support, and to Charlie Morrison for his brilliant eye, endless ideas and general heroism.

WORKS CITED

Aeschylus, *Eumenides*, in the trilogy *The Oresteia*, trans. Ted Hughes, New York: Farrar Straus & Giroux (1999).

Aeschylus, *Choephori* and *Eumenides*, in *Oresteia*, trans. Christopher Collard, Oxford: OUP (2002).

Euripides, *Bacchae*, in *Bacchae and Other Plays*, trans. James Morwood, Oxford: OUP (2000).

Bruner, Jerome, *Making Stories: Law, Literature, Life*, Cambridge, MA: HUP (2003).

Grove, David, online: www.cleanlanguage.co.uk.

Huxley, Aldous, *The Doors of Perception and Heaven and Hell*, London: Penguin (1954).

Jung, C. G., *Conscious, Unconscious and Individuation* (1964), see: *The Essential Jung: Selected Writings*, London: Fontana Press (1998).

Midgley, Mary, in Strawson, 'Against Narrativity'.

Pessoa, Fernando, *Livro do Desassossego: Composto por Bernardo Soares, ajudante de guarda-livros na cidade de Lisboa* (1984); Eng. *The Book of Disquiet*, trans. Margaret Jull Costa, London: Serpent's Tail (1991).

Storr, Anthony, *Feet of Clay: A Study of Gurus*, New York: The Free Press (1996).

Storr, Anthony, *Art of Psychotherapy*, New York: Routledge (1999).

Strawson, Galen, 'Against Narrativity', *Ratio* 17 (2004).

Strawson, Galen, 'I am not a Story' (2004), online: Eaon, excerpted from Zachary Leader (ed.), *On Life-Writing*, Oxford: OUP (2015).

von Franz, Marie-Luise, *The Problem of the Puer Aeternus* (Studies in Jungian psychology by Jungian analysts), Toronto: Inner City Books (2000).

Wallin, David J., *Attachment in Psychotherapy*, New York: Guilford Press (2007).